I0670500

the accidental life of mf ascher

Ivy H. Booker

Burn the Town Down Press

ISBN: 9781965014059 (ebook)

ISBN: 9781965014042 (print)

For our fearless leader, Michele Montgomery,
and all the Write InMates

prologue

It's crazy to think that we fight our whole lives not to be put into some kind of box, and yet, when it's all said and done, that's exactly where we wind up. In this case, a lacquered cherry casket with silver embellishments and a creamy billowy satin interior for a comfortable eternal rest. A nice one, all things considered, but a box just the same.

"Such a lovely eulogy," says a woman blotting her eyes with shredded tissue.

It wasn't. The pace was way off, and at some point, it became a rambling jumble of nothing.

"Yes, it was," I mutter, stepping away, trying harder to tuck myself into the far pocket of the crowd.

A good eulogy can make a bad moment better. It has the power to transform a person from a total piece of garbage into a selfless and loving human being. Small, simple acts in a person's life become larger-than-life events. A eulogy is the perfect example of creative nonfiction. It takes the best parts about someone and blows them up into something even greater. Truth amplified by fiction.

Sometimes, the power of a eulogy isn't in the words but in the presentation. Maybe that's why this one was so awful; the speaker didn't do it justice. Or because I happen to know the deceased well, every attempt to inflate them and their achievements failed.

A band of saturated summer air collects around my neck, and I swipe at sweat percolating under my collar. It's too early in the season for the heat to be this bad. But maybe it has more to do with the whispers floating through the cemetery air.

"How could this happen?"

"Such an awful way to die."

"In the prime of life."

These and every other variation of whys and hows and what-nows fly in from all directions. Everyone agrees that this is just a bad dream. A person like *that* didn't deserve an end like *this*.

If only they knew.

I adjust my shades and turn away from the collective in a futile attempt to block it all out: the voices, but even more, the visions that pour through my head and thunder inside my chest.

No one will ever know what really happened or why.

Except for me.

Except for us.

one
sophia

Two Stars. This book was obviously written by an alcoholic.
  -Goodreads Reviewer

The first thing Sophia did when she arrived at the Lake George house was always the same: check the recycling bin. If she was lucky, the previous renters left something good behind. Once she had uncovered an empty fifteen-year-old single malt scotch. Members of her MFA cohort—she wouldn't call them friends—were her guests that weekend, and they'd been pathetically impressed. Snobs, all of them, yet none of them could tell the difference between "aged in an oak barrel" and "refilled with discount scotch found on the bottom shelf of a convenience store."

She didn't need to pull the same sort of tricks on her visitors this weekend. They were her friends, her soulmates, the writers down in the trenches with her. They wouldn't care how much she spent—or didn't spend—on alcohol for their writing retreat weekends. Still, though, she couldn't help it. That illusion of money, of having it all together, was important to maintain, even in front of people who not only knew it to be a lie but would never call her out on it. They kept each other's secrets.

The recycling bin yielded a treasure: four empty French wine bottles. This would be perfect; one box of cheap red blend would fill them, and they could all pretend together. Talia would post a picture of the bottle on Instagram, with her bare feet close by. That was another thing they pretended about, that Talia had always been a foot model for shoe companies and jewelers specializing in toe rings and not that she used to sell images and toe-licking access to creepy men with money and a fetish. Her perfect, dainty feet paid the rent, and that was all that mattered.

Sophia took the bottles inside to rinse them in the kitchen sink before doing a quick walk-through of the house, making sure it was clean and in good shape. She only got to stay in her own house twice per year: once at the end of winter, once at the end of summer. The offseasons. She couldn't afford it otherwise, forgoing the rental income she depended upon. Someday, her career would take off, but for now, this was all she had.

There were some smudges on one window, and when she counted the wineglasses in the cabinet, three were missing. Not bad. This was far better than the time half the dinner plates were chipped, and since the pattern was discontinued, she'd had to buy twelve completely new place settings. Grandma, rest her soul, never would have approved of mismatched sets. Too messy and improper. That was Grandma, fussy about appearances.

Grandma would have fussed over the smear on the window, too. In her honor, Sophia ineffectively wiped at it, before realizing it was outside, the imprint of a suicidal bird. She could deal with that later, balancing precariously on a patio chair. Or she could leave it. The fall rains would wash it away soon enough. The feathery marks didn't impede the view. Below her, through the slowly reddening leaves, Lake George glistened blue in all its glory. This was the view she wanted to wake up to every day. When she was a bestseller, she would pretend she lived here year-round. The television interviews would take place here, in front of the two-story picture windows. "The beauty of nature inspires my work," she would say.

Her grandfather had built this house himself, in his optimistic youth, thinking one day he would fill the four bedrooms with family. That's all Grandpa had ever wanted, a large family full of children and laughter. He'd raise them in the city, but their weekends would be spent at the lake house. He'd envisioned big family holidays, constructing the house with room for a twelve-foot-tall Christmas tree, and lining the attic space with bunks for the anticipated grandchildren. As he pounded each nail into place, he'd imagined retiring up here, teaching the grandchildren how to fish.

Unfortunately for Grandpa's dreams, Grandma had only been able to carry one of her seven pregnancies to term, and that child grew up to be a disappointment, lost to addiction and eventual overdose. Only Sophia and her brother made up the grand imagined family, and since neither of them would have children— Sophia due to disinterest, Gage due to lack of opportunity—the line would end. Some future unrelated family would have their joyous holidays here, create their own transgenerational memories. But that was a long time from now. Sophia would keep the house as long as she could afford it. Sometime—soon, hopefully —when Sophia was famous, she'd use the property to host writing retreats. Not like the ones she currently hosted, when her friends and their laptops would arrive, and they'd spend the days writing and the nights drinking. No, these would be proper retreats, booked full years in advance, where in the evenings the guests would gather around to listen to Sophia's wisdom and admire her words. She'd sign books for them and thank them for coming, and later she'd see the autographed books selling at a huge markup on eBay, subjected to bidding wars.

Sometimes Sophia feared she was too much like her grandfather, dreaming and setting things in place for a future that would never happen. Somehow, it happened for everyone else. The rest of her MFA cohort had achieved success, even Chadwick, the loser who'd dropped out after a semester and went on to top the *New York Times* list and was currently in talks with George Clooney to star in the movie adaptation of his undeserved bestseller. Chadwick, who made cutting remarks about other people's writing when he was a hack with terrible prose and an inability to use the Oxford comma. His success really just showed how tasteless the publishing industry was, how it depended on luck rather than skill.

She couldn't focus on that. This weekend wasn't about failures and jealousy. This weekend was about friendship, writing, and encouragement. Hadn't it been wonderful three years ago, celebrating Chelsea? They'd all read her Publishers Marketplace announcement so many times they'd committed it to memory, and Max turned it into a song. At the time, they were all heady with excitement. Chelsea was just the first. Success was coming for all of them—they could feel it. The air vibrated with potential. Sophia, obviously, would be next, selling a three-book deal to a Big Five. Then Talia, then finally Max, and with each one, they'd drink and dance and cry together. They would toast their wins with expensive alcohol, not the faux stuff that Sophia created with a funnel and a search of the liquor store sale rack.

Those celebrations hadn't happened yet, and they were all starting to think they never would. The year after Chelsea's big break, their gathering was mournful and angry. They all felt Chelsea's loss as keenly as if it had been their own. They'd never hold Chelsea's book and tell people they knew her way back when. Misogyny and manipulations had taken it away from all of them.

The Lakeview Market hadn't changed since her childhood. Even the proprietor, Mrs. Cooper, had been behind the counter since Sophia's grandfather's days, though her last name had changed four times in the intervening years, and she'd always made a point that one of those times it should have been Aldren. Grandma hadn't been too happy about that implication. Mrs. Cooper—at the time, Miss Harlowe—dated Grandpa first, and in fact, her initials were the ones carved in the lake house foundation. If Grandma hadn't taken a summer job waitressing at the café and stolen Grandpa's heart, he would have had a decidedly different life. Judging from Mrs. Cooper's fecundity, he may have been able to fill the rooms of the lake house the way he'd dreamed.

Despite the animosity between the elderly romantic rivals, Mrs. Cooper had always been friendly to Sophia and to her brother. She'd slipped them free lollipops when they were young and looked the other way when teenage Gage shoplifted a six-pack of beer, though she did bust him when he tried to steal a pack of cigars.

"We're always happy to see you come home," Mrs. Cooper said as Sophia set her purchases on the counter. A box of merlot to match the label on the recycled bottles as well as graham crackers and marshmallows for the s'mores to toast over the remains of the rejection letters that they'd burn tonight. She'd brought the rest of the meal prep up from the discount supermarket she always stopped at along the way, but the cheap graham crackers were sold out. Tourist town markups made the food just slightly too expensive here.

"Oh, I know I should come up more often, but I just get so busy," Sophia said. Busy. Yes, that was it, too busy. It wasn't about the money. Not at all. She liked to maintain the illusion that life in Queens was glamorous, filled with bookish events and literary soirées, and not evenings hunched over her laptop holding back tears.

"And how are your books coming along, dear?" Mrs. Cooper asked her usual refrain, not knowing it was a knife to the heart.

Dead in the water. May as well be burned. Not garnering interest.

"I'm querying my fourth novel." That was an answer that impressed non-writers. They didn't have to know that novels one through three—representing years of her life's work—were languishing unsold, from hundreds of rejected queries all with variations on a theme: Lovely, but not marketable. Not commercial enough. Too cerebral for the current publishing environment.

"We all knew you'd succeed. Your grandfather always said so." Mrs. Cooper misinterpreted the vague query info as good news. "And how's Gage? Still in Kansas?"

"He's in Kentucky now, at McCreary." He'd been in Kansas for a couple of years, but when Leavenworth became medium security, he'd been moved. He'd die out there one day, either of old age or with a shank in him. "He's hanging in there. Reading a lot." And writing letters, full of meandering thoughts and grim poetry, but always ending in words of encouragement for his sister.

Mrs. Cooper shook her head and made sympathetic noises. "That poor boy chose the wrong path in life. Not like you." That was a mild way of putting it. Gage had chosen the wrong path, again and again and again. Sophia wondered sometimes if she had, too, though in a less violent way. Perhaps chasing her dream of becoming a published author was detrimental to her happiness. Perhaps she'd be better off in an office job with a steady salary, or really, a job with *any* salary. Living off of vacation rental income while pursuing her dreams had forced her into a frugal and precarious existence.

"Yes, well, I should be going. I've got guests coming." This conversation was veering into the personal, and Sophia never liked that. She would not gossip to Mrs. Cooper about her brother. It had been bad enough when the trial was going on and her brief visits to the lake house meant dodging questions about evidence and testimony and why he should have pled guilty or whether the detectives had it out for him.

"Your writer friends?" Mrs. Cooper's lip curled in disgust. "Tell that foul-mouthed one she's still banned from my store."

It didn't take long to refill the wine bottles, and just as she finished, Sophia heard the familiar rattling of Max's ancient Mazda making its painful way up the gravel driveway. That was another reason they couldn't come in winter—none of them had vehicles that could survive the journey. Chelsea had planned to purchase a 4WD SUV with her royalties, but those checks never came.

Finally. Sometimes she felt a little silly about how excited she was for these retreats. Kind of pathetic, really, that these three women, her fellow failures, were also her only true friends. Ever since they found each other at that writing workshop seven years ago, where all of their work shone brightly in a sea of pedantic overwrought crap, they'd been tight. All talented, all misunderstood, all rejected by everyone but each other. Someday, though, they'd show the world. They'd have their breakthrough. Future bestsellers, every single one of them.

Sophia took up her grandmother's traditional pose at the door, a gracious hostess welcoming her guests. "Come in, welcome," she called out.

"Outlet, I need an outlet now." Chelsea shoved past her in the doorway, rushing to the dining room, laptop in hand. She didn't even pause to take off her shoes, despite the small sign pleading that she do so.

"Good to see you, too," Sophia snapped, then took a deep breath to calm herself. No need to start the weekend off on a sour note. *Gracious hostess: has it all together. Welcoming. Friendly. Hold the illusion.*

"She's on a deadline," Talia explained, almost apologetically. Talia was too nice, constantly apologizing for everything. She, at least, remembered to take her shoes off, so Sophia wouldn't have to vacuum gravel and dirt out of the carpet later. Underneath her oversized boots, Talia wore thick socks, and Sophia knew that under those was a layer of lotion. Talia's foot care routines were time-consuming and legendary, but like she always said, she had to protect her moneymakers.

"Did you work her deadline into your schedule?" Sophia teased.

"No, but we can move around a few things." Talia had the cheerful let's-do-this attitude of a first-time camp counselor, before getting beaten down by whiny campers and administrative bureaucracy. She whipped out a folder from her enormous hand-bag. "First, we're starting off with—"

"A drink," Max finished for her, already sipping from a large to-go cup that smelled suspiciously not like soda. Max was the most intimidating of the four, the most in-your-face. Secretly, Sophia envied Max's brazen fuck-everything attitude. She wished she'd had an iota of Max's confidence as she moved through the world. Instead, she had to rely on her grandma's training, the perfect polite façade coupled with private internal screaming.

"I have wine ready, but it looks like you've already started."

Max raised her plastic 7-Eleven cup in a cheers gesture. "Started in Queens."

"What? You were drinking this whole time? Max!" Talia looked up from perusing her schedule, which was surely thrown off by this revelation. Drinks probably had an appointed time and duration. 5:30-6:00, one glass of wine. 6:00-6:30, second glass of wine.

"You knew," Max replied. Her eyes were only faintly red. She was the Ernest Hemingway of the group, maintaining a constant level of alcohol in her bloodstream.

"You shouldn't drink and drive," Sophia chastised gently. It didn't matter what she said. Max wouldn't listen. She never listened to anyone.

two
talia

Have you ever read "The Emperor's New Clothes?" This book is the emperor, and I'm telling you it has no clothes. The first two chapters aren't bad, but the excessive narration is a tangled web of confusion. I have a PhD in Calligraphic Arts. I know bad writing when I see it.

-Professor Sue

"Okay, writers, let's get started!" Talia clapped her hands twice, a sign for everyone to pay attention. They'd just finished dinner, a delicious salad Sophia had made. "It's time for the annual burning of the letters. I hope you all printed out your most heinous rejections."

"Your Girl-Scout-leader act is enough to make me throw up," Max said.

"Let her have her fun, Max. This is Talia's big event," Chelsea defended her.

"Exactly." Talia did love this moment. She'd been planning it for weeks. "This is our weekend kickoff event, my favorite part— build the fire, burn the letters, toast the marshmallows, make the s'mores. I bought everyone their favorite chocolate from Trader Joe's."

Talia grinned as if chocolate bars were the greatest of gifts. All she wanted was to please her friends. The women who, despite their personality flaws and periodic nastiness, meant everything to her. The only ones who truly understood her—her writing, her disappointments, her failures.

"I have mine." Sophia raised a black three-ring binder. She always printed her letters out as they arrived and filed them chronologically.

"Good girl!" Talia applauded her friend's organization.

"Mine are here." Chelsea pulled a stack out of her tired army green messenger bag, the same bag she had on her shoulder when they all first met.

"Max," Talia said firmly. "I hope you didn't forget yours this year. And don't tell us you didn't get any because I know you did." She tried to pinch Max's cheeks, but Max slapped her hands away.

"Your cheerfulness is really getting me down. You might enjoy this ritual, but it just makes me mad all over again." Max retrieved a few crumpled pieces of paper from her backpack.

"It's cathartic," Sophia said. "And if anyone needs to let go of some pent-up tension, Max, it's you."

As they filed outside to the patio, Max nudged Talia and gestured toward Sophia. "That's what happens when you're a thirty-six-year-old woman who hasn't had sex in, I don't know—ever."

Talia pulled away. While she didn't mind Max's gleeful descriptions of her own escapades, there was something tasteless about discussing Sophia's sex life, especially since she guarded her privacy. Fictional sex was an entirely different thing. Talia could write sex scenes with the best of them, although she avoided erotica, thinking it a prurient shortcut for writers who couldn't attract readers with decent, well-written stories. Though, "mommy-porn" had earned some authors big money in recent years.

In Talia's estimation, her own sex life had been robust. Men, most of whom she rejected, gravitated to her as if mating hormones leached from her pores. Maybe her body produced some strange come-hither scent.

In childhood, Talia held onto her baby fat as if famine were a constant threat. Her overbearing Jewish mother (who carried a food scale in her purse) put her on a crash diet six months before her bat mitzvah. "No daughter of mine is going to stand on the bimah and read from the Torah with the entire congregation whispering, 'Shame, such a pretty face.'"

By thirteen, her body had transformed. By sixteen, she was modeling for catalogs. By eighteen, she had signed a lucrative modeling contract. By twenty, she had an eating disorder. By twenty-two, she was fat again. And then, "Tsk-tsk-tsk, such a pretty face" followed her like an annoying fly.

The girls formed a circle on the deck to begin Talia's favorite activity. Sophia turned the gas knob to the right, and a low whistle sounded. "Look out!" She dropped a lit match into the fake rock fire pit.

They all jumped back as the flame ignited with impatient fury. A few years earlier, the house nearly caught fire when Talia insisted she knew how to build a campfire out of logs and kindling and "just a squirt" of lighter fluid. The following year, Sophia bought the gas pit from Costco and banned Talia from touching matches.

"Let the burning begin!" Talia said as they seated themselves in wicker chairs. "I'll go first." She withdrew one page from her red plastic file folder and cleared her throat. "'Dear Ms. Goldstein, We are unable to accept your work at this time. As a side note, please consider rewriting your query letter before submitting to other agents. You come across as desperate and needy.'"

"He critiqued your query? What a motherfucking asshole!" Max shouted the refrain that always accompanied the rejections.

Talia pushed a fist into the air and dropped her rejection letter into the fire. "Take that, motherfuckers!"

"Oh, my god," Chelsea said. "Our sweet girl is using the F-word."

"Only on occasion," Talia said, staring at the ashes and sparks floating upwards. "As any good writer knows, profanity loses its impact when it's overused."

"She's right about that," Sophia piped up.

Meeting each other's eyes, Talia and Sophia nodded in agreement and then turned to Max with emphasis.

"You think I overuse the F-word?" Max sat straight as a plank. "Well, then, fuck you!"

They dissolved into laughter.

Sophia stood. "Okay, my turn. You're going to love this one. 'Dear Sophia, Thank you for your interest in our Writer in Residence program, located in the beautiful Canadian Rockies. Our program is limited to authors who have previously achieved some modicum of success. According to our algorithms, you have not. Feel free to reapply in two years' time.'"

"Motherfucking assholes!" Max shouted again, waving her flask and spilling vodka. "Don't they know you have an MFA? I mean, doesn't that already qualify you as having achieved success?"

Chelsea choked on a rare laugh. "An MFA doesn't mean shit."

"Yes, it does," Sophia argued. "I worked my ass off for that degree."

"Oh, please." Chelsea ripped open the marshmallow bag and popped one into her mouth.

"No!" Talia grabbed the bag and twisted it shut. "No marshmallows until we finish our letters."

Chelsea snatched back the bag and tossed marshmallows at Sophia and Max.

"Okay, fine," Talia said, giving in to their teasing. "Can we please continue now?"

"I'll go." Chelsea smoothed a crumpled sheet of paper. "'Thank you for giving me the opportunity to consider your work. While I thought your angle was intriguing at first, upon further reading, I found it too unoriginal. I'm looking for a unique and fresh voice. Of course, writing is very subjective, and I'll be cheering your future proposals on with gusto! Don't stop writing.'"

Talia cocked her head. "That's weird. Didn't your letter last year also reference unoriginality?"

Chelsea balked. "I don't remember. I burned it."

Talia had an uncanny memory for such things. "If it did, it's probably a coincidence. And it makes no sense. Your writing is the most original I've ever read. Alright Maxi, your turn."

Max always went last because she received the best rejections.

"'This is a doozy." Max read with a squeaky, cartoonish voice: "'Dear Ms. DeLeon, I'm sorry it has taken us over a year to get back to you. Unfortunately, the agent who had requested a full manuscript from you has passed away. I've shown your query and sample pages to our other agents, but unfortunately, none has expressed interest. Best of luck, Joyce Vandever, administrative assistant.'"

Max spit into the fire. "*Unfortunately*, Joyce Vandever, FUCK YOU!" She laughed and howled at the moon.

Talia prepared her squeamish ears for the closing ceremony, hoping there were no families or children within hearing distance.

"Writers rise!" Max shouted and lifted her arms like the rabbi at Yom Kippur. "Prepare to place all remaining sacrificial letters upon the flames!"

It was serious business, a cleansing, a catharsis, a twisted and ridiculous way of trying to control one's fate in an industry that worshipped the almighty dollar at the expense of creativity.

In one clean motion, they simultaneously ignited one corner of their papers, allowed them to burn until the flames licked their fingertips, then dropped them into the pit. They watched with hypnotized focus as the remaining shreds curled and fell into the crevices between the cement logs.

"MOTHERFUCKING ASSHOLES on three," Max said. "One, two, three!"

Four shouts of "motherfucking assholes" echoed. Even Talia hollered at the top of her lungs. She exhaled a huge breath and fell back into her chair, ready to comfort herself with sweets. "And now we toast with flaming marshmallows!"

Max raised her flask. "And vodka."

They settled in and concocted their s'mores. Talia tore open two sleeves of crisp graham crackers. She toasted her marshmallow with extreme patience, taking extra time to make sure it would be soft and creamy all the way through.

Max stuck her skewer directly into the flames and allowed her marshmallow to catch fire. She raised it like a burning torch. "I will lead the way out of darkness!"

Chelsea, who barely toasted hers before squishing it between two graham crackers, snorted. "Yeah, just what we need. A drunken leader with a superiority complex."

"Please don't bicker," Talia said, passing out the carefully selected candy bars. Dark chocolate for Sophia, salted caramel for Chelsea, hazelnut for Max, and pure milk for herself. "This is bonding time. And we're supposed to uplift each other."

In addition to repression, uplifting her friends was her other happy place.

"Okay, Miss Sunshine," Max said. "What good news do you have to brighten our dreary dispositions?"

"My little sister's getting married."

Rumblings of disgust and "that sucks" made her feel somewhat better.

"Oh, wait!" Chelsea grabbed Talia's hand. "I saw your feet in an ad for toe rings on my Instagram feed."

Sophia chortled. "You've gone from 'such a pretty face' to 'such a pretty foot,' huh?"

Talia's friends laughed. She joined in.

"It pays the bills, at least. The funny thing is, ever since I gained weight, my feet are even more plump and pretty. They're really in demand."

Max's lips curled into a snarl. "That is so sexist."

"Not really," Talia said, licking a sticky chocolate-marsh-mallow spot off her thumb. "Feet with a little extra padding have smoother skin and usually better-shaped toes. Besides, I'm blessed with an Egyptian foot. Perfect symmetry and a slanted toe line. Although, I might be prone to bunions later on, and if that—"

"Enough about your fucking feet!" Max ate a burnt marsh-mallow, dusting her face with gray ash. "I have shitty news. Remember that disgusting pig, Alec?"

"That lawyer who had a crush on Talia?" Chelsea asked.

"That's the one," Max said, giving Talia a knowing wink.

"Alec Pendergrass did not have a crush on me." Talia recoiled, hoping her friends couldn't see her blush. "Well, he sends me 'U up?' texts on occasion, but I never reply."

"Too bad," Max said. "I heard he just signed with a huge agency."

"You're kidding." Sophia gripped the arms of her chair. "He writes nothing but implausible, overwrought legal thrillers. And they're awful. I had to critique his pages once, and I swear I could not find one positive thing to say."

Chelsea groaned. "And there you have it. That idiot gets an agent, and we get nothing but rejections."

"It's going to work out for all of us one day," Talia said, directing the conversation away from Alec. "I just know it."

"Fuck you, Mary Sunshine."

Talia's eyes burned. She loved Max but hated the way she tried to tamp down her optimism for all of them. "Yeah, well, fuck you, too, Mean-Max!"

"Mean-Max?" She spit crumbs of graham crackers along with her laugh. "Is that the best you've got?"

"Okay, stop. This is getting us nowhere," Sophia said. "I'm thinking about a change. Maybe we need to leave our chosen genres and try something new."

Talia couldn't imagine any of them writing outside of their chosen genres. Sophia was brilliant and wrote literary master-pieces. Chelsea could spin a psychological thriller that would someday make her the next Gillian Flynn. And Max, well, her words came out like a tidal wave hitting the beach—beautiful and terrifying and ominous all at once.

As for Talia, she loved her own romantic women's fiction. Ideas came to her as if lined up on a conveyor belt. No matter where she went, a person or situation or event stimulated her imagination, giving birth to a new story. All she had to do was plug it into her outline method and let the plot unfold. Easier said than done, of course. But she knew her manuscripts were better than average. And her readers were out there. She just needed to get published to find them.

"No," Chelsea said. "Changing genres won't work. We need to write what we love. Besides, once AI replaces writers, none of this will matter. Creativity and artistry in all forms will be dead."

"Artificial Intelligence? Don't even say that!" Talia refused to consider the idea that a bot could write an email, let alone a novel.

"Yeah," Sophia said. "AI can't create original ideas."

"Neither can Chelsea." Max poked her friend's shoulder. "At least not according to that extremely well-written rejection letter."

Chelsea chucked a marshmallow at Max.

"Here's what really bugs me," Talia said. "Agents say they want originality, but most of what's published is just tried-and-true reruns of something that's already out there."

"Exactly." Chelsea ate the last three marshmallows out of the bag. "Why do you think most of the blockbuster movies are sequels? *Star Wars, Jurassic Park, Harry Potter*. Once something proves to be a money-maker, it's wash-rinse-repeat. And hey, who doesn't want to make money?"

"Money is the ultimate validation," Talia said. "Because god knows we don't get validation from our mothers."

Sophia stood and shut off the gas to the firepit. "Enough. Let's go inside and drink more wine."

Talia pushed herself out of the rickety chair, mesmerized by the flames as they flickered and faded away. She hoped tomorrow would bring renewed spirits. After all, it was writing day. If they didn't cheer up and find a little hope, none of them would accomplish anything.

In the kitchen, Talia pulled on yellow rubber gloves and commenced the next exercise—the cleaning of the kitchen.

Chelsea, who refused to clean, opened her laptop.

"I thought you were done with work." Sophia said.

"I am. I wanted to try out AI. I've heard it can create an entire story with only a few parameters."

"Seriously?" Talia asked.

"Let's try it," Max said, leaning over Chelsea's shoulder. "Tell it to write a short story. We each get to put in one instruction."

They huddled over the keyboard as Chelsea typed and spoke. "I'll start us off," she said. "Write a five-thousand-word story with an ambitious hedge fund manager who borrowed millions from his clients and can't pay it back."

"That's not original," Talia said. "It's Bernie Madoff. Oh, how he embarrassed the Jews."

"No, no, we can use it." Sophia stepped in closer. "Add this: one of his clients broke into his house, tied him up, and made him watch as he spray-painted his priceless artwork, including a Picasso."

"A Picasso?" Max said. "Come on!"

"Doesn't matter, keep going." Chelsea looked up at Max. "You go."

"As the client, a fucking lumberjack with broad shoulders and a dick like a—"

"NO!" Talia said. "I will not be party to any kind of erotica."

"Fine," Max said again. "Delete the dick part."

Chelsea backspaced ... click click click.

Max began again. "As the client, who looked like a lumberjack," she paused and flicked the edge of Talia's ear. "Okay with you, Miss Prissy?"

"Yes. Good."

Grinning, Max continued her directive. "... sliced the paintings with a box cutter, a vicious dog the size of a cow tore through the house—"

"My turn!" Talia shoved everyone out of the way. "The lumberjack-turned-vandal spun around, in fear for his life. But to his amazement, the dog knocked him down and slurped kisses all over his face. It was the dog he lost two years earlier that he believed had been snatched. 'You stole my money and my sweet Twinky?' Lumberjack guy said. 'Shame on you!'"

"Shame on you?" Max groaned. "I'm gonna barf."

Chelsea finished. "The lumberjack took his dog and left the hedge manager strapped to the chair, hoping he'd starve to death." She pressed "enter."

They watched, eyes wide, as AI spun their hideous ideas into a story. It flowed. It had pacing, decent dialogue, intrigue. Its punctuation was impeccable.

"Holy shit," Max said.

Within minutes, to Talia's horror, a robot had written a work of fiction that did not suck.

three
max

Five stars. Oh my god, this book was incredible. I feel seen for the first time. I so identified with the main character. She is complex and beautiful and damaged and her storyline is unforgettable. Really, she is every woman.

-readingforwomen

Max moved away from the circle of women to get a better look at them. She rarely harbored positive feelings for other people. They often repelled her. Their imperfections and hypocrisy reeked like sweat trickling from their pores. The smell of it made her nauseous.

But these women—Sophia and Chelsea and Talia—they didn't have that stink. They smelled of struggle and hope intermingled. They hungered for the same thing: to write out of passion, out of love for books and words that flowed from their tongues like perfect songs. They were just like her. Talented writers, powerful storytellers, their words buried in manuscripts that got no recognition from traditional publishers.

"It's just not fair," she whispered, not realizing the phrase came out of her mouth until they all turned away from the computer screen and tossed her a quizzical glance, their eyes still dancing with joy and drink, lightheaded, lighthearted as they took turns typing more directions into the AI machine to see what it could do.

"Sorry," Max mumbled. "Just thinking out loud." She emptied the remaining drops of Sophia's red wine into her glass and gulped it without savoring its taste. She opened another bottle and filled their glasses, a chorus of "thanks" absentmindedly reaching her ears as they continued to laugh and add more twists and turns to the story that had no end.

Dangling the wine stem between her fingers, she smiled at her friends. She didn't have many of those. The only people who came in and out of her life were men she picked up at a bar whenever she had that empty feeling she didn't know how to fill with any sort of permanence. Sometimes the men were younger, sometimes older, but always they were strangers. She drank with them until her defenses and self-loathing were at bay, until her limbs felt light and unencumbered by the weight of her pain, and she offered them her bed.

Sometimes she knew their names. Sometimes she didn't. What did it matter? They were just men, and in the end, after a night of lying beneath them, they still didn't see her. They didn't love her. They didn't know her. And every single one of them failed to fill her, to satisfy her in the way she needed—whatever way that was.

After all these years, she still didn't know what she needed. She only knew what she wanted. To be a goddamn writer. A full-time writer, not a freelancer who had to pitch a hundred ideas a week just to get one piece that paid less than three hundred dollars. Not even her evening job teaching creative writing classes at the community college in Brooklyn added enough to pay her bills. She was in debt, living in a crappy one-bedroom apartment in Queens, German roaches crawling out of her air vents, and water stains seeping from her ceiling like a slow, cancerous tumor.

None of it mattered. Only her writing meant anything to her. Max was a writer even if the traditional publishing industry did not consider her one. She spent hours writing, pitching, and querying agents who said "no thanks" in form emails they sent to everyone. The least they could do was personalize their rejections. But they didn't care. So neither would she. Fuck them. Mother-fuckers.

She didn't need them. They could keep their Britney Spears and Michelle Obama and Prince Harry of Sussex, those celebrity posers who didn't even pen their own memoirs. They had ghost-writers. The so-called celebrity authors didn't know how to craft a story, structure a memoir, or develop a voice. This was Max's genre. It was a hard one to write and sell. You had to be introspec-tive. To dig deep into your soul and expose the rough and silent bones of your life without fear or shame.

Max snickered at the thought of ghostwriters being hired to write celebrity memoirs. She looked at Chelsea and wondered if she had penned any of those stories. The nondisclosure agree-ments she signed when hired for the jobs prevented her from telling her friends, but Max hoped that someday with enough cajoling—and alcohol—Chelsea would eventually break.

Of the four of them, Chelsea was the coolest. Not cold. Just cool. She had been touched by masculine control and manipula-tion, and she buried any warmth she had been born with deep in her veins, hiding it there in case another bastard came along to rip more hope out of her. Chelsea didn't offer a lot of information, not since her reputation as a writer had been destroyed when her then husband took her book and sold it as his own.

But one thing about Chelsea, Max nodded as she took another sip of her drink. That girl was a fighter.

Chelsea had been working on that novel when they first met, during the weekend writing workshop seven years earlier. In the women's bathroom. Chelsea was having a hard time pulling the paper towel out of the dispenser, and Max had helped her with it. And that was it. They clicked, walking out of the restroom in peals of laughter, meeting Sophia and Talia at dinner. They were seated together at a round table all the way in the back, like outliers, and since the waiter was meticulous about filling up their glasses with cheap wine, they kept drinking, giggling like school-girls in the back of a church. They were so loud, so obnoxious, that the workshop organizer asked them to keep it down.

"Bitch, please!" Max yelled at his retreating back. If they could not enjoy themselves, be themselves at a writing workshop where they were asked to find their voices and write their truths, then what was the point of it?

Sophia was not a woman Max would ever have sought as a friend, but she was glad the stars and their hopes had brought them together that night. Sophia was lovely and charming, but Max saw beneath her posturing, the alter ego she had constructed to fend off disappointments and rejections. Every time she looked into Sophia's brown eyes, Max was able to reach in and pull out the little girl she found there. Just like the many girls she had discovered in the foster care system. Discarded girls, abused girls. Girls who had to build iron shields around their hearts to protect them when fear, or men, unexpectedly struck with malice.

She knew little of Sophia's background. She was guarded, but Max liked that about her, the way she looked down at everyone, her jaw clenched with pretense, her eyes full of distaste for those she deemed beneath her. Max envied that kind of confidence, that kind of quiet, covert fuck-you attitude that seemed to come so naturally to Sophia. There was no guilt or remorse.

And Sophia was the best struggling writer whose work Max had ever read. Her prose was lyrical, and every word existed to complement the next one. Reading her sentences aloud was like taking a bite of the most perfect dessert. It was filling and fulfilling at the same time. It was downright enviable. After all, Sophia was the only one among them who had her MFA in Creative Writing. And it showed.

All Max knew was that she just had to write. It was what kept her in this life, alive, awake. Otherwise, she would've drowned herself somewhere a long time ago. In a tub. In the fathomless mouth of the sea. In a lake, her pockets filled with jagged rocks weighing her down to the bottom until she breathed her last liquid breath.

But now she had her friends. These women who called her at the lowest moments in her life, just when she had been preparing to swallow a glass of wine and a bottle of pills. It was like they had a sixth sense. On several occasions, they'd brought her *back* from the dark folds of despair that cradled her every few months. Whenever the struggle of living overwhelmed her.

Sophia's lake house was the best place to celebrate their friendship, their writing, and the hopes that the world kept stomping on. There seemed to be a willful disregard for women who fought to tell their stories despite the industry that corrupted writing and discouraged pure talent.

"Fuckers! All of them." Max drew herself out of her thoughts long enough to spit into the sink, a habit she had formed every time the negative thoughts about traditional publishers and agents showed up in her mind.

"Those motherfuckers!" shouted Talia.

Max smiled when Talia squealed those words, her words.

Talia was perhaps Max's favorite writer-friend. That weekend workshop had marked them as kindred souls. Max felt responsible for her. Talia was naïve, the kind of girl who fended off hardship as if it were an STD she contracted simply by sitting on the toilet seat. But the complexity she discovered in Talia on the night they first met cemented their friendship.

Unable to sleep, Max had gone to the hotel bar to down a few shots. Talia was in one of the corner booths with Alec, a guy from the workshop. Max had detested him from the moment he'd first opened his mouth, bragging about law school and writing thrillers and the success he was on the verge of achieving. He had dark hair, a strong build, and a not-disgusting face, but he was still another fucking pig on the inside.

The way he leered at Talia reminded Max of the rage she felt as a child when her foster dads had given her the same lustful look.

Her heart sank, and the scars on her wrists throbbed with the aching memories of her childhood.

Max wondered at the innocent girl she had just met who couldn't even say "shit" or "fuck" without blushing, yet she allowed this pig to stroke her shoulder and whisper what Max imagined were acrid words into Talia's ear. Did she lack the ability to see through this guy's bullshit?

She nursed her drink and kept a low profile, her eyes and limbs aware of every movement Talia and Alec made. She felt her bones grinding with irritation when she caught his fingers sliding up Talia's arm. His lips drawing closer to Talia's ear. His tongue lapping at the lobe.

Max couldn't take it anymore. She leapt from the stool and plopped herself down in the booth. "Well, hello, you two."

Talia's plump cheeks turned bright pink. "Max? Um, hi. What are you doing here?"

"Just making sure you want this pig's filthy hands and tongue all over you." She had seen too many girls like Talia reduced to nothing in the wake of a man's selfish desire. Too many souls broken by it.

The asshole withdrew his arm from around Talia's shoulders, boring his gaze into Max in a lame attempt at intimidation. She didn't flinch. He didn't know she wasn't like Talia or most other women. She wouldn't back down and let her new friend fall victim to his drool and false promises.

He reached into his jacket pocket and took out a billfold. "Such a shame, Talia. We were in for a good time. Let's try to meet up again, someplace more private for our ... session." He dropped a twenty on the table and slid out of the narrow booth.

"What the fuck was he talking about?" Max crumpled the twenty-dollar bill. "And twenty bucks? Barely enough for one drink. Fucking asshole."

"Would you be quiet, please?" Talia said. "And don't take this the wrong way, but I just met you. We hardly know each other."

Max's shoulders sank with the realization that Talia was right. They had just met. They didn't know each other.

"I'm sorry. Maybe you know what you're doing. When I saw him plying you with drinks, touching you, it triggered me. I've known guys like that my whole life, and I guess I thought you were in danger. But that's just me. My shit. I misread the situation."

Talia sighed. "I appreciate that you wanted to protect me. But I'm fine."

Max sat back. "It didn't look that way. Aren't you afraid to be alone with a dirtbag like him?"

"Alec? He's harmless, like all the others I've connected with." Talia tucked her head low, the way a turtle withdraws into its shell. For protection. "It's—it's sort of a side hustle."

"A side hustle? You mean for money?"

Talia leaned in closer. "A long time ago, I was a fashion model, but I gained weight, and that was the end of that. Then one of my modeling friends told me about men who have foot fetishes. And my plump, perfect feet could be a hot commodity. You'd be surprised how much men pay to lick honey or chocolate or peanut butter off women's toes."

Max knocked back what was left of her vodka. "That asshole was going to pay you to lick your feet?" She couldn't understand how Talia, this sweet, unassuming girl, could have such deep, dark layers. Everything to Max was black or white. Everyone was good or bad. There was no murky middle.

"A hundred bucks."

"Fuck me," Max said. A million warnings pulsed through her head. She wanted to argue, explain the dangers Talia could be inviting, but she bit her tongue, not wanting to embarrass the young woman sitting across from her. The shame was already embedded in her features, in the pink hues of her flushed cheeks.

"Anyway," Talia cleared her throat and perked up. "I need a good friend ten times more than a hundred bucks. And I think you will be the one. I'm sure of it."

Max smiled, intrigued by her new friend. In that moment, she knew she would need to keep an eye on her, protect her. She didn't want Talia to experience any of the things she had when her own innocence had been snuffed out of her. She didn't want the sweetness in Talia's character, even the gullibility, to be replaced by bitterness and self-loathing, the way hers had been.

Max shook away the images of the past, peeled herself away from the dark thoughts, and forced herself to stay in the present, back in Sophia's kitchen, her friends giggling, still bent over the laptop.

Looking over at them, she saw raw talent, wondering how all those agents and editors failed to see them, their skill, the light and power they brought into the literary world through the stories they told.

The publishing industry was just like the foster care system that took in kids, one after the other, and didn't give a shit what happened to them. There were abuses and rapes and bullying that made children tougher than they needed to be, while foster parents pretended to be good citizens giving back to society, the needy, all the while collecting the cash and going out to the bars. They exploited children's pain and losses for a dime, in the same way the publishing industry exploited writers for the tears and pain of crafting new texts, creating vast interior lives and complex characters one could only imagine.

It was a bankrupt system that abandoned its wards, like Max, who tried to flee life every few months. And like Chelsea, whose work was stolen by a man who said he loved her, the editors likening her to a charlatan, a plagiarist, while taking his word over hers. And like Sophia, who spent hours and years doing everything she was supposed to be doing, getting an MFA, attending writing retreats, networking with teachers for support, and editing journals, all for nothing. And Talia, a romance writer who lived in sweet small-town stories but used to sell her feet for male pleasure because writing didn't make her any money.

It was all a scam, and Max was drunk with vengeance. She

wanted to expose this industry that made her feel just as poor, just as dejected, just as invisible as the foster parents had made her feel as a child.

Here with her friends, her comrades, forged into writers by the fires of rejection letters and desperate persistence, she felt a surge of power blossom in her chest, pulling itself out of her throat to form words of resistance.

She inched closer and placed her arm around Talia's rounded shoulders. "Let's see how good AI really is."

four
chelsea

Jesus Christ, this book is depressing. The characters are stupid and keep trying even when the hits keep coming. If you aren't a raging alcoholic by the end of this book, you aren't doing it right. Five stars.
  –Goodreads Goddess

The sliver of light slipping between the blinds roused Chelsea from an alcohol-infused sleep, one that she planned to remain in because she never got to stay in bed these days. There were always deadlines. Research to sort through. Clients to appease. But not this weekend. After she hit "send" on her assignment the night before, she was free. She sighed and sank back down into the folds of the bed, the weight of demand lifting.

And then came the humming. "You Are My Sunshine" interspersed with the clanking of metal, the smacking of wood, and the screech of drawers all reverberated through Chelsea's hungover head. Sure, the lake house was the perfect respite from her dingy Newark apartment, but it also came with a huge downside—Talia.

Not because her friend was bad. She was far from it. Chelsea admired the way Talia moved through life. Positive, with a bright takeaway in the face of abject darkness. Even her foot modeling, as weird as *that* was, didn't tarnish Talia's shiny view of the world.

No, the worst part about Talia was how fucking cheerful she was in the morning.

Chelsea huffed and hurled the covers away. Hell-bent on putting an end to the noise, she flung the door open, squinting against the light.

"A-ha! I knew this would get you up." Talia beamed, stopping her with a bright smile and an outstretched cup of coffee with the just-right shade of cream swirled in.

Fine. So the worst thing about Talia also came with an upside. Chelsea accepted the peace offering.

"She's like the damn Pied Piper," Max said from just beyond her, a bottle of Bailey's lifted. "Want a hit?"

"Why the hell not?" she said, holding her cup out for Max to flavor.

"Hey, careful. Don't drink too much," Talia scolded in her melodious way. "We have a full day of writing ahead."

Writing. That's what they were here to do. Right. Chelsea sipped her coffee and swallowed the dread. A flash of them all hovering around her laptop last night prompted her to cast an uneasy glance around the kitchen.

"Anyone seen my laptop?"

Sophia's slick ponytail swiveled toward the living room. "It's probably out there somewhere."

Chelsea high-stepped her way between the minefield of blankets and pillows they'd abandoned. When she spotted the dead laptop open under the coffee table, a quick wave of panic rushed up about what her friends might have seen in their drunken writing orgy. She brushed the thoughts away and plugged it in.

One teeny tiny thing her friends didn't know was that Chelsea hadn't written a word for herself in over two years. The rejection letters she burned last night were recycled from previous years before the words—the magic—fell silent in the aftermath of humiliation at the hands of her ex-husband.

Fucking Rick. God, if Chelsea could go back, remove the blinders from her younger self, shake her, and tell her to listen to her gut and run the hell away from the narcissistic bastard, she would. He was incapable of validating her, of seeing her. Of making her feel like she was enough just the way she was.

She had never been enough. Had never reached her "true potential" in the eyes of any number of teachers, therapists, and certainly not her parents. Only here in the safety of this group did Chelsea feel like she could let go of all those unmet expectations long enough to be herself and breathe.

So why hadn't she told them she hadn't written? Why was she pretending? If anybody would understand, these three would.

Chelsea pondered this as she dressed for the day. Her friends would hold her up, empathize, do what they did for each other. But that was exactly why she didn't say a word. She was sick of needing so much from them.

She returned to the kitchen for the Talia-allotted thirty minutes for breakfast, a board of fruit, muffins, and cheese. "A charcuterie of writing fuel," Sophia proclaimed as she adjusted the cardigan strapped over her silky tank and jeans. Both she and Talia dressed like they were on their way to an author's talk. Chelsea and Max shared the same view of writing clothes—soft oversized shirts and comfy joggers.

Between bites, they talked like they hadn't spent a night catching up. Theirs was a comradery Chelsea hadn't experienced before. They were a far cry from her med school peers, everyone in it for themselves. The fake friendships and hookups to gain an advantage over one another. That entire scene disgusted Chelsea in a way no disease-ridden cadaver ever had.

She had hated med school and didn't know what she was going to do about it. Until the night she passed by that flyer about a short story contest. She went back to her apartment, and instead of studying anatomy until four in the morning, she drafted a thousand-word story all about a med school student who murdered her nemesis and got away with it.

It won the contest and the three-hundred-dollar prize attached. It couldn't pay for a single textbook, but it was enough to slam the door on med school. She found her voice and true calling. And while writing came easily to Chelsea, telling her parents did not. Their reaction was visceral and swift. They screamed about how useless and worthless writing was. How humiliating her decision was for them. It confirmed what Chelsea always suspected: what she wanted or felt or needed didn't matter. She had always been the invisible child, and she always would be.

Chelsea spent seven years developing those thousand words into eighty-five thousand, a debut novel she'd entitled, *The Secrets We Keep*. Part thriller, part psychological suspense, part social commentary about bullying and the lengths some entitled brats went to in higher ed. The manuscript was snatched up by an agent and editor within months of her first query. It was a dream come true ... until a single phone call turned it into a nightmare. Her editor and agent confirmed that they'd received credible information about a movie well into production with the same title and plot. She would find out later that her estranged husband, Rick, had stolen it before they split and passed it to his mistress—a twenty-two-year-old model Chelsea didn't know existed until that moment—whose dad owned the production company. It broke Chelsea and triggered a financial tsunami that swallowed her whole, one that she was still fighting to get out from under.

When she'd walked away from medical school, she had to pay back every scholarship and grant. Her parents could have written the check. It was a fraction of what they made in a year, pennies compared to the millions in their portfolio. But as a last act of teaching her a lesson, they cut her off and removed her name from the family trust she would have been entitled to on her thirtieth birthday.

Heap onto that the hundred-and-fifty-thousand-dollar advance she had to repay. The one that Rick was thrilled to spend in the months before he left her. All while hiding studio money from the same story—*her* story—whose eventual box office success turned into a three-picture deal for him after the divorce. His success left her far worse than broke. It blackballed Chelsea from every publisher in the world.

Talia's alarm chimed, and the four friends moved into the living room, assuming the same writing positions they occupied every year. Sophia on the loveseat, Talia on the recliner, Max on one end of the couch, and Chelsea on the other. She picked up her laptop, the weight inconsequential, the burden anything but.

Chelsea wanted the magic to return so she could repay her friends. They had rallied around her when everyone else turned their backs. And unlike the rest of the world, they believed in her. She owed it to them to do something so big that they would all come away with so much more than the breadcrumbs they shared now.

She wiped the past away and turned toward the screen as it flickered to life with some sort of document that wasn't any program or writing she recognized. Chelsea opened her mouth to ask if anyone had used her laptop to work on something, but then the memory of their drunken AI experiment clamped it shut.

She moved her cursor to the corner X when something caught her eye. Five minutes later, she was still reading, disbelief rattling around in her head. This AI program had written an entire book. Impossible, and yet, there it was. Before she could figure out what she had here, she needed to save it.

"After what Sophia suggested last night, I'm thinking about dipping a toe into another genre," Talia announced. She shifted in the recliner and adjusted her lap desk.

"As opposed to chocolate?" Sophia said, eliciting a snort from Max.

"Erotica?" Chelsea asked, juggling the conversation with copying the text into Word.

Talia's complexion deepened to match the apple pattern dotting the upholstery. "You know I couldn't do that." She cast a look over her shoulder like someone else might be listening. "I draw the line at writing porn."

"It's not porn if it's written well enough," Sophia said.

"Whoa," Max said, nudging her laptop to the side to lean forward. "They taught you how to write sex in MFA school?"

Sophia appeared unbothered, as Sophia usually did. "I can write a sex scene."

"Behind the door doesn't count," Talia shot back. "And how does one write sex in literary fiction?"

This set off a diversion where they all took turns tossing out what might be literary ways to describe sex, things like pulsating tumescence, unmerciful male machine, flesh flaming fellatio, a cunnilingus cornucopia, a welcomed intrusion. A side quest that only ended when Sophia flung a pillow at Max.

"As I was saying," Talia continued as if their commentary had never happened. "The market is kind of saturated with lumberjack romance right now, but you know what's hot?"

"Literary porn?" Max snickered.

Talia continued again, unfazed. "Sasquatch romance."

The room fell silent until Chelsea made the mistake of glancing at Sophia, her face scrunched half in disbelief, half in disgust. It was the same what-the-actual-fuck look they shared across the table at the writing workshop after one of the men read a portion of his chapter where he described a woman's breasts as "bobbing boobies." But now, unlike then, Chelsea couldn't contain herself and burst out laughing, triggering a chain reaction of guffaws throughout the room.

"Is that actually a thing?" Max heaved out between breaths.

"Apparently." Talia shrugged.

"Like people," Sophia started, revulsion dripping from her voice, "want to read about sex—"

"With Bigfoot?" Chelsea finished as Sophia devolved into another fit of laughter.

"I know it sounds ridiculous. But it's a thing, I swear. And, at this point, I'll write anything that might sell. Almost anything."

Talia raised her hands in defense, and the conversation continued a little longer until Chelsea noticed the AI text was copied and saved. She considered sharing her discovery, but it would only serve to further the procrastination the writers in the room were happy to partake in.

"Let's just get back to work before this block of time is over. We will *not* continue this discussion later." Talia reset herself on the recliner, and they resumed their respective writer poses without another word.

Chelsea started at the beginning of the book. It wouldn't take long to read through it. Thanks to the speed-reading she'd mastered in med school, she could finish a three-hundred-page book in about two hours. With each page, a new sprig of excitement sprouted from the hollow of her chest. This wasn't fluid given all they shouted into it the night before. Outlandish, sure. They'd been attempting to one-up each other. But it wasn't outright awful.

"Why are you smiling at your computer?" Talia asked.

Chelsea shifted her gaze to Talia. "No reason. Just thinking."

She could tell them all now about what they'd created together, but something told her to wait until she tweaked it, made the voice as unique as their friendship, and shaped it into a real book. She could upload it, slap on a cover, and order a copy for each of them. A hilarious souvenir to commemorate their weekend and their friendship. Something they could laugh about. They all needed more of that.

It wasn't like she was working on anything for herself. And this little jolt of magic buzzing through her head was nice. What could it hurt?

five
talia

The least cohesive novel I've ever read, but something kept me going. A mix of so much nonsense that somehow managed to come together —like a recipe with too many optional ingredients. 3.5 to 4 stars, a solid B-minus.

-Randy-the-reading-machine

Talia had just finished her nighttime ritual of soaking her feet in warm coconut oil, covering them with thick cotton socks, and crawling into bed with her laptop when her cell chimed. She groaned at the caller ID: *Mom cell.* Why did her mother always call at the worst times? It had to be a special skill acquired in Jewish mothering school.

Talia considered not answering. She'd only just returned from the wonderful, productive, self-affirming weekend with her best friends. Couldn't she have one day to revel in the afterglow of their retreat? But if she didn't answer, her mother, who had been texting nonstop all day, would jump to the logical conclusion that there'd been a catastrophic accident and Talia was lying dead in a ditch.

"Hi, Mom." Talia forced a hint of cheerfulness into her tone.

"I've been texting you for hours. It's rude not to respond. What was so important that you couldn't reply to my messages?"

So much for her mother being worried. Riva Goldstein was not exactly a bad mother. Just a cold fish.

"I was in Lake George. My retreat was this weekend."

"Oh, your little writers' meeting, hmm?"

It irked Talia how her mother used a diminutive to describe something so important, so meaningful to her.

"I hate how you refer to it that way, Mom. It's way more than a *little meeting.*" Talia didn't want to have an argument, but her mother was so annoying.

"Don't get all persnickety with me, Talia! You're so reactionary. Why is it that every time we ..."

Talia lowered the volume on her phone so she could barely hear her mother's rant. Besides, she didn't want to disturb her neighbors.

The walls of her studio in Harlem on the Upper West Side were paper-thin. As her mother yelled, Talia gathered her coziest blanket around her neck, one of several ways she soothed herself. Having suffered from anxiety since childhood, she'd decorated her apartment with the aura of a spa. Soft blue paint, fluffy white bedding, an abundance of throw pillows. No clutter. It was one of the few things she could control when the rest of her life was a roller coaster of mental stress.

As for the neighbors, she hardly knew them, except for one thing. Every Wednesday and Saturday like clockwork, at 10:03 p.m., the couple engaged in sexual activity so routine Talia could make the groan-grunt-ugh rhythm right along with them. Then, *oh god, oh god—UHHHH!* Sometimes, if it had been a while, she used her vibrator and joined in the fun. It kind of mortified her, but what the hell? One of the advantages of living alone.

"Are you done, Mom? I need to get to bed. Busy day tomorrow."

"Are you working?"

The disbelief in her mother's voice set off a new annoyance.

"Of course, I am. At the theater box office. You know that. And, um, I picked up some freelance assignments, so yeah. All good. We'll catch up soon." Her finger hovered over the red end-call button.

"Wait! I haven't even gotten to the reason I called in the first place."

Why, oh why, had she answered? "Okay, what is it?"

"Your sister wants you to come wedding dress shopping with us. Isn't that sweet?"

Talia threw an arm over her eyes. The idea of wedding dress shopping was about as appealing as shoveling shit in the camel cage at the Bronx Zoo.

"She's so excited," her mother continued with overblown enthusiasm. "And she definitely wants your opinion on brides-maid dresses. We've already selected a few colors and styles, and you get the deciding vote. You know, try them on and we can see which might be most flattering."

"On my plus-size body. Gotcha."

"Now, Talia, don't be that way. You could be so pretty, and we just want you to look your best."

And not humiliate you with my fat ass.

"And then you'll know where to go in case your dress needs altering."

Talia gritted her teeth at the not-so-subtle hint that it would be dandy if she shed a few pounds before the wedding. If only it were as easy as her mother—a svelte size six—made it sound.

"Sure, Mom. Just let me know when and where. I'll make it work."

"Excellent. I love our mother-daughter outings. And we can talk shower details, too. You'll be giving it, of course, being that you're the maid of honor. Don't worry though, I'll plan it and pay for it. But it'll be your name on the invitation."

Talia's mom was an expert at keeping up appearances, forever putting on display the façade of a perfect family. Riva Goldstein turned herself inside out to show off, to make it known to her many acquaintances that her daughters adored her, her husband was the love of her life, and her home was a bastion of joy. Talia wondered if she'd be living with these falsehoods for the rest of her life.

"Okay, gotta go. Talk soon, love you, bye." She ended the call without waiting for a response.

A moment later, after her ire subsided, loneliness set in like winter snow in Central Park. The end of weekends at the lake with her friends was like the end of summer camp—a letdown. The high she had been on all weekend crashed the moment she arrived home, sort of like drug withdrawal.

Talia padded into the kitchen, a mere three steps from her twin bed, tucked into the corner. The top freezer of her too-small refrigerator was full of single-serving ice cream cups, the kind kids ate at birthday parties. Chocolate, vanilla, and strawberry. She took out one of each flavor and returned to bed. Something about peeling off the top and using the flat wooden spoon soothed her.

While eating ice cream, she read through the story she'd worked on over the weekend. Although the Sasquatch romance genre had real sales potential, she wasn't feeling it.

Small-town, feel-good women's fiction with romantic subplots was her favorite to write, but unoriginal. They all took place in idyllic locations—Nantucket, the Pacific Northwest, California Wine Country, the deep South. She'd never been to any of those places and had no extra money to travel for research, even if such expenses were tax-deductible. Not that she needed to. Creating a fictional small town was one of her writing superpowers. But the truth was, she could never compete with all the *New York Times* bestselling authors whose series were optioned by Netflix and Hallmark the minute they were published.

Talia dragged her wooden spoon over the ice cream, curling it like a ribbon, and set it on her tongue. She continued reading about her new idea.

It had been an epiphany of sorts, inspired by an article about teen depression and social media—how damaging it was to young girls (duh!) who could never live up to the photos their *friends* posted—the beautiful clothes, the perfect bodies, the hunky boyfriends, the weddings in Italy.

Even Talia, at thirty-six, felt the vitriol, the poisonous messages that shouted, "Look at me! My life is great and yours isn't!" Maliciousness dripping from cell phones like blood from the arm of a girl who cut her own skin.

To be clear, Talia was not a cutter. She'd tried it once in high school when someone she knew described it as the most *exquisite* relief to feel physical pain. Talia had to find out for herself. She'd just turned sixteen, and the desperation to maintain her perfect figure was becoming an obsession. One night when her parents were out and her younger sister was in bed, she slipped into the kitchen. With a small paring knife, she made a not-so-shallow cut in the delicate skin on the underside of her left arm. It hurt like hell, and then the blood rose slowly, dark and rich, the color of wine. Exquisite relief, it was not. It was just horrible and messy and stupid. She let the blood flow, waiting for the delicious taste of calm. It never came. The kitchen floor looked like a scene out of a slasher flick.

Returning to her outline, she typed: *Everyone's life is perfect on Instagram.*

Everything staged and choreographed, truth be damned. Blur the lines, fake it 'til you make it, never let them see you sweat. The new concept unfolded in her mind (writing in her head was much easier than actual writing, but that was where all ideas started). A young woman in her twenties, desperate to be the person she's pretending to be online. Then, something happens, not sure what, but the pretense is ripped away, the truth revealed, her life destroyed—until, until what? Talia didn't know yet, but it would come. Just thinking about writing dark truths with painful revelations, brooding secondary characters, and heart-wrenching plot twists boosted her confidence and motivation. She couldn't wait to tell the girls, to let them know she was moving on, trying something new, something that really excited her. Fuck the gatekeepers!

Talia had polished off the vanilla and the strawberry, saving the chocolate for last. But suddenly, she didn't want it. She returned the ice cream cup to the freezer, wiped down the counter, brushed her teeth, and got back in bed.

Exhaustion took over. Calm sleep swept her into its warm embrace. She drifted toward it with a wide yawn as she settled against her pillows and tucked the thick comforter under her chins.

Then—*thump, thump, thump* on the wall.

Groan—grunt—ugh over and over and over.

"What the hell?" she shouted, smacking the wall. "It's Sunday night! There's no fucking on Sunday!"

six
sophia

One star. There were no dragons.

It was bad enough that Sophia was late, breaking her perfect streak of punctuality, but she also forgot her shoes. She'd stopped exactly one block from the restaurant to switch her practical and comfortable commuting sneakers for her I-belong-in-Manhattan knock-off Louboutins, and they weren't there. She dug through her vintage Goyard St. Louis tote, the one she specifically chose to carry, because after lunch with her real friends, she had a happy hour with her MFA cohort, and she needed to impress. *I just love vintage bags, they're so fun to collect*, she always said, pretending she hadn't inherited her grandmother's collection. *Just picked this one up at auction, can you believe it?*

But now she'd have to attend both events in *sneakers*, like she fell off a Midwest church group tour bus, another hick from flyover country come to gawk at the big city. This was her brother's fault. She could picture exactly where she left her shoe bag—on the kitchen table right next to the travel coffee mug that she also forgot. She'd been gathering her things when he called. Gage was the reason she maintained her grandparents' landline, the only place she'd accept collect calls. Well, maybe there was another reason, too. The telemarketers still called for Grandpa, and every time they asked for him, she felt like she wasn't the only one left to treasure his memory.

Gage usually called on a specified schedule, as long as he maintained his phone privileges. Unexpected calls were reserved for when his commissary money was running low, like the time his cellmate destroyed his toiletries—the man actually *ate* Gage's toothpaste and soap—and he wanted a refresher deposit early. This time was different. He wanted a bigger favor.

"You know those true crime books," he said, and her heart dropped. Someone was going to be poking around, telling his life story, spinning it for maximum drama.

"Please don't," she said, fearing the publicity it might bring. They had different last names, and the few articles that mentioned her used her given name, Emma, rather than the middle name she went by, so she had plausible deniability. *Gage? Gage Williams? Yes, we grew up in the same neighborhood, but I hardly knew him.* A novelization of his crimes would surely share too much about their childhood, draw unwanted attention to her. She wanted fame, but she wanted it from her own writing, not her brother's notoriety. Bad enough when crime tourists stopped by to photograph her house, morbid paparazzi who took turns posing in front, even though Gage never—*never!*—harmed anyone there.

"Some podcaster keeps contacting me. He put money in my commissary to try and get me to talk. I've been thinking about it, Sophia. If someone is going to make money off my story, shouldn't it be you? You're a great writer and ..." His voice dropped into a whisper. "You're the only one who would tell it with nuance, you know? You're the only one who knows the other side of me. The real me."

People can be more than one thing, that's what Grandma had said when she explained why she spent her life savings on failed rehab for her daughter. *Your mother*, she'd assured Sophia, *had a loving side, a good side. She wasn't just a junkie.* And that's how

Sophia felt about her brother. He was more than one thing. News articles called him evil, a psychopath. The painful, powerful statements from the victims' families portrayed him as a remorseless monster. And yes, he was those things. But he was also the best big brother. He taught her how to ride a bike, protected her from bullies, had given her a box of chocolates every Valentine's Day and signed it from a secret admirer. He enrolled her in Krav Maga classes and taught her how to keep her drink covered at bars, and he made sure she always had a safe ride home. He read everything she wrote and gave her nothing but encouragement and compliments. She loved him.

Writing about him, though? Pouring her actual heart onto the pages for a mass audience? That wasn't the story she wanted to tell. She wanted to write fiction, perfectly crafted characters with lyrical language and emotional journeys that tugged heartstrings. A slice of life, one that never existed, not her real life. Not the violence. Not the blood. Not the truth.

"Think about it," he begged when she told him she couldn't write *that*. And she did, which was why her heels were at home, and she was running so late to meet her friends that she saw perpetually-indifferent-to-clocks Max arriving ahead of her, entering the restaurant in a rush. She paused for a moment to smooth her ponytail and check her reflection in a store window. If it weren't for the shoes, nobody would know anything was wrong.

⸺

Talia was the one who spotted her first and waved frantically, as if Sophia couldn't find them. She raised a hand back, *hi, yes, I see you*, and made her way to the table.

"I never thought I'd beat you anywhere," Max said, raising a glass in triumph. Lunch was too late for drinking mimosas, the brunch beverage of choice, so there were four afternoon-appropriate martinis on the table instead.

"I ordered for us," Talia said. "I couldn't wait, not after spending yesterday shopping for a bridesmaid's dress."

"I'm surprised you didn't order anything stronger." Sophia slid into the open seat and took a sip. She hated the taste of martinis but loved the way they looked, the deco design of the glass. Martinis made her feel like she belonged in a vintage advertisement, selling illicit liquor in the 1920s.

"Who says I didn't?" Talia's cheeks were already pink.

"How was shopping?" Sophia asked, not because she was overly interested, but because she was still trying to distract herself from everything. It wasn't just Gage's phone call. The roof at the Lake George house had leaked two weeks ago, and while insurance covered the repairs, it didn't cover the weeks of lost income from canceled rentals. Money was tight, and as much as she hated to admit it, writing a true crime story might help her finances. Could she debase herself? Maybe under a pen name? No. Pen names were for authors with something to hide. She would only write work she herself was proud to stand behind.

"My mother ..." Talia said, and that was all they needed to hear. Talia's mother was the overbearing kind, the sort of woman who loved to point out the flaws in others while ignoring her own, and Talia was her favorite target. Sophia had once considered using Mrs. Goldstein as the inspiration for a character but had to dismiss the idea. She was too much of a caricature to be believable, and Sophia's literary style had no room for comic relief.

"Motherfucking asshole," Max finished the sentence for her.

"Motherfucking asshole," Chelsea echoed.

"Everybody but us, right?" Talia said.

"Nah, we're assholes, too." Max raised her glass. "To all of us, mother—"

"Please keep it down." The waiter appeared next to her, frowning. "My manager said to tell you you're disrupting the other diners."

Talia squealed out an apology. Max looked like she was going to continue her toast but thought better of it. No sense in getting kicked out before they could eat, though based on how quickly the waiter speed-walked to the kitchen, Sophia suspected their orders would be bumped to the front of the queue and they'd be ushered out the moment they put forks down, with no chance of ordering dessert. Didn't matter. She couldn't afford dessert, anyway. She could barely afford the soup she'd ordered with an apologetic *I'm not that hungry.*

Since they wouldn't be having a long lunch, Sophia thought they should get right to it. Chelsea was the one that called them together, which in the writing world could only mean one thing: publishing news. Sophia tried to hold back her jealousy as she asked, "Well? Let's have it. I haven't seen anything in Publishers Marketplace yet. I've been looking."

"I saw something," Max said. "You remember that guy who gave a talk on character development and how if you want to write female characters, just write a man but give him boobs? Significant deal to a Big Five. Can you believe that?"

"Given the state of the industry, yes I can." Chelsea was probably reflecting on the one time her name appeared, and how quickly it had all gone away.

"I meant I've been looking for Chelsea's name. Isn't that why you invited us to lunch and said you had something to share?" While watching others get book deals was a bitter experience, Sophia could swallow her jealousy for a friend. She knew the moment Chelsea said she had something to show them, that it would be a contract, and that, once again, Sophia was being left behind, ignored, while others achieved their dreams.

"It's not a book deal." Chelsea dug into her ever-present messenger bag and extracted three tissue-stuffed gift bags.

"Yay! I love presents!" Talia snatched hers excitedly. "Oh. A book."

Sophia pulled the book from her own gift bag and examined the cover. It was vague and generic, the way so many were these days. The trend of having a flower as the focus was over-saturating the market, but she supposed it must sell. This one included additional popular design clichés, a drop of blood oozing from one petal and what appeared to be an eye peeking out from behind a leaf.

"*Deep Within the Discontented Dreaming of Dorian Dimwitty* by MF Ascher? I haven't heard of this one." Probably yet another poorly written, dumbed-down trope-filled piece of consumer fluff that would sell a million copies, while other, better books languished on the shelf and on discount bargain tables, or, as in Sophia's case, in agents' inboxes.

"Is this one you ghostwrote?" Talia asked.

"Finally!" Max said. "You're violating a non-disclosure! I knew you would. So who is MF Ascher? Are they famous for something?"

Chelsea laughed. "*We're* MF Ascher. Ascher, asshole, get it? It's the one we wrote with AI."

Sophia turned the book over in her hands. This is what they made—not wrote. She'd never call shouting ideas at a computer writing. She'd always thought that the first time she'd hold her own work in her hand, she'd feel a sense of pride, joy, achievement. Chelsea had taken that moment away. She was a contributor to a scam.

"You published it?" Sophia tried to keep the annoyance from her voice. "You didn't put our names anywhere, right?" What would her MFA cohorts think if they knew? *You can't write, can you? Can't succeed, so you cheat?*

"Of course not. We're the"—Chelsea dropped her voice so the waiter wouldn't hear—"motherfucking asshole this time. I just put it on Amazon as a joke. It's not connected to us in any way. I thought it would be funny."

Talia started flipping through the pages. "We did this?"

"Our ideas did this. It's all just for fun." Chelsea shook her head. "Don't overthink it."

"I love it!" Max shouted. "This just proves that anything can get published."

"Anything can get *self-published*," Sophia corrected. If anything could get published, she'd have at least four novels in bookstores right now. They all would.

"Self-publishing is awesome! It spits in the face of the industry gatekeepers. It proves people don't need their validation. *We* don't need their validation," Max said. "Maybe there's something to this."

"I will never give up my dreams," Sophia told her, but a little voice inside asked, *are you sure*? It could be so easy, uploading a file. Slapping a premade cover on and telling people she was finally a real author. No, she couldn't do that.

"Well, I love it," Talia said as she flipped through the pages. "Where'd you get this beautiful cover?"

Chelsea snorted. "I used an image editor on my phone to combine a bunch of royalty-free pictures. It took less than five minutes."

Max opened her book and snorted aloud. "You signed these as MF Ascher? Where's the inscription? You're supposed to write something fucking stupid. *May this book inspire your sense of wonder. Read this with bliss*, that sort of shit."

"You're just supposed to cross out the author's name and put your signature below it," Sophia pointed out. She'd already planned out her author signature, a beautiful legible swirly one, not to be confused with the messy legal scrawl on her driver's license and credit cards. All she needed was her own book—and a Montblanc fountain pen. Both would come in time, hopefully.

"Let me see your copy." Talia snatched it from Chelsea. "This one isn't signed."

"I wasn't going to sign my own book. That would be pathetic."

"I'll do it." Max tried to take it from Talia with one hand, while pulling a sharpie from her purse with the other.

"No, you'll put profanity. Someone give me a pen." Talia held the book out of Max's reach, giggling as her friend almost knocked over both of their martinis.

"Stop it before you get us kicked out of here," Sophia hissed at them. She was too late, though.

"Ladies, we're going to ask you to take your book club meeting elsewhere." The manager appeared at their table, bill and card reader in hand. "Immediately."

seven

everyone

The only thing this book is good for is holding up the uneven leg on my coffee table.
  –@JesusJunkie

TALIA

Still chuckling over their *published* book, Talia boarded a bus and headed uptown. Whenever she had extra time, she opted to ride the bus instead of the subway. Staying above ground in the daylight, where she could watch people coming and going and avoid rats, was preferable.

The afternoon sun warmed the window, relaxing her. She reached into her purse, a large tan boho bag, and removed her copy of *Deep Within the Discontented Dreaming of Dorian Dimwitty*. It looked and felt like a real book with its intriguing cover image, clever title, and heavy cream pages. Even the "author," *MF Ascher*, sounded legitimate. Only they knew what those initials stood for, and it tickled her to no end.

She fanned the pages, and they fluttered with a pleasant release of air. Talia reread the dedication:

To wine, s'mores, and burning it all down.

Chelsea's words were the only honest thing in the entire book. And she was speaking directly to her three closest friends.

The bus jolted to a stop, and riders pushed their way into the already crowded space. Talia scooted over to allow someone to sit beside her. She offered a polite smile, then returned to the book and scanned the first few pages.

"What are you reading?"

"Excuse me?" Talia looked at the older woman arranging bags at her feet.

"I'm an avid reader and always looking for something new. Is it good? What's it about?" The woman showed such sincere interest that Talia couldn't help but warm up to her.

"Actually, I just started it."

"The title is quite intriguing." The woman reached into her bag and removed a sandwich, which she unwrapped without regard to passengers who might not appreciate the smell of tuna and onions. Talia's momentary sense of affection wavered.

"You know," the woman said, her mouth full, "people don't read books like they used to. I remember when reading was everybody's favorite pastime. Now all anybody does is stare at their phones. It's criminal, don't you think?"

"I guess so."

"May I look at the book?" The woman extended her hand as if her request had already been granted.

"Oh, um, sure."

She studied the cover and scanned a few pages, nibbling on her sandwich. "Maybe I'll pick up a copy at the bookshop. Do you think it's appropriate? I do not approve of gratuitous sex or violence, and I find foul language quite offensive."

A wave of nausea struck without warning. "I have no idea." Talia gathered her things and crossed in front of the annoying and smelly seatmate. "My stop is next. Have a nice day."

She pushed her way through the crowd to the back door and

clung to the pole. Whether it was the woman's nosy questions about the book, the drinks at lunch, or the smell of tuna, Talia had no idea, but if she didn't get into the fresh air soon, she surely would vomit on someone's shoes.

The moment the doors opened, she stumbled down the steps to the sidewalk. Ducking into the first bodega she passed, Talia bought a cold ginger ale. She took a few sips and waited for her stomach to settle.

With an hour to spare before her shift at the box office started, Talia strolled the twenty or so blocks toward the theater district. She checked in ahead of schedule and worked until seven p.m.

By the time she got home, Talia was exhausted. She filled her tub with lavender scented bubble bath and water as hot as she could stand, anxious to wash away the city stink. There was no way she'd ever eat tuna again, which was too bad because she'd always loved a good tuna sandwich.

As she lowered her body into the tiny tub, water sloshed over the edge.

After a good soak, Talia heaved herself up, slathered her skin with scented body oil, and stepped out of the tub. She wrapped herself in a fluffy white bath sheet and then sat on the toilet to check a painful spot on her foot.

The walk that afternoon had caused a small blister on the back of her left heel. "Shit," she said, applying Neosporin and a bandage. She had a photo shoot on Wednesday. If the blister didn't heal completely by then, she'd have to cancel it, which she could not afford to do.

Talia set the concern aside as she put on her pajamas, excited to read *the book*. She spread a cozy blanket over her legs and reached into her oversized purse, feeling for it. The deep bag was such a pain, everything fell to the bottom.

She dumped the contents onto her lap. Wallet, keys, small notebooks, pens, lip gloss, gum, random snacks, a half-consumed water bottle. It was all there, except for the book.

SOPHIA

There were charity shops on the Upper East Side. That's where Sophia stood the best chance of replacing her heels with something—anything—that wouldn't get her judged by her more successful classmates. Lucky for her, there was a pair of Jimmy Choos, not quite in her size, but she could curl her toes for an hour or so. And extra lucky, the deep scratch that caused them to be marked down to a price she could afford was hardly noticeable if she kept her feet together.

Finding the shoes helped reset her emotional equilibrium. She was, if not happy, at least content when she arrived at the designated bar to await her MFA classmates for their quarterly gathering. She still had no news to share, so she would sit politely through all the announcements and humble brags: "I thought my novel was terrible, but I guess the *New York Times* disagreed, and while the advance wasn't what I wanted, I did get enough to put down a deposit on a condo." "It took me three weeks to hit the bestseller list. I was so afraid my publisher would drop me, but since the movie deal came through, I guess they'll keep me on. I'm so fortunate that they're so understanding."

She wished she didn't have to attend, but her absence would be noted as a sign of defeat. So she sat at a table, thumbed through the strangely compelling AI novel that Chelsea had so unceremoniously dumped on her, and waited.

Chadwick was the first to arrive. He did his usual thing where he looked around the bar, vaguely nodding at complete strangers and pretending that they were all watching him. He thought he was so superior, with his movie deal and his trashy thrillers that could be picked up in any supermarket checkout line. Nobody actually recognized authors in person unless they were superfans or worked in the industry.

"Sophia, I'm so happy you're still coming to these," he greeted her. His voice always made her skin crawl. "I hope it's not demoralizing for you."

"Just because I can't share details of my work doesn't mean I'm not interested in hearing about yours," she told him politely. She'd made a few minor embellishments over the years, borrowing stories from Chelsea about ghostwriting. Let them think she was a private success. They didn't have to know the truth.

"I'm sure one day I'll be reading some celebrity memoir and recognize your style," he said, but it didn't sound supportive in her ears. More condescending, like he was sure he never would, that she'd never amount to anything. "Look, Adabel is here. I heard her agent is shopping around a trilogy that's garnering a lot of interest."

Soon the table filled with bragging former classmates, each trying to one-up each other while simultaneously being self-deprecating. There was Georgiana, who somehow hit the best-seller list with a novel that opened with the protagonist waking up in bed and then standing in front of a mirror to describe her physical features; Tobias, whose poetry had been read at the White House, despite it being what Sophia would consider an ode to the mediocre man; and, of course, Nyla, who grew up in luxury as the wealthy scion of one of the most prominent New England families, yet somehow was known for her #ownvoices urban grit.

Sophia kept a smile on her face, made passing remarks implying the success of her ghostwriting and mentioning that she was out on submission with her own work. Her headache pressed down on her, made worse by the way Chadwick put his hand on her thigh.

When he leaned over and suggested they get out of there together, that was her cue to leave. Without him. She had no interest in him whatsoever, as she had informed him on numerous occasions over the years. He took her rejection as playing hard to get, but on her part, it was sheer revulsion. She'd had sex exactly twice. Once, in college, with a man reputed to possess great bedroom skills, and once with a woman known for the same. Those interactions confirmed what she'd always believed: sex was disgusting, unnecessary, and wildly overrated.

"Sorry, I have to catch my train," she said, shoving past him and heading out into the night. She walked the best she could in her too-small shoes until she made it around the corner and was able to change into her sneakers. It wasn't until she got home that she noticed the book wasn't in her bag.

CHELSEA

Chelsea's phone pinged.

RICK

Here

Her head fell backward with a groan. She had just gotten home from lunch with her friends, and Rick dampened her mood. She tossed her bag on the kitchen counter next to the box.

Rick the Dick.

For reasons unknown, Chelsea still had a box of his things. Although he'd been officially gone for two and half years (not counting the year he spent banging that producer's daughter behind her back), he called her out of the blue, whining about all that he had already lost in the divorce—a complaint that made Chelsea choke on her coffee. He insisted on picking up the box after his usual Friday fish-fry lunch at Montague's Italian Ristorante, (not to be confused with Capulet's Pizzeria across the street).

The obnoxious knocking cut through her head, and she would give just about anything to return it to his skull.

"Hey, Chels," Rick said, leaning on the doorframe like he propped it up and not the other way around. He tried too hard with that dimple. "You look good."

Fucking Rick. "Your stuff is over there." She gestured without turning her head or making any kind of move to abandon the door.

His brown eyes scorched her from toe to head. "Why such a quick in and out?"

"Because it's something you're good at, as I recall." Even Rick, as fake as he was, couldn't hold a grin in the face of that insult. God, that felt good. He returned to full RDF (Resting Dick Face, bless Max's filthy mouth) and loafed past her to the counter.

"You know, Chels," he began. "You can do a helluva lot better than this place. I could hook you up with Elaria's brother. He's a realtor."

None of this deserved a response. Chelsea had never, would never, call Rick's wannabe movie star girlfriend for a damn thing.

Her phone rang from her bag. Rick stood sideways to let her get to it; the cologne he bathed in gagged her. She knew from the timing of the call that it was a potential client she couldn't afford to miss.

"I have to take this," she said, hustling towards her room.

"Working on anything new?" Rick asked, still not moving to leave.

Wouldn't you like to know, you thief.

"Just take your box and go." She slammed her bedroom door and hoped like hell he would break his neck going down the stairs.

MAX

Max loved Astoria. It was a writer's gateway to cultural differences and creativity, packed with people from different walks of life. She enjoyed writing at the local Greek coffee shop that served iced frappés. The strong coffee with the foamy layer on top made her feel like she was in Greece, a traveling writer sitting at a local taverna, scribbling in her notebooks, describing faces with bulbous noses and deep-set eyes that spoke of poverty and generosity and lived experiences full of hardship and struggle.

But she couldn't afford to travel to Greece or Italy or Spain. Her own poverty restricted her to the crowded corners of Astoria, living among the diverse bodies of immigrants who planted their roots on American soil but lived their individual lives, going to their churches, speaking their own languages, and opening restaurants that sold their food to the masses. She could only go as far as the Greek café a few blocks away, order a drink, and fire up her laptop for a few hours of uninterrupted writing.

She was writing another essay on the foster care system, hoping to pitch it to *USA Today*. It would mark her 90th rejection from their editors, but she didn't give a fuck. She would submit her work again and again, because that's where her work belonged. In motherfucking *USA Today,* with or without an agent or any literary connections to get her published there. Eventually, her writing would make it, and they would suffer the shame of knowing that they had rejected her for years.

"Fuckers," she smirked, and it was at this time that her brown gaze met the twinkling blue eyes belonging to a ruggedly handsome man. He was staring right at her, not even attempting to hide his interest.

"What are you looking at?" She closed her laptop and challenged him. Men did not scare her. They did not intimidate her. But once in a while, she felt the tingling, a charge of electricity running up and down her spine when she met a man she wanted in her bed. Like now.

He laughed, his head thrown back, the brown threads of his hair bouncing off his forehead so that he had to push them back with his fingers.

No ring. Just a silver watch to help him tell time.

She smiled at him, pointed to the chair beside hers, and then watched as he rose from the table a few feet from hers and sauntered over. The smile was lovely. Deep. Sexy.

An hour later, they were in her apartment, completely naked, his tall, lean frame covering her smaller one, his bones pressing against hers. A gentleman through and through. He had even tried to make her come, his fingers toying with the layers of her girl parts until she moaned. Not many men cared if she came or not. They didn't ask what pleased her and they didn't attempt to please her.

Coming was too intimate, anyway. It's why she didn't care.

She preferred it when they crushed her, came inside her, and then left.

When he was finished, she rolled over onto her right hip, turned on the light by her side of the bed, and grabbed the book she and her friends had ordered AI to write for them.

She punched three pillows behind her until they formed a puffy cocoon and leaned against them as she began to read.

"What are you reading?" he asked, leaning against the headboard.

Max felt his eyes on her and glanced into the mirror on the opposite side of the bed to see what he was looking at. All she saw was a girl with disheveled dark curls cascading over her pale shoulders, reading as if he weren't there, her breasts and face unmasked and perhaps even beautiful. She looked wild, raw. Untamable.

She turned her attention back to the man who lay beside her, a curious expression on his face.

"A new book."

"Oh, yeah? What's it about?"

"Well, I haven't finished it yet, but the first chapter alone has everything it's supposed to have. A hook that grabbed me by the first paragraph, humor and emotional tension in perfect balance, conflict that propels me to keep turning the pages ... and the characters ..."

She turned to him with the excitement of a child, an uncorrupted one who had discovered the wonders of life for the first time and insisted on living in it—not withdrawing from it. Like she had just found love and wanted to revel in it.

"The characters are all complex and full of contradictions," Max explained, not wanting to reveal too much lest she let it slip that it was all a farce. And that she was part of it. She lowered her eyes, but not in shame. She was proud, because she was part of the sham that could oust the system.

"Sounds interesting," he said. "So what books would you compare it to?"

She paused, considering how far she should take this. It might be fun to see how over-the-top she could get before he called her bullshit. She scoffed to herself because men never called her on her bullshit, especially ones who lay naked in her bed.

"What a great question!" She put the book down, pushed the loose curls away from her face, and turned to look at him. She was suddenly conscious of her nakedness, aware of his, the taut muscles of his abs, the brown hair on his long legs, the way his hip bone begged to be touched.

She flushed and pulled the covers up to her chin, looking into his blue eyes for the first time since a few hours ago when they had met over her frappé and laptop.

"It's like everything. Everything good you've ever read. It has the feminist leanings of *Lessons in Chemistry*. The suspense of *The Silent Patient*. The complexity of Roxane Gay's *Hunger*. The rawness of Adrienne Rich's work. The darkness of Audre Lorde's poetry. The conciseness of Hemingway. The brutality of James Baldwin. It even sings with the insightfulness of Brené Brown's research on human connection." She stopped to take a deep breath, her brain running down all the authors the AI generator seemed to have used to create this novel that almost made her feel jealous for not being brilliant enough to write it on her own.

"You must read a lot."

"I'm a writer. But not like ... this." She lowered her gaze to the cover of the book and trailed her fingers over the name of the author Chelsea had created for this masterpiece.

MF Ascher.

What a writer. What a racket!

She sensed him watching her again. He had this way of caressing her with his eyes that made her feel exposed. So she did what she always did when she felt men getting too close for comfort.

"So you want to fuck again? Or you can leave. It's up to you."

She lay on her back, pulled the covers off her body, and closed her eyes. She knew he would stay. And there was a small part of her that wanted him to. Maybe even through the night.

The next morning, she opened her eyes to find him gone. On the pillow beside hers, there was a business card with a hand-written note.

I hope you don't mind. I borrowed your book. If you want it back, give me a call.

Max flipped the card over to see his name: Brad Harrison, *The New York Times.*

eight
max

What is it called when you laugh and cry at the same time? Craugh? I craughed my way through this book. MF Ascher is my new favorite author. I can't wait for the sequel! Write faster, pretty please!
    -Goodreads Reviewer

Max pulled into Chelsea's apartment complex in New Jersey forty-five minutes late.

Shutting off the engine, she turned to Talia, the reason for their lateness. The girl was always running around with her head half screwed on, reminding Max of those little bobbing hula-dancing girl toys people put on their car dashboards. She had a smile on her face, her cheeks flushed with excitement, but she was all over the place.

"Why do you think Chelsea's holding this emergency meeting?" Max asked Talia, who was freshening her makeup in the small mirror behind the visor. "It all sounds fishy to me. I don't like it."

"Well, let's go inside and see. We're not going to find out anything sitting in the car," Talia sang in a high falsetto that made Max's bones tense. She shot her a dirty look and reached beneath her seat to take a much-needed swig of vodka from her flask. When nothing came out, she tossed it in the back and reached for her spare bottle beneath the passenger seat, moving Talia's feet to get at it. This one was half full, and the liquid slid down her throat as if it had finally made its way home.

"Are you freaking insane?" Talia's squeal almost made Max spill her treasure, and she licked the drops of vodka before they traveled from her mouth towards her chin.

Talia stared at her, lips formed in a pretty pink O, and Max arched her eyebrows with impatience.

"What now?" Max's gruff voice filled the space between them, sharp and full of the rancor that came from driving all the way from Queens and then to Harlem to get Talia and then to New Jersey in bumper-to-bumper traffic.

"One of these days you're gonna get pulled over and arrested for drinking and driving."

"Who's driving? I'm parked, and the key is out of the ignition." Max grabbed the keys, still in the ignition, and pulled them out. "See?" She put her hands in the air, the keys dangling from her fingertips, the bottle in plain sight.

"When you get arrested, I'm not bailing you out. I don't have that kind of money."

Max shrugged, took another sip, and tucked the container beneath her seat this time, for easy access when she needed it. She knew it would be soon. She sank into her seat, letting the alcohol numb her, and joined Talia in scanning their surroundings—a run-down apartment complex with unkempt lawns and graffitied walls.

"Poor Chelsea," Talia said, breaking the silence. "Rick sure did a number on her. Someone should take him to the cleaners, or stick a knife into his car tires. Something. Chelsea doesn't deserve any of this."

They got out of the car and made their way to their meeting with Chelsea and Sophia. Max's gut was telling her that only bad news was going to greet her at the door. She trudged behind Talia, wondering how this girl walked with a slight skip in her step when life was such drudgery and people were so fucked in the head. She was almost envious of the bubbliness she exuded.

"Fuck!" Max exclaimed as they entered the building, its interior as gray and decayed as the exterior. The elevator was broken. Max spit at the sign plastered on the split doors.

"Ew." Talia's fingers reached out as if to push Max away from her with disgust. "Keep your spit in your body. No one wants to see it, hear it, or smell it."

"Oh, please. Get over yourself. You're no princess. I know what you've done with your toes," she said as they started up the stairs.

"Just shut it, okay?" Talia's cheeks were flushed and pink, either from exertion or embarrassment. "We agreed you wouldn't talk about my toes. And besides, you know I don't do that kind of thing anymore."

Max noted Talia's deep, short breaths and half-smiled at her friend's discomfort with the truth. She'd promised she would never bring the toe thing up again, but once in a while, like now, when Talia put on airs that reeked of pretense in front of her, she couldn't help but remind Talia that she knew the truth.

Max paused at the third-floor landing, wishing she had worn her sneakers. They were lighter than her combat boots, which weighed her down from one step to the next as if they were chained to an anvil.

"You're right, I'm sorry. I'll never bring it up again." She tossed Talia a grin—the open, toothy one that they both knew meant she was being insincere.

"You have way too much fun at my expense." Talia pouted.

"Oh, please. You know I love you."

They finally reached the sixth floor, and Max yanked the door open to the hallway, looking for 6B. In the three years since Rick's betrayal and Chelsea's fall from grace, this was the first time she'd invited them over. At least to this dump. Max understood. Chelsea had gone from having it all to having nothing, because she had trusted the man who had vowed he'd love her in sickness and in health. But no one said anything about greed. When that yellow-eyed villain showed up, Rick the Dick revealed his true colors.

"Prick," she mumbled under her breath and knocked on the door, afraid the wood would crack and fall apart at the touch of her knuckles.

The door swung open. Chelsea, her face ashen, stood beside Sophia.

"What's going on?" Max demanded, dismissing false pleasantries.

Talia elbowed Max. "Geez, give her a minute. We just got here."

"Sit down," Chelsea said. "Please."

They did as they were told, taking their places on the couch. The three exchanged glances as they watched Chelsea—the one who always held it together and was in control of every situation—appear more unsure than Max had ever seen her. She regretted leaving the vodka in the car.

"What the fuck is going on, Chelsea? Why the emergency meeting?" Max jutted her chin out with frustration. She could feel something in the air. A stink.

"Something happened. I can't explain how ... yet. But ..." Chelsea dug a sleeve of antacids out of her pocket and chucked one in her mouth. Talia's hand braced against Max's thigh like she was waiting for the bottom to drop out.

"Are you dying or something?" Max asked.

"What? No. It's this." Chelsea grabbed her laptop off the counter and set it on the coffee table, the screen open towards them.

They craned their necks to look at an Amazon page with a graph. But Max couldn't make sense of it except for the sharp uptick in the line.

"What the fuck are we looking at, Chels?" Max asked.

Chelsea drew in a sharp breath. "So you know how I got us all paperbacks of the book? I had to upload it to Amazon to do that, and well, something crazy happened."

She paused.

Max wasn't sure if it was for dramatic effect or because she couldn't find the words. "Spit it out," she raised her voice. She hated being in the dark, and her stomach was churning with anticipation.

"It started selling. The book went viral." Chelsea's words came out in a hush.

"What book went viral?" Talia asked.

"Our book," Max answered, rolling her eyes at Talia's confusion.

"Oh my god," Sophia exclaimed with horror. "You had no right to publish that book. No one agreed to it."

"*Our* book?" Talia asked, still confused.

"Yes, Talia." Sophia snapped. "What don't you get? It's the one that AI wrote and Chelsea decided to put on Amazon. Without asking any of us." Her fingers ran through the loose tendrils of her ponytail with irritation.

"Oh." Talia sat back. "That's not good. Is it?"

Sophia turned her attention to Chelsea. "How did this happen?"

"I don't know. But it's selling five, ten, twelve *thousand* copies *a day* and the numbers just keep going up. And there are thousands of reviews. Some people hate the book. Others love it. I thought it was a mistake, but it's not."

"Holy shit. Holy motherfucking shit." Max let out a laugh that was deep and robust. "This is fucking crazy!" She leaned over and read a few of the online comments. "'Wow! I can tell when an author is trying too hard to be clever, but Ascher isn't trying at all —he's just brilliant. The Obnoxious Book Blogger.'"

Chelsea nodded towards the screen. "'*Deep Within the Discontented Dreaming of Dorian Dimwitty*, by MF Ascher, is a titillating and scintillating story that breaks every writing rule in all the right ways. It is poised to become the gold standard by which every other work of fiction is held to.' That's the *Post*."

A snorting giggle erupted from Talia's lips. "Listen to this one. 'I guarantee this guy wears tweed jackets with elbow patches and smokes cigars unironically. We get it, you're a writer, you own a thesaurus and know how to use it. Personally, I prefer sci-fi. Two stars.'"

"Bitch!" Max's gruff response brought out another dusting of giggles from Talia. But Sophia had the expression of someone who had just gotten T-boned and stumbled out of the car in confusion. The only time she ever looked like that was when she —or anyone—brought up her MFA peers.

"I don't know why you're laughing," she cried out. "This is disastrous. It's going to ruin my career as a writer."

Max turned to Sophia and gave her a knowing smile. "Sophia, don't you see? This can work for us."

"What? How exactly will this work for us?"

Max understood Sophia's concern, what she was afraid of. If any of this came out, that she had been part of using AI to write a book, one that became a sensation, she would never be taken seriously as a literary writer. Her MFA classmates already thought she was a washout, but if anyone found out about this, then it would be true. They would have been right about her. She was already a failure in their eyes. But now she would also be a cheater.

Sophia put her face in her hands and let out a groan of disbelief.

"This proves exactly what we already know, how awful and screwed up the publishing industry is," Max explained, her hands waving wildly, in tandem with her words. "It's a fucking joke where money talks and art is corrupted. The so-called critics can't tell a fake from the real thing. And neither can readers or book bloggers. Our book has stripped the veneer from an industry that says it wants art but really only wants what sells. We can use this to show the world the truth. To expose it all as a lie." By the end of her tirade, she was standing, triumphant, ready to lead them into battle.

"You're an agitator, Max." Sophia stood, shaking her head. "You want a revolution. But that's not what I want. I want to write and to make it with my talent. This AI book, it's not me. I had no say in any of it."

Sophia turned and glared at Chelsea, pointing at the laptop. "Take it down. You do not have my permission. I have a reputation to maintain, and if my work goes viral, it will be because of me. My gift as a writer. Not because I cheated. So take it the fuck down. Now."

There was a long pause, pregnant with unvoiced feelings and emotions among the women. They were each trying to make sense of this. To understand the full weight of what was happening to them as writers. As friends.

"There's more." Chelsea cleared her throat. She moved around Sophia and went to her small desk. She pulled out three envelopes from her drawer and brought them over. "There's a check in here for each of you. From your share of the sales. I have concerns that we need to talk through, but I wanted you to have these beforehand."

Max, Sophia, and Talia accepted the envelopes and opened them slowly.

Talia gasped. "Is this for real?"

"Holy shit." Max looked at the number on the check made out to her. "$83,422.36?"

"Yes," Chelsea said.

Max whistled. "We all made the same?"

"Yes, of course. I split it four ways."

"This changes things a bit, doesn't it, Sophia?" Max couldn't help rubbing it in.

For all of Sophia's high and mighty talk of art and ownership and making it on her own, Max knew money would change all that. Sophia tried to hide it, but Max knew the truth. Her livelihood was hanging by a thread, just like the rest of them.

Sophia didn't respond. She stared at the check, folded it, and tucked it into her purse. Her features revealed nothing of her thoughts.

"This is amazing. No more foot modeling or writing stupid content for companies I don't give a crap about." Talia's words came out in a throaty hush, as if she were trying to hold back tears, her fingers outlining her name and the numbers on the check.

"I know what this money means to you guys. What it means to all of us," Chelsea said, her voice reserved.

Max wondered why Chelsea didn't appear happier. She should be elated.

"Got any champagne?" Talia's voice broke through the quiet, a musical note that rang with joy in this one space, in this one moment. "We should celebrate. Shouldn't we?"

nine
chelsea

I liked the book, I really did, but the fact that it is vague really irks me. This would've been five stars if the writer had given more details. The showing didn't tell nearly enough.
—C. Dawson, Writer

Chelsea rinsed her empty glass under the tepid water, the chatter of her friends filling the room behind her. It gave her a minute to steady herself after unloading such a heavy weight.

She'd been dealing with this development since the email from Amazon two weeks ago. She dismissed that and the next one as spam. But after the third, she took thirty seconds to log into her old, basically defunct account.

The numbers on the screen were wrong. They had to be. Someone at the multibillion-dollar company had made a mistake. She fell back in her chair, shook off any possibility that this was real, and closed her browser. Chelsea had been on a tight deadline and didn't have time to waste on an Amazon glitch. She rebooted her computer and kept plugging away.

But there was a nagging voice in the back of her mind urging her to check one more time. So after she finished the assignment, she logged back in, certain there would be a fresh set of zeroes awaiting her. And there were zeroes, but they were preceded by actual numbers. Dollars that made no sense.

Publishing the book was fun. A way to cheer up her friends and herself. To give them all a little ray of sunshine, pretending they were holding their own book babies in their hands. This book was a fake and never meant to make a penny.

She returned to the living room and the conversation. Now that her accidental co-conspirators were here, she felt the opposite of comfort. Their reactions did nothing but break open the dormant ulcer that clung to the lining of her stomach. Talia's eyes practically burst out of her head at the prospect of having (and spending) that money, right alongside Max's rousing fuck-them battle cries and correlating victory dance. The two of them were delighted—thrilled—about what it meant for their respective situations.

Chelsea didn't want to give them the money. And not because she didn't want to share it with them, but because she was afraid of what would happen once they had it. Money brought out the worst in people, even those who purported to love each other. She'd experienced the fallout from greed firsthand and didn't want the same fate to befall her friends.

She'd been wrestling with it for days, trying to reason her way around it. In the end, she couldn't stand keeping the secret. It was a book they had created together, for better or worse. And though she would caution them as best as she could, she couldn't control them. Really, she didn't want to. Not exactly, anyway.

"You know the best part about this," Max said. "When the time comes for us to tell the world what we did, they're all going to look like idiots. How amazing will it be when they have to admit that they don't know shit? Not about readers or writers or books."

"I don't think we need to take it that far," Sophia cautioned from across the couch. She was the only other one who seemed to understand what this might cost them if the truth came out.

"We don't have to do anything yet. We can just enjoy the

money, can't we?" Talia's voice pinched the way it did when she had an opinion that she didn't quite want to share with everyone.

"That's what we need to talk about." Chelsea inhaled, knowing that what she was about to suggest might not go over so well. "I don't think we should spend any of it—at least, not yet."

"Why not?" Talia rebuked.

"For starters, this may be a fluke. There's no guarantee it'll continue. Spending it all at once would be foolish." Though, if she were being honest, Chelsea had a feeling this was going to be the first of many large checks. The book sales showed no sign of slowing. But she needed to set the tone for her friends now. The stakes were too high for her—and them.

"We aren't children," Max said.

Chelsea knew Max would be the hardest one to wrangle. "I know, sorry. But if we go throwing a ton of money around, it might draw suspicion, and *that* will lead to too many questions."

"Getting caught using AI will taint our reputations." Sophia said. "And ruin us."

"Right. Plus, while I'm confident that no one can connect the money to me, if someone really wanted to figure it out, they probably could." Chelsea had learned from a ghostwriting client, an infamous financial guru, all about how to hide money. She never imagined she'd have to put that knowledge to the test.

"And you don't want this to bounce back to you. Got it." Max pointed her fingers like a gun and pulled the trigger.

Irritation started to get the better of Chelsea, but she pushed it aside. She needed to keep herself together before things really went off the rails.

"I don't want this to come back to any of us. That's why I'm suggesting we don't spend much until we get a better handle on the scope of things."

Max raised her hand and waved it around like a know-it-all third grader. Chelsea rolled her eyes, which apparently was all the permission Max needed.

"Why give us the money if you're so worried we'll spend it?"

It would have been so much easier if she had kept it under wraps.

"I couldn't keep this from you. It wouldn't be right. You'd find out about the book's success eventually, and then what? I casually announce that I've been sitting on all this money? You'd never trust me again."

Her friends nodded while they contemplated her words. "So all I'm asking is that you not spend much of it." Memories of Rick tossing her six-figure advance around like it was rice at a wedding rushed through her head—

Rick.

Chelsea glanced toward the kitchen counter where his box had been the day she returned from lunch with the girls. The day she'd given them the books.

"Shit." Chelsea pulled her phone from her pocket, her heart punching her chest as she filtered through the missed calls, the texts, and the voicemails.

Rick had sent her twenty-six texts she'd ignored. He'd called her almost as many times.

"Oh, fuck!" She paced back and forth behind the sofa. She did this. She screwed everything up for herself and her friends. Of course it was her. Of course it was *him.*

She unloaded the air from her chest in one exasperated exhale. "Rick has my copy of the book. That has to be why it went viral."

"Are you sure?" Talia twisted her hands with concern.

"Positive. The day I gave them to you, he came over to pick up a box of his stuff. It was right there" —she pointed to the counter — "and so was the book. He must have taken it after I went into my room to answer a call from a client."

Rick. Fucking Rick.

"Why don't you call him?" Sophia offered, her voice smooth, with no hint of the exasperation filtering through Chelsea. "See what he wants and whether he actually has the book."

"Good idea. You may be going down this rabbit hole for nothing," Max seconded.

"We'll all stand here with you." Talia placed a shaky hand on Chelsea's shoulder.

It probably scared them, seeing her like this, so contradictory to her typical confident self. They rallied around her as she called Rick and tapped the speaker icon.

"Jesus, Chels, took you long enough to get back to me," his voice rasped from the other end of the line. "I was going to come bang on your door."

"What do you want, Rick?" She asked, forcing indifference and irritation into her tone.

"I'm great, thanks for asking," he scoffed. "Listen, I need to know where you got this book."

Chelsea was fairly sure that all four hearts in her living room had stopped.

She cleared the disgust from her throat. "What book?"

"The one that was in your bag. By MF Ascher."

"So you stole my book?"

"I borrowed it."

"Sure you did. Just like you borrowed my *other* book," Chelsea said. Rightful ownership had never stopped him before.

"Let's not get into that right now. I've been trying to get in touch with the guy who wrote it. He's a damn ghost."

Chelsea's friends were staring and waiting for her to ask the bigger questions. "Why do you want to find him, and what makes you think I know?"

"Well, for one, you have an autographed copy, so you've met him or someone who knows him."

The memory of Max grabbing Chelsea's copy and signing it at the table between fits of laughter raced through her mind.

"And two," he continued. "I want the film rights for my production company."

Talia gasped and clamped a hand over her mouth. Chelsea scanned her friends, each dealing with this news in various ways. Sophia's skin drained of color while Max's face remained unchanged.

"I don't know what to tell you," she said, fighting to regain her I-don't-give-a-shit voice. "I'm too busy for this."

"Just point me in the right direction. I'm not asking you to do the work for me."

"It worked out well for you the last time." Chelsea held her back a little straighter.

Fuck Rick. Fuck publishing. Fuck her agent and the editor who dumped her without even considering that *he* could be the thief. Fuck everyone who underestimated Chelsea at every step of her life.

"Chels—"

She hung up the phone and gazed at her friends with renewed determination. She had a mission. She needed to make sure Rick didn't get another thing of hers—and even though she didn't write it this time, it sure as hell belonged to her. And to her friends.

━━

As it turned out, Chelsea wasn't the only one who'd lost the book. Sophia confessed that her copy disappeared after her cohort meeting but insisted it could've been anyone at the bar; Talia, scattered as usual, might have lost hers on the bus, the bodega, or the box office; and Max's latest one-night-stand, who happened to be a fucking *New York Times* reporter, "borrowed" it. In the end, it didn't matter how it got out. All that mattered was what they were going to do next.

But the gravity of the situation still hung around her shoulders, especially when it came to Max and Talia.

After the two wild cards left, Sophia hung back.

"You're worried about them spending all the money, aren't you?" Sophia sat cross-legged on the couch.

"I'm more worried that they'll tell the wrong person about it and that'll become a whole other thing." Chelsea sat beside her and hugged a pillow into her chest.

"Talia for sure is going to blab," Sophia said. "She can't help herself."

"That gives me absolutely no peace." Chelsea chuckled and shook her head. Her friends were wonderful, all of them, but Talia could be easily swayed, and Max was the person who usually did the swaying.

"It's why I wanted to stay behind. So we can talk about what we're going to do. And them."

Chelsea nodded and leaned in. "What are you thinking?"

"If it ever got out that I had something to do with a book written with AI, any hope of publishing something legitimate would be gone forever," Sophia reminded her.

"Agreed. But it's my name on the line. Not yours. I know my reputation doesn't mean shit at this point." It hurt to say it because it was so true. She'd lost all credibility, and while her friends supported her, dancing around the subject of her inability to get anything published again, they knew the truth.

Sophia shook her head. "We're all complicit in creating the book. I know it's not my name, but it is a consequence that I can't have happen. Even though ..." Her eyes softened, and for a moment, Chelsea saw a flood of emotion welling within them. This was very un-Sophia like, which reinforced Chelsea's belief that her friend was good at creating an image of herself she wanted the world to buy into. "Even though I could really use the money." Sophia choked on the words, as if it hurt to utter them.

All four of them were broke. The one piece of this whole fiasco that provided any kind of comfort was the money. Chelsea was so far in debt that she could work the rest of her life and die still owing money.

Perhaps this was divine intervention, the universe trying to right wrongs—not just for her, but for all of them. Chelsea had learned after Rick's betrayal to prepare for the worst. So when that financial guru hired her to ghostwrite his book last year and offered her a numbered account in his Cayman bank, she took it.

And until last week, that account had never contained more than twenty-five bucks.

Chelsea sighed. "We can't let the AI thing get out. Ever."

"You won't tell, and I won't tell," Sophia said. "But unless something happens to Talia and Max, like they suddenly lose the ability to speak—"

"Or get hit by a bus on their way home tonight, there's no way to stop them from talking," Chelsea finished.

The two stared at the brazenness of this statement before they burst out laughing, shaking off what passed between them.

"God, I would feel awful if that happened!" Chelsea exclaimed, covering her face with her hands.

"Yeah, and I'll make sure to tell everyone you're the one who willed it." Sophia snorted, which sent both women spiraling into a teary fit of laughter.

It felt good to have someone to laugh and conspire and vent with. Sophia had always been that person for her, even though they didn't spend much time alone together.

"We need to figure out how to cover our tracks and make ourselves completely invisible in all of this," Chelsea said. "Plenty of people have pen names and ghostwriters. So maybe we play that out and see what happens."

Sophia bobbed her head and smoothed the ponytail between her fingers like a satin ribbon. "So I have a thought. That guy, Alec Pendergrass."

"The skeezy lawyer who claimed he had an agent when all he had was a connection to an intern to the assistant of an agent?" Chelsea chuckled. "He was delusional enough to believe he was going to be the next John Grisham."

Sophia nodded. "I bet we can ask him how to do it."

"You think we need a lawyer?" Chelsea hadn't considered this, but perhaps it was a good idea.

"Definitely. There's no way to cover up the identity of MF Ascher without a representative. With a lawyer, we can remain anonymous."

"You're right," Chelsea said. "I'm sure he'd jump at the chance. Especially since he had a thing for Talia." A flash of him slurring all over Talia's shoulder at a character arc workshop they'd attended zipped through Chelsea's brain.

Bringing in another person would be tricky, but if they hired Alec, he'd be bound by legal ethics of confidentiality, like doctors and HIPAA. He would be the safest to loop in because of it, but bringing this up to Max and Talia might set off a firestorm.

"I say we contact him," Chelsea said. "But we keep it between us, at least for now."

"Agreed," Sophia nodded. "The less they know, the better."

ten
talia

Max accelerated as though they were being chased by bad guys.

"Could you please slow down?" Talia said, perspiration dripping between her generous breasts. "On top of everything we've been through today, you want to get pulled over? Or worse, cause an accident?"

She reduced her speed, but only a little. "What's your problem? And why are you saying *everything we've been through*, as if something awful has happened? I think this is the greatest day ever!"

"It just makes me nervous."

"Everything makes you nervous." Max merged onto the highway, a smile playing on her lips.

Talia could practically see the wheels spinning in Max's head. She loved anything that smacked of sticking it to the man or taking down the established order. If she'd lived 250 years ago, Max would've been a revolutionary, the first to dump tea into the harbor. Talia worried about her propensity for acting without thinking.

As Max drove and nattered (every third word being some variation of fuck) about how Chelsea's little mistake was the best thing that could've happened to them, Talia's mind wandered. Her friends were in predicaments, just like she was. And she understood the position of each of them.

Sophia was obsessed with her reputation as a literary writer with an MFA; Max was consumed with blowing up the industry that didn't respect or embrace her; Chelsea was desperate to regain control after having suffered profound betrayal and humiliation at the hands of an egotistical, unscrupulous ex.

As for her, Talia craved acceptance. That's why she loved her friends with a deep longing. They were the opposite of her family, especially her mother, who saw her as a disappointment and an embarrassment.

But money could change all that.

Talia glanced to her left. Max was still blathering, but she blocked out the sound. Max was volatile, like a firecracker dancing beside a lit match. She had a finger hovering over the proverbial red button at all times, ready to start a nuclear war without consulting advisors. Thank god she didn't have political aspirations. If anybody could stir the lunatic masses, it was Max.

And now, with money in the bank? She could be dangerous. Talia wanted to take her hand, calm her down, and help her develop a broader perspective.

While Max felt it her mission to protect Talia from the cruel world and evil men, Talia needed to protect Max from herself. Out of the four of them, Max was reckless and unpredictable—the one who could self-destruct at any moment.

"Jesus, Talia! Are you listening?"

Talia jerked herself out of the reverie. "Oh, sorry, what did you say?"

"I asked why you're crying."

"I'm not crying."

"So those are fucking raindrops on your cheeks?"

Talia touched her face. It was wet with warm tears. "Wow, weird. I didn't even realize."

Max frowned. "What were you thinking about?"

"You."

"Me?"

Talia switched gears. She couldn't tell Max how much she worried about her. Max would just laugh and dismiss it and tell her she was an idiot.

"Well, all of us, really. And the money. I think Chelsea's right. We can't spend too much of it. And believe me, I'd love to. If my mother knew I'd made this kind of money, she'd shit her pants."

Max laughed with too much enthusiasm. "I would pay to see that! And now I can. I can afford fucking anything. We all can."

"No, we can't. Do you have any idea how to handle this much money? You know how many lottery winners are broke again within a year?"

A new worry sprung to life. What if the book kept making money? Sudden and unexpected windfalls were a risky business, and Max, with unlimited funds, would be disastrous. She was much too impulsive.

"Fuck that, Talia. I can handle money. I'm as responsible as any of you."

They were back in Manhattan now, a few miles from Talia's apartment, when the car sputtered and stopped in the middle of the street.

"Oh, shit."

"What's wrong?" Talia asked.

"We're out of gas."

"*Seriously?* We're out of gas in the middle of Harlem, in the dark?" Talia couldn't believe they hadn't checked the tank before leaving New Jersey. She should've thought of that, because Max wouldn't.

Horns blared as cars swerved around them, drivers flipping them off.

"Yeah! Fuck you, too!" Max gave her middle finger a workout. "And you, too!"

"Shut up, Max," Talia said. "You want to get shot?"

Max grunted. "I hate people."

"Hate all you want, but we can't just stay here blocking traffic. I'm going to push while you steer."

"Really? You can push a car? Are you superhuman now?"

Talia released her seatbelt. "We'll find out."

Traffic whizzed by. Christmas lights that should have been removed weeks ago were wrapped around some of the streetlamps and hung haphazardly inside of shop windows. Talia zipped up her parka, placed both hands on the bumper, and pushed with all her might.

Max stuck her head out of the driver's side window. "We're not moving!"

Talia let out a wail that would rival Tarzan's and pushed again. The car didn't budge.

"Can I help?"

She looked into the face of a Prince Charming. Tall and broad and wearing a black suit. She had to be dreaming. This would be the "meet-cute" in her next novel. The dialogue unfolded in her mind:

"I'd hate for you to get your clothes dirty."

"It's not my clothes that are about to get dirty."

The heroine gasped at his suggestiveness. "So very kind of you to offer assistance."

"I may have an ulterior motive. Your beauty has capti—"

"Who the fuck are you?" Max jumped out of the car.

"Calm down, Max. He just offered to help." Talia was mortified by her friend's overreaction.

"Did you put it in neutral?" the potential leading man said.

"Of course I did!" Max looked at Talia. "Just push the fucking car."

"I assume you're out of gas," the man said.

"Why else would the car conk out?" Talia asked.

"Could be a dead alternator or bad coolant system or clogged fuel line, just to name a few causes."

They stared at him, Talia captivated and Max annoyed.

"Are you two wasted?" he asked.

Talia gathered her wits. "We're fine. And yes, please help. Max, get back in the car."

"And be sure it's in neutral." The man grinned at Talia. His teeth sparkled in the lamplight.

With Prince Charming's strength and Talia's adrenaline surging, they managed to push the car all the way to the curb.

"There you go. All set," the man said, dusting his hands together. It was then that Talia noticed the gold band on his left ring finger. The story in her head took a dark turn. How would she get rid of the wife?

"Thank you so much, sir. I wish there were some way I could—"

Before she finished her sentence, the man jogged into the street and waved down a cab. He jumped into the yellow car as if he couldn't wait to escape. Probably because he couldn't.

Max got out and stood beside Talia as the beautiful, strong, solicitous man disappeared around a corner. Definitely not the happily-ever-after Talia had hoped for.

"Alrighty," said Max. "Let's take a cab to your place. My treat."

eleven
sophia

If I see one more basic bitch carrying around this awful book, I am going to scream. I read literature, not trends. Follow me on TikTok: @JaneAustinIsAHack and @EssentialOilsSale

Two things Sophia did not like: trudging through dirty snow and traveling all the way out to Brooklyn to do so. But she didn't have much choice. She knew exactly two lawyers. One was the public defender who thought he'd make a name for himself by taking her brother's case to trial. With a plea deal, Gage might have had a chance at parole one day. Losing at trial and getting consecutive life sentences meant he'd never see freedom, but at least his attorney got to make an impassioned closing argument.

The other attorney she knew, the one that she and Chelsea were scheduled to meet, was Alec Pendergrass, a failed writer. Just like them. He'd had the same dreams, attended the same workshop where they'd all met. She'd run into him many times over the years after that. They all had. They went to the same seminars, sat through the same author talks, commiserated over cheap beers after book signings when they had to listen to mediocre writers tell glowing stories of their own miracle successes.

He was a failed attorney, too, from Sophia's understanding.

He'd been so cocky when they met. The writing workshop had been his indulgent reward to himself while waiting for his bar exam results. Alec announced he was going into entertainment law and he'd happily represent them later. But then he failed the bar exam—twice. When he finally passed it, he repeated the lie that everyone always told each other, that his dreams had changed. He was happier, he said, getting hired on as an associate at a personal injury firm in Brooklyn. "I'm helping people get what they deserve," he told them, though Sophia recognized the look in his eyes. It was the same look Talia got when she said she enjoyed foot modeling, or when Chelsea was trying to convince everyone that this current ghostwriting assignment was fulfilling. Liars, all of them. All but Max, whose unflinching honesty might bring this whole AI fiasco crashing down on their heads.

Sophia waited by the Robert F. Kennedy Memorial bust in Columbus Park, stomping her feet to keep them from freezing. She should have worn warmer boots, but these thin leather ones matched her outfit better. *If Chelsea doesn't get here soon, I'm going in without her. We're going to be late.*

While she waited, she thumbed through her copy of *Deep Within the Discontented Dreaming of Dorian Dimwitty*. Not her original copy. That one was long gone, accidentally abandoned at a bar and carried off by one of her MFA cohorts, most likely. Or, in her preferred scenario, it could be sitting in the bar's lost and found, and she bore no responsibility for the book getting out into the wider world. This copy was one she'd picked up from a bookstore, feeling furtive and embarrassed, hiding it in a stack she carried to the register, where she'd paid in cash. It wasn't a bad book. The fact that AI could write a decent, somewhat compelling novel stung. Sophia spent years pouring her heart into her work, yet four women shouting random ideas at a software program could produce an entire work in one night. It hurt.

"Great book," a man walking by shouted, and she gave him a half wave of acknowledgement. That was a mistake; he took it as an invitation to stop and talk. "I've read my copy a dozen times and keep finding new insights. Ascher is a master."

"Indeed." Sophia pointedly tucked the book back into her bag and checked the time on her phone. *Come on, Chelsea.*

"I'd love to chat about it when you've finished it," the man suggested, holding out a business card. "Call me."

Thank god Chelsea finally arrived. Sophia rushed off to meet her, leaving the man and his card behind. Max would've taken the card, called him, and made him buy her top-shelf drinks before taking him home for a night she'd surely tell them all about in way too much detail. Sophia had no patience for such things.

—

Sophia and Chelsea rode the elevator up to the ninth floor in silence. They'd talked it all out the night before, after looking up costs. Alec would probably charge them hourly, but he might ask for a cut of the profits as well. If—big if—they sold the movie rights, he could likely claim twenty percent, a small price to pay to keep their names out of it.

Alec welcomed them cheerfully enough, escorting them to his tiny, windowless interior office. His framed diploma and bar admission certificate hung on the wall behind the client chairs, a strategy Sophia would have employed as well. Clients wouldn't have time for more than a quick glance, keeping them from noticing the year that passed between graduation and licensure.

"How's Talia doing?" Alec's first question was no surprise. "Chelsea, when you made the appointment, I thought you said she was coming."

Sophia hid her smile. Chelsea had made the appointment for herself and a friend, knowing that Alec's not-so-secret crush would get them in much sooner than their names alone.

"Talia's great," Chelsea said. "Working hard, as she does. I just had her over last week."

"Yeah? Did she talk about me?"

"I think your name came up." Sophia interjected, figuring she might as well feed his ego. "How's your writing going?"

"Great, I just got two requests for fulls. Things are finally happening." He smiled proudly, but did not bounce the question back to them. Sophia realized he probably assumed that neither of them was close to success. They'd had too many similar conversations over the years.

"So ..." Chelsea took the reins. "Alec, is this conversation confidential? Lawyer-client privilege?"

"It is," he said slowly. "But I'm also obligated to inform you that I have ethical obligations."

"Yes, we expected that. That's why we're here. We know you're very ethical." Chelsea appeared to be taking the same tact by flattering him.

"I just want to make that clear. I mostly handle slip and falls. You both walked in here just fine; I'm not going to send you out for X-rays or to some shady chiropractor to boost up a claim for you. I only take real cases."

"You think we're here to fake a personal injury case?" Chelsea got that annoyed look on her face, the one usually triggered only by mentions of her ex-husband. Sophia placed a warning hand on her arm. They needed this meeting to go well.

Alec shrugged. "It wouldn't be the first time. One little slip on an icy patch and people see dollar signs. If you aren't here because of neck pain, and I know it's not a social call, why did you make this appointment?" The unspoken question, Sophia suspected, was why isn't Talia here? And also, why won't she date me? And could you put in a good word?

Chelsea nodded at Sophia. It was time. Sophia pulled the book from her bag and set it on Alec's faux-teak desk.

"Have you read this?"

Alec laughed dismissively. "Not my genre. I know, I know, everyone's raving about it. This guy is turning the literary world on its head. But honestly, I looked at the first chapter. It's garbage. The man's a hack."

"So, if given the opportunity to represent the author in *her* dealings with the public, you wouldn't be interested?" Chelsea asked.

"Her?" Alec's eyes darted back and forth between the two women. Sophia kept her face impassive, but next to her, Chelsea was not as controlled. She grinned.

"Her?" Alec repeated. "Meaning ... you?"

"This conversation is completely confidential," Sophia reminded him. "No one is to know what we talked about here."

"Which ... who ..." Alec flipped through the pages. He stopped and narrowed his eyes. "Chelsea, this isn't your voice. I know what's going on. This is one of your ghostwriting pieces, and now that it's made it big, you want more money. A larger share of the profits." His expression grew calculating. "I'll need to see the original contract. We might be able to renegotiate."

"It's not ghostwriting," Chelsea corrected him. "I wasn't the only one who wrote it."

"It was a group project," Sophia added. "We all—the two of us plus Max and Talia—co-wrote it. We never thought it would go viral." She tried to take a relaxed pose, but her body was thrumming with nerves. There were too many layers to this mess, too many secrets to keep.

"You all wrote this? I thought Talia was writing romance." He began to skim it again, as if hoping to parse out which words were Talia's, perhaps to get a glimpse into her psyche. Too bad this wasn't the Sasquatch romance they'd joked about. Alec probably would have shown up at Talia's door in costume.

"We collaborated during a retreat. It was all in good fun," Chelsea said, the same argument she'd used on all of them when she'd given them the books and the checks.

The dollar amount on her check was seared into Sophia's brain. It was so much money. She could have *savings*. She could *invest*. She could buy new clothes without having to spend hours combing through thrift shops. That's why this meeting had to go well.

"This is the kind of thing you write for fun? It's on the bestseller lists!" Alec turned away from them, tapping away at his computer, calling up their book on the screen. The number of reviews had increased since Sophia had last checked. "You've hit number one everywhere! You ... I can't believe the four of you wrote this."

"We've been having writing retreats together for years. Why wouldn't something come of it?" Sophia asked. She was being very careful with her phrasing. She didn't want to lie to an attorney, but she and Chelsea had already decided they couldn't tell him the full truth. Not now. Not ever.

"Wow. This is ... wow. I could ... wow. What exactly do you want from me?" Alec's face started turning red, and a vein pulsed in his forehead. It was the money, Sophia was sure of it. Maybe they should have asked if Alec had any terrible heart conditions before dumping this on him. If the excitement caused him to drop dead in his office, they'd probably have to explain to somebody else why they were here, and the news would spread.

"We need someone to represent our interests, but keep our names out of it. Entirely." Chelsea leaned forward, pointing at him decisively. "Alec, we think you're the perfect person to do it."

He stopped his nervous tapping. "Why don't you want your names on this? It's huge! You'll have agents knocking down your doors."

"We have our reasons," Chelsea told him. This was another thing they'd agreed on last night over the phone. Minimal details. The less he knew, the better.

"I get it," he said. "The plagiarism scandal, am I right? You can't have your name on anything. Why not use Sophia as a spokesperson? Or better, Talia?"

"This isn't my voice, and it isn't Talia's either. Agents who read this won't like our real work. We don't want to confuse the market. It'd be like if you wrote something like ... Sasquatch erotica. You'd never be able to sell a legal thriller under your own name," Sophia explained.

"Sasquatch what? That's not real, is it?" Alec glanced at his computer screen and Sophia instantly knew what search terms he'd be using the second they left.

"Our names cannot be attached to this project. We need someone to represent MF Ascher," Chelsea repeated. "Alec, if you can't handle it, we can go elsewhere. We came here out of respect for your literary talent. This is a golden opportunity for you as well."

Privately, Sophia thought Chelsea was laying it on a little thick, but appealing to the male ego seemed to work.

"Ladies, I'll be proud to represent you. Now, let's talk money."

twelve
max

DNF. This is bullshit. I'm a tenured university professor and all this drivel is plagiarized from the classics. It's like that disgusting book that went viral—the one that was written poorly and full of explicit sex. And everyone fell for it. It's disgusting that anyone can go online and publish a book and everyone thinks it means something profound. It does not.
-@profsmarts

Max pulled up in front of Talia's apartment complex in a hot red Mustang convertible with the top down and the heat ramped up, her curly tendrils frazzled by the icy wind.

"Hey, good looking. Wanna ride?"

"Max, what the heck?" Talia squawked.

Max grinned, feeling playful, which wasn't often. In fact, this side of her only came out when she was around Talia. There was something about her that made Max feel more like herself than anyone else, including Chelsea and Sophia. They were guarded, holding their thoughts and feelings close to their chest in case someone would use the information to hurt them, take advantage of them.

Talia wasn't like that. Even though her own family criticized her, which pissed Max off, Talia was still true to her nature. She maintained the lightness that made Max want to protect her.

Max hated family. She didn't grow up with a family the way others did, with mothers and fathers and siblings. Just selfish bastards who exploited the foster care system and its wards for money.

But she saw how family treated each other. Parents had unrelenting expectations for their children, like Talia's mother, who looked down on her. For what? Not being thin enough? A real parent would love Talia, see her light, and want to shield her from harm.

Like her, Talia was alone in the world, sort of. This was the bond that kept Max bound to her. If anything happened to her, she knew Talia would notice and do something about it. She would do the same for Talia. She would wage war on anyone who hurt her.

"You like?" Max asked. "Her name is Ruby."

Max gunned the engine, and it grumbled beneath her feet, vibrating like a lioness purring after a feast of gazelle flesh and entrails.

"Not really." Talia's mouth hung open as she lowered herself into the cushy leather seat. Her eyes surveyed the navigation system that lit up in red and orange flames on the dashboard. "Please tell me it's a rental. Or that you stole it."

"I'm no thief." Max's grin widened as she pulled on to the main road and headed to the highway towards Chelsea's apartment. This time, Max didn't mind the long trek from Queens, with or without traffic. She was riding in style. One she could buy for herself, without anyone's help or empty promises. "I just came into some money and couldn't help myself."

"We talked about this. Chelsea said we could spend a little, like a hundred dollars or maybe a thousand. Not tens of thousands!"

Max's skin tingled with irritation. But her stubbornness swept that small spasm of wasted feeling back where it belonged. Into a deep void.

"Say something, Max," Talia insisted, her fingers fighting to calm the long tresses of dark brown hair being pulled and tossed around by the wind.

She stayed silent, pretending to look at the side mirrors, then the rearview mirror as she switched lanes, gunning her sports car along the left lane of the highway, doing at least twenty miles over the speed limit.

"Did you spend it all?" Talia asked in disbelief.

When she still didn't answer, pretending to play with the music buttons, Talia reached over and pinched her arm.

"Jesus!" Max yelled over the noise of the thrashing wind and the cars whooshing past them.

"Will you put the top up, please? It's freezing. And I can't hear you!"

Max looked over at Talia, noting her exasperation, and rolled her eyes with irritation. She got off at the next exit ramp, stopped at the corner, and flipped the button that rolled the top over them, enclosing them in the small space of the car, promising to entrust their secret.

"Okay. Fine," she relented as the quiet grew pregnant between them. "I deposited my check and then spent about half of it on this car. But I needed it, okay? Mine was old and kept breaking down. So why not? Why not make my life a little fucking easier? It's my money."

Irritated, she gunned the engine and sped along the side roads. The car grumbled in response. She felt like a child who came home after curfew and had to explain to her mom that she deserved to have some fun. Some liberties. Something to make her existence feel grounded and secure in this life that seemed to want her to leave quietly as if she had never been there, had never breathed its toxic fumes, had never wept over its unfairness to people like her—without money, without power, without a home full of loving people and loving ... anything.

"I won't apologize for it." Max said. There was an edge in her voice, not intended to hurt Talia, but to set a boundary that needed to be put between them, to justify her decision. It was, after all, her decision. Her money. Her fucking car. "Are you telling me you've spent zero money?"

"I'll admit," Talia said in a small voice that forced Max to lean toward her to hear. "I spent a couple thousand dollars."

"You did … what?" Max took her eyes off the road for a second to look over at Talia, whose hands were gripping one another on her lap, like a schoolgirl admonished for cheating on a test.

"I used it to buy flowers for my sister's bridal shower."

Max choked on a laugh. "What am I going to do with you?"

"What do you mean by that?" Talia arched her eyebrows. "Stop laughing at me, or I'll pinch you again. Besides, the flowers cost a fraction of what you spent on this car!"

"Oh, good god, girl!" Max wiped tears from her eyes. "You have all this money and you spend it on your stupid sister. The money is for you. Not for any of them."

Talia remained silent, as if contemplating Max's words. Then she said, "It was for me, so I could prove to my mother I'm not a failure. And it worked. Her eyes popped out of her head when I said I'd cover the cost of the ridiculously overpriced flowers she'd ordered for the stupid over-the-top shower she planned."

"I get that." Max reached over to squeeze Talia's fingers in solidarity. In kindness, really. "But I need to teach you how to be selfish. To do something just for you. Like I did for myself by buying this car."

"I admit to being a teeny bit selfish."

"Explain," Max ordered with a knowing grin.

"Well, I went to a spa and got a hot-stone massage, a facial, and a mani-pedi. I drank expensive champagne and ate caviar on toast, too. And the whole time, I was thinking, is this what rich people do? It was incredible. I want to be rich."

"Woo-hoo! Good for you. I mean it," she added when Talia

gave her a dubious look. "You deserve to spoil yourself. Think about it. No one else spoils us, so we have to do it ourselves."

"Yes," Talia replied, her voice low and thick with emotion. "I know you're right."

Max gave her a thoughtful glance and patted her arm before turning up the music, both women left to their own internal musings for the rest of the ride to Jersey.

When they finally reached Chelsea's apartment complex, neither moved a muscle to get out of the car. They sat quietly and listened to the music for a bit until Talia shifted out of their trance and filled the space between them with words.

"What do you think they're going to say?"

"Who?" Max looked over at Talia, noting the worry lines that pulled at her round cheeks, all pink and flushed.

"Chelsea and Sophia. You think they're going to be mad at us? I mean, I know we had permission, but we both went overboard. Especially you."

Max's mouth formed a smirk. "I bet you anything—half my earnings from this crazy book—that they also spent some of the money. We're all human. All selfish. All self-serving. Some of us are just better at hiding it."

She refused to conceal her cynicism for people. Even if those people were her friends—and now fellow conspirators. It was her lived experience with humans, weak ones, strong ones, all of them the same in some form or another.

"I don't agree with everything you said, but you're probably right about the money. I mean, how could they not spend at least a little?"

"Exactly," Max mumbled, a sadness hanging low on the branch of her words. How we each deal with that culpability is yet to be seen, she thought to herself, keeping that bit of wisdom from the most innocent of her friends.

Max stretched her arms and legs and motioned for them to get out. "Now let's go see what Chelsea has for us this time. I hope it's another check!"

Her eyes twinkled with excitement, and Talia laughed aloud.

thirteen
talia

Dear New York Times, how how how how how did this book make it onto the bestseller list? If this is where literature is headed, humanity is doomed.

-SamanthaQ

"Wait." Talia tugged Max's arm. "I think we should park around the corner."

"Why?" Max pulled away.

"I don't want Chelsea and Sophia to see your car."

Max scowled at her. "That's ridiculous."

"No, it's not. I agree that Chelsea and Sophia might have spent some of their money, but probably small amounts. You have to admit, a new car is above and beyond." Talia softened her tone. "Can't we keep it under the radar for now?"

"Fine." Max gunned the motor and swerved out of the perfect parking space they'd been lucky to find. "You're really taking all the joy out of this." She drove down the block until the car was out of view from Chelsea's dingy windows. "Happy now?"

"I just want to be careful, Max. And you know I don't mean to spoil your fun."

Max threw open her door. "Well you're sure doing a good job of it. You're so fucking cautious and intimidated by them."

"I know I am." Talia pretended to agree. "But as long as you and I are on the same page, I feel like nobody gets to have the upper hand. That's why I think it's best if we keep the money we've spent between us, at least until we know for sure that they're splurging a little, too." Talia paused and analyzed Max's expression. Her friend's tight lips relaxed, and she let out a breath of air. Talia needed to wear her down in minuscule increments.

"All right, I won't mention the car."

"Good," Talia said as she stepped onto the curb, already conflicted about ruining Max's giddy mood. Max had so little that made her happy. As they fell in step beside each other, Talia grabbed her hand like they were two girls on the playground. "But," she said with a conspiratorial grin, "your new car is fucking fabulous!" It always cheered her up when Talia said the F-word.

By the time they climbed the stairs up to Chelsea's apartment, they were out of breath and sweaty. Talia's anxiety increased with every step toward the door.

"Jesus, Tal, relax. I can practically smell how nervous you are."

"That's rude," Talia said. "I'm wearing deodorant. The good kind, too. I went to CVS and bought the name brand instead of generic."

"Oooh, spent another ten bucks, I'll bet. Wait 'til Chelsea hears that. You'll be in big trouble."

Talia giggled. Max could be such a character.

The minute they walked in, Talia sensed they weren't there to collect their second checks, as Max had hoped. Both Sophia and Chelsea stood in the kitchen with grim expressions, as if they were making a condolence call.

"Is something wrong?" Talia asked. Fear seized her. What if everything had fallen apart? What if the algorithms had picked up the fact that they'd used AI and they were about to be arrested for violating some "terms of service" agreement? There was no way

Talia could come up with two thousand dollars to pay for the flowers she'd ordered for the bridal shower.

"Nothing's wrong," Chelsea said. "Sophia and I were just talking about her brother. She's worried about him."

"Yeah," Sophia said, taking a tray of mini pizza bites from the toaster oven. "He's, um, he has the flu, a bad flu."

"I'm so sorry," Talia said, relieved and then guilty for her selfish concerns. "I hope he'll be okay."

"Me, too," Max said with a genuineness she rarely showed to anyone other than Talia. "That sucks."

"He's in the infirmary; he should be fine." Sophia shook her head as if to straighten out her thoughts.

As usual, she was close-lipped about her last remaining family member. Talia could only imagine how painful it was for Sophia to be worried about her disabled brother all the time. He was in some sort of care home far away, but she showed such sisterly devotion. He must be a good man, Talia figured. Hopefully, the influx of money will help her care for him—perhaps move him to a better facility with more resources.

"Anyway, let's get down to business." Sophia flashed a raised eyebrow at Chelsea as if their brains were in sync.

A fleeting flicker of worry (or was it anticipation?) fluttered against Talia's chest. She put on her bright smile and popped a pizza bite into her mouth. Her New Year's resolution had been to break the habit of stress eating. It was *not* going well. But since it was midafternoon, a few pizza bites could be considered lunch. Shoot, she might've eaten lunch right before Max picked her up. Talia tried to remember what she'd written in her food diary. Oh, yeah, nothing. Another failed resolution. Never mind. She'd skip dinner.

Chelsea, in her big sister way, wrapped an arm around her, sensing Talia's nerves, perhaps. A sudden burst of comfort warmed her. Maybe she needed to switch best friends. Nah, Chelsea and Sophia were too connected. Talia would have to keep her role as beloved pet.

"We have news. Well, kind of news, more of a topic to discuss. And a major decision to make together."

"Do you have anything stronger than wine?" Max asked. "I'd like a shot of tequila."

"Me, too," Sophia said out of character. She opened Chelsea's liquor cabinet, a sorry shelf that was almost empty. "Look at that, *Jose Cuervo*."

Max gagged. "I'm buying you good tequila with my next royalty check. Meantime, gimme a shot of that piss-water."

There was just enough for four shots. They all drank. It burned Talia's throat. "I forgot how much I hate cheap tequila."

They took seats in Chelsea's tattered living room. Talia sat on the edge of a straight-backed chair popping pizza bites into her mouth while Sophia and Chelsea took turns *informing* them of their secret mission to engage the help of Alec Pendergrass.

"I fucking hate that guy!" Max shouted. "How could you even think that would be a good idea? He's a no-talent scumbag. Plus, he practically stalks Talia! No way, no fucking way."

Talia cringed at the mention of Alec Pendergrass, especially in front of Max, but she wasn't about to argue. "Calm down, Max. Let's hear them out."

Max sneered. "Why do we need a lawyer, anyway?"

"We need a person who ..." Sophia paused and pursed her lips. Talia liked the way Sophia chose her words carefully. "A person who is ethically bound to keep our identities secret but can represent our interests when it comes to appearances, contracts, taxes, financial decisions."

"Decisions *we* make," Chelsea said. "Nobody else."

Max blinked rapidly, as if her busy brain were trying to absorb this information. "How much did you pay him?" she asked.

"Nothing," Chelsea said. "Not yet, anyway."

"The four of us have to agree to take this step," Sophia said. "It needs to be unanimous. No matter what happens, we're all in this together. Chelsea published our drunken manuscript for fun, but we *all* lost our copies of the book. And we're *all* reaping the rewards—at least for as long as they last."

"What does that mean?" Talia asked. "You really think this is just a—a fluke? A case of the emperor with no clothes waiting for someone to speak the truth?"

"What truth do you mean?" Max got giddy. "That we reveal it's AI now? Because I'm all for that!"

"Are you all for *your* reputation being shredded?" Chelsea shot back. "Because that's what'll happen if it gets out that the book was written by AI."

"You trust Alec not to tell?" Talia asked.

"He doesn't know that part. And he never will." Sophia narrowed her gaze at Max. "Unless somebody tells him."

"Come on!" Max jumped up and paced the room. "Can't we just use this to blow up the industry? To prove that the gate-keepers who reject our work year in and year out don't know shit and can't tell fake writing from real?"

"That was our first reaction," Chelsea said. "Before the money started rolling in. Our royalties this month are already more than last month's."

Talia gasped. Her right knee bounced and her hands trembled. Money changed everyone in ways they couldn't predict. "I agree. We're like lottery winners. The first thing they're supposed to do is hire a lawyer, an accountant, and a financial advisor. You think we should get a financial advisor?"

Chelsea rested a hand on Talia's jumping knee. "One step at a time. It's not like we're into the millions—yet."

Talia struggled to breathe. The amount of money they could make was beyond comprehension. But money was a drug to some people. The more they got, the more they wanted.

"But why Alec?" Max planted herself in front of Sophia. "We can't stand him. He's an idiot."

"He's actually not an idiot." Sophia's levelheaded tone calmed Talia's nerves. Her voice was soothing. "He's smart, he's hungry, and he's tired of being an ambulance chaser. We're giving him an opportunity he can't resist, which means he'll be malleable. He will love being the face of MF Ascher. His ego will keep him in check. He won't ask questions. He'll do what we want him to do. No more—no less."

Talia watched as Max's expression changed. Her pursed lips relaxed, then tightened up again. She looked closely at each of her friends, as if sizing them up.

"Think about the future, Max," Chelsea said. "We need to ensure we're protected from any of this getting out. We've got to keep our identities a secret—and protect the money, for however long it lasts."

"Okay." Max sat on the coffee table. "I agree, but on one condition."

"What?" Talia blurted out. The more they talked, the more anxious she became. "What condition?"

"That at some point, we let the world know that the brilliant book that fools all around the world are fawning over was written by a fucking machine!"

Talia attempted to read Chelsea and Sophia's expressions. Man, they had excellent poker faces. She and Max were hopeless when it came to hiding behind blank stares. While Chelsea revealed nothing, her face and body unchanged, Sophia gave away the slightest indication of—of what? Trepidation?

Finally, Chelsea spoke. "I think we can work with that. Don't you, Sophia?"

Talia was half insulted and half relieved Chelsea did not ask her, too. It was no secret that Talia would go along with Chelsea. While she loved Max and admired Sophia, Talia idolized Chelsea as if she were the senior counselor at summer camp.

When Sophia didn't answer, Talia jumped in to break the silence. "I'm fine with that. I mean, eventually we'll have so much money socked away it won't even matter, right? And now that we have a lawyer, he can make sure it's all, you know, on the up and up, right? Like, set things up so that even if everything implodes, none of us have to pay anything back. He can do that, right?"

"Be quiet, Talia," Max said. "And quit ending every sentence with 'right?' It's fucking annoying."

Talia clamped her jaw shut. Another nervous habit—repeating certain words.

"I think," Sophia said, twirling her ponytail between her fingers, "that can work."

Talia fell back onto Chelsea's tattered couch. The tension in the room dissipated like a nasty odor. Everyone seemed happy, or happy enough, which was all Talia could hope for at this point. Still, a slim thread of apprehension tugged at her, like a faraway yellow light flashing in the distance, warning her, warning them all, to proceed with caution.

fourteen
chelsea

I absolutely need a movie version of this book, though once it happens, I'll be pissed that they screwed it up. Still, I would love to see Dwayne Johnson and Kevin Hart take a run at it.
–The Cozy Reader

With each tick of the second hand, Chelsea's stomach squeezed tighter. She had to focus on keeping the dread at bay because today of all days, Rick absolutely could not see it. If he even got a brief whiff of weakness, he'd pounce, and their entire plan would go up in flames.

"I still can't believe you're good with this." Alec sat on her left, scrolling through his phone and straightening his blazing red tie. Fitting choice for a power play.

She gazed around the lobby of Rick's production company. He insisted on keeping it East Coast-based. Why, she didn't know. Probably because here he could still be a big fish in a smaller pond, while the ocean in Los Angeles would swallow him whole.

The office reminded her of a mausoleum with stone-faced walls and gilded picture frames in symmetrical rows, the plates below etched with what Chelsea could only surmise were relevant names and dates. It was a shrine to Rick, his dimple-pitted smirk featured in every single one within sight.

"Why wouldn't I be good with it?" she asked, monitoring the tremor in her voice. "A deal's a deal. And money is money." She fished out the roll of Tums she bought on the way over. Her stomach had been giving her hell, her lifelong ulcer flaring back to life.

"Yeah, but this is your ex. A slimeball that, as I remember Talia mentioning, totally fucked you over."

Talia. Sweet, lovable Talia. God, she loved that woman and her big mouth. But Talia wasn't the only one Chelsea worried about at this moment.

She leaned closer to Alec, the overpowering cologne or body spray—did he actually use Axe like a middle-school boy?—squeezing her throat.

"We got divorced. That typically means someone got fucked over." She righted herself, inside and out. Alec shrugged and went back to his phone, scrolling through pictures of women on a dating app. Chelsea bit her lip when she realized they weren't faces that he was interested in—he was zooming in on the feet.

She cleared her throat and turned her attention back to the *People* magazine she had picked up from the side table. Her brain ran through every scenario of what might happen with this meeting, as it had been doing since Rick called to confirm it yesterday. She had slept maybe twenty minutes since then between the client deadlines and her racing thoughts.

Her mind now returned to Talia and how easily she could vomit information to the wrong people at any moment. But her heart was in the right place, and she never did anything with a hint of malice. And Max was a time bomb. Chelsea couldn't stomach the thought of her outing them though she pretended to be on board. The stakes were too high for her with what she had already been through. Even after the first two waves of money, and the total amount climbing, Chelsea hadn't spent it. When Max's explosion brought it all crashing down, Chelsea would need it to go into hiding. For good.

But the night after the four agreed to let Max expose the book at some point, Chelsea's head filled with the most delightful and devious notion. A story played out, from beginning to end, curling her lips at the corners, igniting that spark in her chest that had flickered back to life in the cabin all those months ago. She didn't dare spring out of bed to write it down. Instead, she swam in the details, the possibilities of one scene flowing into another. The connective tissue was flimsy, but it could all build to a glorious and masterful ending that included the takedown of the bastard who had screwed her out of the thing that made her who she was. The mere consideration that this Revenge Story might work cracked the iced-over pieces of her creative heart.

She just needed to make sure all the characters did what she needed them to do, including her three best friends.

"Chels!" Rick said from the doorway, arms parted wide as if he expected her to fall into his embrace. Like hell. Chelsea was not the woman she'd been nine years ago when they'd met, the woman who let herself get swept away in his good looks, his charm, his unyielding attention and affection. She was so taken back then that she'd ignored the red flags, the times he feigned concern. His emotions were an act, things he wore like masks and paraded around for minutes and hours when the situation called for it until those people—including Chelsea—no longer served him. Then he slithered out of his fake skin like a snake.

But now Chelsea knew exactly who and what she was dealing with.

"Rick, this is Alec Pendergrass, Esquire. He represents MF Ascher."

Rick dropped his arms and moved forward, right hand proffered, fake-toothed smile gleaming towards Alec. Chelsea fought off the reflexive eye roll.

"It's a pleasure to meet you, Alec." The two men shook hands and beamed at each other. Chelsea couldn't help but notice that

Alec seemed to grow two inches taller. Being in Rick's presence did that to a person.

"The honor's all mine, Rick. I'm eager to see what you've got to offer us."

Chelsea's breath caught at Alec's slip, but Rick didn't bat an eye. Instead, he clapped Alec on the back, guiding him down the hall while leaving her to trail behind. She regretted in that instant not having Sophia here. The stench of overgrown male egos flooded the air. But they agreed it would look too suspicious if anyone other than Chelsea took this meeting.

The trio ended their short walk in Rick's office, three times bigger than it needed to be, with a breathtaking view of the Hudson River.

"That's a beautiful sight," Alec said, his eyes wide, glimmering at the Oscar posed front and center on the desk.

"Isn't it? Go ahead," Rick said, sitting back in his seat, eyes black from nabbing his prey. "Touch it." Chelsea swallowed the hate-filled boulder that bounded up into her throat, as Alec caressed the award for best screenplay that was the ultimate symbol of Rick's betrayal. Her unblinking eyes brushed around the room, pausing on the framed poster for *Murder and Other Secrets* (the title being the only change Rick made between her book and his movie) and its sequel, *The Buried Past*. She wanted to rip that statue out of Alec's hands and send it crashing into Rick's skull until there was nothing left but shards of bone and black blood.

But she didn't. Her friends were depending on her to do the right thing for them, not the right thing for her. This plot of hers needed to be written with a happy ending for all of them.

She cleared her throat, breaking Alec's spell with the Oscar. He placed it on the desk and settled back into his chair.

"I understand that you may be interested in speaking to MF Ascher about film rights for the book," Alec said, his professional tone returning.

"I am. Very much so."

"I represent Ms. Ascher in all matters, so consider whatever you say to me a direct line to her."

Rick nodded and moved his eyes to Chelsea, who remained stoic. "What part do you play in this thing, Chels?"

"You asked how I got the book. This"—she gestured to Alec —"is how. MF Ascher is a mutual friend of ours." She understood Rick and the way he worked. She also recognized the narrowing of his eyes, the flicker of something dancing around the edge that flooded her with delight.

She leaned toward Alec and placed her left hand softly on his shoulder. She did her best to counteract the stiffening of his body under her unexpected touch, and when Alec shot her a confused gaze, she let her fingers dance down his arm and squeeze his hand. He stared in disbelief, but then, like a puppet in her show, he lifted her hand to his lips and doused it with a kiss.

The scene lasted maybe ten seconds, and by the time her theatrics were through, she knew that Rick had not only bought it, but that his jealous streak would overpower his rationality. It lit her up from head to toe, this newfound power that she might hold over the man who destroyed her. She was going to need every bit of it if her story was going to play out as she intended. Because Rick's demise *was* her happy ending. If Max had her way and took them down, Chelsea would take Rick with her. But she needed every piece to fall into place. The plot in her Revenge Story was complicated, and every character had to do her bidding.

"Right. So, Rick," Alec started again, drawing the meeting back on track. "Shoot straight with me. What's your best and final offer? A savvy man like you already knows what you want."

"I do. I'll give Ascher two million for the rights to the book."

Alec knit his brows and shook his head. "No good. Do you have any idea how much money this book has already made?"

Of course, he didn't. But neither did Alec.

"It's hit every bestseller list. Has over 280,000 reviews. Was just picked by Oprah *and* Reese for their book clubs. I'm fielding calls from every major news outlet and production studio you can think of. And if that is your best and final, we'll excuse ourselves and get back to our day." He reached over and squeezed Chelsea's knee in a way that indicated Alec was going to take full advantage of her ploy and play up the nature of their relationship.

If there was one thing she knew better than anyone, one message she repeated to Alec when they prepared for this meeting, it was this: Rick Stafford did not like to lose. If they played their cards right, Rick would give them every single thing she wanted—and more.

Rick stared down at his desk for a moment, like he was playing out a conversation in his head. Alec moved his palm up to Chelsea's bare thigh, an advancement she halted by covering his hairy hand with hers.

"Ten million for the exclusive rights," Rick cleared his throat. "Plus, fifteen percent of box office and streaming residuals on every penny."

Alec remained silent, as if weighing the offer.

Rick continued. "And I'll guarantee twenty million for the next book and double the box office residuals."

Rick slid his gaze to Chelsea, attempting to read her expression. But she wouldn't give him a damn thing, and so she waited for Alec to answer, locked in an impasse with her sworn enemy across yet another battlefield.

"That beats some of the numbers I'm hearing from your competitors," Alec said.

She was impressed by his nonchalant business tone. It tore Rick's attention from her and gave her a small victory.

Alec stood, prompting Rick to do the same.

"So, does this mean we have a deal?" Rick pushed his hand back out to Alec, and Chelsea caught the glimpse of a shake running through his arm.

Alec regarded him for a few moments, drawing out the climax like Chelsea told him to. Until his face widened into a smile, his hand accepting Rick's and pumping it the way two men do when they believe they've done something extraordinary.

"We do. I'll need the contract within the next forty-eight hours. Otherwise, my client will insist I move on."

Rick chuckled. "I like your style, Alec. You'll have it by the end of the day."

Chelsea stood, smoothing her skirt down to hide her shaky knees. She needed to get out of this toxic air.

"Chels," Rick said, nodding at her. He ran his eyes over her like he always did, but the weight of his gaze had eased. She turned her back, leading the way to the elevator.

She fought against the smile that teased her lips. It wasn't so much about the money, the breadth of which was incomprehensible to her at this moment. No, it was something else. It was the joy that filled a writer's chest when her characters did exactly what she wanted them to do.

"That's a lot of fucking money," Max said between bites of her burger. "And you're sure you want to give this to Rick?" The four of them were sitting in a crowded diner a few blocks from Rick's office. Chelsea had met them twenty minutes ago and immediately launched into a summary of the meeting.

Chelsea shrugged and put on her not-a-big-deal face. She figured Max would bring this up again.

"It's the best-case scenario for *all* of us. That's what matters."

"But can you trust him?" Max pushed.

"That's why we have a lawyer. Rick craves money and fame, both of which this deal gives him. And regardless of how much we dislike Alec, the guy knows how to cut a deal. He'll make sure everything is legal and enforceable." She tamped down the concern that her friends might question her motives or trust her.

Thankfully, Max appeared satisfied for now and took another sip of her drink.

"Do you think he'll actually send the contract to Alec?" Talia chased her fries with a gulp of mimosa.

"I'm sure of it. Alec did a good job of making it sound like the book was an even bigger deal than it is."

"So this is happening. A movie?" Sophia hadn't done much more than sip her ice water since Chelsea arrived. The two of them had already agreed to talk alone afterwards and hash out the finer details. Talia and Max required special handling to ensure the plot advanced as she needed it to.

Max leaned across the table. "We need to start figuring out how and when we can expose this whole fucked-up scheme. I think now that we have a deal with Hollywood—"

"Not quite." Chelsea stilled her voice to make sure it didn't have a hint of desperation. Max's intention to blow up the system would work for Chelsea; however, it couldn't happen this soon in the story.

"The contract isn't even signed, Max," Sophia continued. "Until that's done, we don't have anything."

"Right, but I'm so excited!" Talia squeaked. "I love the idea of having a movie credit to my name."

Before Chelsea could intervene, Max pounced. "It won't be your name, Talia. It won't be any of our fucking names. It'll be MF Ascher, the robot genius! Those pricks who hold all the cards don't know shit about creativity. About art. About what people like and don't like. They can't even see that a machine wrote something they want so much."

"Oh, right." Talia blinked back tears at Max's harsh tone. None of them were used to it being directed at her.

Chelsea steeled herself, sick of Max hurling the same charges against the industry over and over.

"Max, the time will come. We all agree that it needs to happen, and I promise, it will." Chelsea placed a gentle hand on Max's shoulder.

The table remained silent, wrapped in tension. Chelsea wanted to shake Max by the shoulders and make her see that she needed this to right the wrong Rick caused her. Sure, she could probably just say it, but she was tired of the constant pity party of support anytime his name came up. Max might tell her to get the fuck over it and move on. No, she couldn't tell any of them yet. That way, if her plan failed, they would never know she was attempting such a long shot.

"God damn it," Max said, slamming her hands on the table, rattling them all. She leaned back in her chair, arms crossed against her like a shield while she huffed. "Fine. You win. But just remember, at some point, this all comes crashing down."

"None of us will stop you when the time is right," Chelsea said, as another plot point in her Revenge Story fell into place—for now.

fifteen
sophia

I wanted to love this book. I really did. I mean, the title itself. Come on! But I just didn't. Love it, that is. The setting was hard to pin down, and the characters were unbelievable. I know it's fiction. But still. Characters have to be believable, and I just didn't believe anything about her. Sorry, Ascher, whoever you are. I give this book 2 stars.

Gage's phone call was late. Sophia sat at the kitchen table, waiting. She couldn't leave the house until he called, and whenever his calls were late, she worried. Minutes, a half hour, no big deal. There were long lines of inmates waiting for the phones. But on days like this, when it was two hours past the time he'd promised, that familiar fear crept through her. Would this be the day he stopped calling? Was his body already buried in the field behind the prison?

It wouldn't be unprecedented. Sophia had once joined a support group for family members of federal prisoners. It was way out in Jersey, so nobody would recognize her. She'd shown up with a baseball cap pulled low over her forehead and never used her real name or Gage's. A man there spoke of how he had spent months sending letters to prison, desperate to contact his son, and heard nothing. The letters weren't returned, there were no phone calls, and after seven months, he'd finally received the news and the bill for the burial. Sophia never wanted to be in that position, but she always feared it. Someday her brother would lose his temper with the wrong person, someone bigger, stronger, someone with a shank.

"Call me, call me, call me," she whispered, and to her relief, the phone rang. She pressed zero before the recorded voice finished the usual spiel, call from inmate, do you accept, blah blah blah.

"You maxed out my commissary, baby girl," Gage said, his voice returning warmth to her bones. He was alive and sounded happy. "Does that mean we have something to celebrate?"

The optimism and hope broke her every time. Her brother was her biggest fan. He was the one who encouraged her. When her rejections piled up, it was Gage's voice in her head, telling her to give it another shot. *Don't quit, baby girl, you have the magic.* That's what he said to her about everything, though. When she tried out for the school volleyball team and got cut, he told her they didn't see her potential. When she wasn't cast in the school play, he told her it was because the director was afraid her star would shine too brightly, showing the rest of the cast to be talentless hacks. She never once believed him. Except about her writing. That was her magic, or so she'd always thought. Too bad AI could put her to shame. Who needs magic when you have technology?

"I came into a bit of money," she said. "Not a big publishing deal."

"It's coming. You'll get one. Have you thought any more about writing my story?"

"Instead of writing your story, what if we change it?" That was what she'd spent countless sleepless nights thinking about lately. She'd checked her bank balance so many times since depositing that check from Chelsea. Even though the desperate little fashionista that lived inside her brain screamed at her to rush to Bergdorf's and make some salesgirl's monthly quota in an afternoon, she hadn't spent a penny on herself. Not yet.

"Change it how?" Gage asked. "I want to tell *my* truth."

She could picture him in his neat prison khakis, gripping the phone with both hands. That's how he'd always held it as a child, as though afraid of dropping the receiver. Even as a teenager, talking to one of his many girlfriends, he had paced the kitchen with both hands holding the phone tightly to his ear.

"I meant, what if I changed the ending? What if ... what if I could afford to help you file an appeal? I could get you an attorney. Maybe ... maybe we can get you out." Bring him home. He could have his childhood bedroom back, the room she'd converted into her cozy writing space. Her dream of one day being photographed there, profiled for a magazine, "When bestselling author, Sophia Aldren, is at her second home in Queens, she writes on a vintage Royal Quiet Deluxe typewriter, the same model used by her idol, poet Anne Sexton," was over. Those profiles would never come. Gage could have the space back. All a writer needed these days was a laptop and AI.

"Get me out?" Gage scoffed. "Don't waste your money. I'm guilty. I'm the only man in here honest enough to admit it. The rest of them, ha! I'm surrounded by innocent men steamrolled by the system. Talked to a guy yesterday, tackled by the cops, gun in his hand, girlfriend's blood all over him, and he says he was framed. They're all innocent."

"Gage, these calls are recorded. Never admit guilt." He was already screwing up her plan. How could she invest all her money in an appellate attorney when all the DA would have to do is play this recording?

"Baby girl, my only mistake was not taking the plea. I'd have been out in sixty, fifty if I behaved. You and me could have lived in an old folks' home together. It's too late for that. There's no appeal that'll work."

"Prosecutorial misconduct? Maybe evidence tampering? It's worth looking into, isn't it?" Sophia hated the desperation in her voice. Deep down, she knew Gage was right. She'd known it since the moment the SWAT team busted through their door. Her brother didn't deserve to ever leave prison. But it still hurt. The first thing he'd ever stolen was baby formula to feed her. The first time he'd been *caught* stealing, it was diapers. Those early petty childhood crimes set him on the path to committing his horrifying adult ones, and she still often wondered if he'd ever had a chance at a different life. Had this always been his future, written in stone from the moment Sophia was born and his eight-year-old shoulders had borne the burden of caring for her in their mother's cockroach-infested drug den?

"Forget it, Sophia. They got me. I know it, they know it, you know it. Why are you talking like this, anyway? What's changed?"

"I ... I was ... ghostwriting. I made a little money." She hated lying to her brother, but, like she warned him, prisoner calls were recorded. Someday someone might tell the truth about where the money came from, but it wouldn't be her. "I wanted to help you."

"Help me by keeping my commissary funds topped up. But don't put too much in at once—they take thirty percent off the top for my restitution."

"What if I pay off your restitution? Would that help?"

"The whole amount? Don't you dare. If you have that kind of money, invest it in yourself, or come visit more often. I'm never going to be able to pay all my debts, but that doesn't make you responsible for them. They don't bother me, anyway. I make seventeen cents an hour, and the government takes six. I don't miss that extra six cents, especially if I've got your deposits."

"How does anyone pay that off?" She couldn't imagine it, not just the weight of the debt on the prisoners, but how awful for the victims, receiving pennies per month in restitution. It would take decades to make back the funeral money, not to mention the medical bills for survivors.

"Buddy of mine just had his wiped clean. The trick is, you need an accomplice with joint and several liability. Then you get them to cover. My buddy's co-defendant's wife won big in Vegas; the Feds swooped in and took it all. Restitution paid in full, and he didn't have to do a damn thing."

"They took ..." She paused to consider the connection. "Wait, was she involved in the crime?"

"No, it was a white-collar embezzlement case, and her only involvement was not being smart enough to divorce her husband when he got locked up. It's community property plus joint and several liability. The Feds'll get the money wherever they can."

━━━

Sophia could not get her brother's words out of her head. She couldn't fathom the disappointment of that woman, celebrating a casino win, dreaming of buying a new car or retiring early, and having that money ripped away to pay for a crime she didn't commit. She picked up her phone, intending to call Chelsea. The two of them had discussed the penalties for committing fraud. But was using AI actually fraud? Did that count? Sure, when Chelsea uploaded the file, she had checked off the box saying the work was hers alone, but that was a white lie, hardly a criminal act.

No matter how she tried to justify it, Sophia couldn't shake the concern. If they were found out, they might have to pay it all back. All the booksellers would claw back the royalties, because using AI went against their terms of service. The movie deal, too. Every penny they'd received was earned through fraud.

And what about Max? She was ready to gloat, to upend the publishing industry, to punish it for denying them the respect they deserved. What then? They certainly wouldn't get that respect. They'd be pariahs in the publishing world, a cautionary tale against claiming computer-generated work as one's own. Their names would become synonymous with deceit. The rage of the readers, the ire of the book distributors, would turn into lawsuits. They'd lose everything.

Instead of dialing Chelsea, Sophia called Alec. "I've got a legal question for you."

"I'm always ready."

"What does jointly and severally liable mean?" After a pause, she added, "It's for my next book. I just want to make sure I'm getting the terminology right."

"Is your character an attractive lawyer, perhaps six feet tall with a chiseled jaw and piercing eyes? Are his initials AP?"

"You don't have a chiseled jaw," she corrected. Alec was a typical man, always assuming everything was about him. The male ego was a powerful yet fragile thing.

"Yes, I do. You just can't see it under my beard."

He called that scraggly thing a beard? He was probably stroking it as he spoke, so proud of his god-given ability to grow hair on his face, as though it required some level of skill. Big deal. Sophia could do that too, just in small, isolated, quickly plucked spots.

"No, it's the story of a woman falsely accused of a crime. I came across the term and wanted to understand it fully."

"Crime thrillers are my territory, not yours. You should stick to your flowery literary prose. Or another Dorian Dimfuckery book; that would sell."

"Never mind, I'll ask another attorney," she said, knowing that would make him answer her question.

"Fine. I assume your character has some co-conspirators? Allegedly? Jointly and severally liable means that if the defendants are collectively sued and owe money, the plaintiff can go after them individually for the full amount."

"Hypothetically, could they collect the full amount from each person? So four—or six, in my book—people committing real estate fraud means the victims can get six times what the jury orders if they make each person pay?"

He chuckled, an indulgent sound that made her blood boil. It was so condescending. "No, my dear, that would be what we call unjust enrichment. The total amount can and will be collected from the defendants, but that means that, for example, if one of them is dead broke, the others have to pay his share. If you're writing this from the plaintiff's point of view, best-case scenario is one of your defendants is a millionaire and covers the whole thing. Worst case—and better for your plotline—they're all poor and judgment-proof."

When Sophia hung up, she had to sit and digest what she'd learned. Her fingers were already shaky. How much had Max and Talia already spent? What if, down the line, everything fell apart, and they had to pay back every penny? Her friends had hardly any assets. Sophia was the only one who owned anything of value. If Max blew it all up, the Lake George house could be lost forever.

sixteen
talia

For the life of me, I don't understand the hype this book is getting. Part literary, part trashy, part YA Sci-Fi, with a mystery thrown in for good measure, as if a desperate chef is throwing spices into a failed soup. Save your money.
– TamiR@home

Talia stood beside her mother in the foyer of a French bistro with white tablecloths and English china, waiting for Jenna, the guest of honor.

"Well, this is a different look for you." Talia's mother scanned her up and down. Then she smiled. "That is a beautiful dress."

"Thanks," she said. "It's new."

Talia smoothed the front of her dress, an A-line floral print that hugged her bodice and made the most of her generous, smooth cleavage. The saleswoman at Bloomingdale's was now her personal shopper and friend. She'd spent two hours curating the perfect shower-hostess, maid-of-honor, older-sister ensemble that not only flattered Talia's plus-size body, but made her look downright sexy. The best part was her new sparkly gold, four-inch heeled, strappy sandals that cost more than the dress. Even the expert personal shopper noticed the unusual beauty of her feet and insisted that if she bought nothing else that day, she simply must purchase the sandals. And the advice had been correct. Adding four inches to her short frame allowed her to look down at her mother.

Talia bent a knee and turned one foot onto its toes. "New shoes, too."

Riva, a stylish woman in her late fifties, admired them. "They are pretty. Do we still wear the same size?"

"Actually, Mom, we never wore the same size."

"Hmmph, too bad. Maybe your sister could borrow them. They'd be gorgeous with her wedding dress, don't you think?"

Talia wanted to remove her shoes and hug them to her chest, protecting them from abuse. "I'm probably going to wear them myself."

"No, the bridesmaids' shoes are cobalt blue satin to match the dress."

"Oh." Talia's brain clicked into gear, formulating the story. The day of the wedding, she would claim she'd worn the shoes to a party and had caught a heel in between some bricks, scraping the gold leather all the way up the back. Of course, she'd rushed them to the repair shop, but sadly, they would not be available in time for the wedding.

"Make sure Jenna tries them on when she gets here," Riva said.

Over my fat dead body. "Absolutely. Nothing but the best for my little sister."

"Now don't be snippy, dear. Jenna is nervous enough."

Talia summoned all the fake sincerity she could muster. "I'm not being snippy, Mom. I genuinely mean it."

"That's very sweet." Her head snapped up. "Oh, look, there she is!"

Jenna, the second and favorite daughter of Riva Goldstein, swept in wearing a white knee-length dress with a full skirt and appliqué petals, like a mini version of her bridal gown. To Talia, she looked like a human wedding cake.

"Wait, go back!" her mother demanded. "I want to video your entrance."

"Okay!" Jenna flitted back out the door and repeated her entrance with additional flair, like a ballerina spinning onto the stage.

"Beautiful!" Riva could not contain herself as she gushed over her younger daughter.

"What do you think, Tal?" her sister asked.

"You look fabulous."

Talia had to admit that her sister was kinder to her than their mother was. Yes, she allowed herself to be paraded about like a cherished doll, but ever since the wedding plans began in earnest, Jenna had rolled her eyes many times at Riva's over-the-top management and extravagance. The day they'd gone shopping for Jenna's wedding dress—a mere eight thousand dollars—Riva had remarked to the sales associate that it probably would be the only wedding gown she'd have to buy. Jenna and Talia were out of sight in the fitting room and overheard their mother's comment.

"Don't pay attention to her, Tal. Mom says stupid shit all the time. You know how she is."

Talia now knew that if she ever did get married, she'd be able to buy her own fucking gown. And she'd for sure elope to a remote island with only her groom and her three closest friends. And their husbands or lovers, if they had them.

"Jenna, look at Talia's sandals. Try them on. You could wear them for the wedding."

Jenna peered at Talia's feet. "They are pretty," she said, scrutinizing them. "Do you mind?"

"Of course not. For sure. You're welcome to borrow them." Talia practically choked on her words. Max would want to smack her. She sat and removed her shoes.

A man walking by practically fell over as her stunning foot was laid bare. When he looked up and his gaze stopped at her breasts, Talia got a little satisfaction from his clumsy titillation.

She handed one golden sandal to her sister, who gingerly

slipped in her foot and buckled the delicate strap. It gaped in the back and drooped in the front.

"It's too big," Jenna said.

"Maybe we could put an extra hole in the strap," Riva said.

Talia snatched the sandal away. Like Cinderella's glass slipper, the shoe would only fit its true owner, even if that owner had the bigger foot.

"Mom, could you stop? I have my own shoes. I don't need to borrow Talia's." Jenna returned her too-small foot to her own pearly white pump.

"Excuse me, Mrs. Goldstein?" The restaurant manager approached Riva. "What did we decide on the bottomless mimosas?"

The moment Talia had been waiting for. Her heart thumped with anticipation. She stepped in front of her mother, almost pushing her out of the way.

"Yes," she said. "Bottomless mimosas, and here's my card." She stood tall on her four-inch heels and withdrew her credit card from her red leather clutch.

The manager accepted the card with a polite nod. "I'll bring the receipt to you after the event. And may I start you off with the mimosas now?"

"Yes, please," Talia said, reveling in the power and satisfaction money brought. For a split second, she thought about Max, who wouldn't approve of how she was spending her ill-gotten riches.

"Wow, Tal, thanks. I thought Mom was footing the bill for the shower."

"I got it," Talia said, as if dropping over three thousand dollars for a ladies' luncheon was child's play.

Riva pulled Talia to the side. "What's going on?"

"It's okay, I can do it," Talia's satisfaction with herself was beginning to falter. "Aren't you pleased that I can afford it?"

"Can you really? I mean, it's a lot of money. And after this outfit you splurged on ..." Riva waved her hands in a circular motion at Talia's dress.

"I've been earning money, Mom. I can't believe you're not, I don't know, proud of me." The thrill of flaunting her ability to pay in front of her mother and sister failed to meet expectations. And she hated that she sounded desperate for mommy's approval.

Riva pursed her lips. "Proud of you because you have a job, Talia? You should have a job. And at thirty-six years old, you should be able to afford to give your sister a bridal shower. This isn't about my being proud."

"Then how about appreciative?" The shower hadn't even begun, and Talia was already at odds with her mother. "Your friends are arriving, Mom. Enjoy yourself."

With her fancy heels clicking, she scurried into the restroom to compose herself and unload her frustration, but her best friend wasn't around. "Shit." Talia listened to Max's familiar message: "If you want a call back, leave your fucking number."

"Hey, it's me." She could tell she sounded weepy, so she coughed to mask it. "Sorry, just choked on my drink. I'm at the shower. All good. Talk to you later. Bye."

Leaving Max a message only exacerbated her loneliness. Talia had no friends attending the shower, nobody who could commiserate or even joke with her. But she couldn't hide in the bathroom all day. She gave her second choice a call.

Chelsea picked up after one ring. "Hi, Talia."

"Are you busy? You sound busy?"

"I'm always busy," Chelsea said. "What's up?"

Talia wondered if she'd made a mistake calling Chelsea. Maybe Sophia would've been the better option. "Not much. Well, that's not true. My sister's shower is about to start. And I—I kind of got into it with my mom."

"Ahh. Couldn't reach Max, and you need a little pep talk?"

"I do." Talia appreciated that Chelsea understood her and was less critical than Max regarding her family.

"I suppose I can help. I know a thing or two about difficult families. So where are you?"

"In the bathroom. In a stall."

"Jesus. Okay, let's FaceTime. I need to see what you're wearing, and I hope it's not all black."

Talia wavered, then she tapped the button. Chelsea's face appeared.

"Lighting's bad. Get out of the stall."

Talia obeyed. Bright lights above the sink illuminated her. "I bought a new dress," she said, setting the phone on the counter and stepping back.

"You look amazing. Dress is beautiful, and those shoes ... So what's the problem?"

Talia glanced in the mirror. She'd slept in sponge rollers to give her dark hair soft wavy curls and even had her makeup done at the Sephora near the restaurant. "My mother, as usual. She's so —so unappreciative."

"Of what? The dress?"

Talia paused. She hadn't meant to expose her spending to Chelsea, but her friend wasn't stupid. Obviously, Talia's new outfit had been purchased with the AI money.

"Well, I sort of sprung for the flowers. I know we aren't supposed to spend much of the money, but I guess I wanted to impress my mother." Oh, what an understatement that was.

Chelsea didn't react at first, her face seemed frozen in the same position. She was mad. Or aggravated. Or worse ... disappointed. Another person Talia had failed.

"I'm really sorry. I didn't want to tell you because I knew you'd be mad at me. But honestly, with what Max spent on her new car, I figured—" Talia gasped and slapped a hand over her mouth.

Chelsea sighed and shook her head. "I know about the car. Sophia and I both know. I figured you were going to spend some of it. It's fine."

"Thank you." Talia's tense shoulders fell forward with relief. She was off the hook and Max's mega-spending was out in the open. Keeping that secret had put Talia on edge for weeks. Permission from Chelsea was a gift. She wished she could jump into her phone and hug her.

Good thing Max hadn't answered her call. Coming clean with Chelsea meant way more than hearing Max's "fuck 'em all!" encouragement.

"Have a good time, and don't let anyone intimidate you. You're stronger than you know. And you're nice. People like you, Talia. Even if you're the odd woman out with your family."

Chelsea was right—Talia didn't fit with her family. She knew she wasn't adopted because she and Jenna had the same hazel eyes and straight nose with a slight bump on the bridge, but she was the outsider. Thanks to Chelsea, at least for today, she didn't care.

"I'm glad I called you," Talia said.

"As Max would tell you, fuck them."

Talia laughed. "That's exactly what she'd say."

With Chelsea's reassurance pushing her forward, Talia swept into the private room to greet the guests and behave as if she truly were the doting older sister and successful, confident daughter of Riva Goldstein.

seventeen
max

Max couldn't stand the hammering throb above her eyebrow. This was the fifth day she'd woken up with a migraine. Nothing seemed to appease it, dull it. Not even vodka. She noted the empty bottle on the floor. The clear liquid had escaped its glass container and rested in a large pool on her newly finished hardwood floor.

Her new apartment.

She hadn't told the girls yet, not even Talia. As much as she loved her, she knew the information would get to Chelsea and Sophia, and Max didn't want to deal with that shit. Not from them. She was trying so hard not to rage at them. It boiled inside her like a loosened electrical wire untethered from its poles.

After all, they were her friends. Her fellow conspirators. Without them, without Chelsea, really, Max would not have been able to buy her dream convertible, the car with an engine that rumbled beneath her whenever she stepped on the gas, or move into an amazing new apartment in Forest Hills. For once, a place that did not reek of piss and poverty or have roaches hissing behind the walls as she slept, creeping into her bedroom through the air vents in the middle of the night. She even had a doorman, a nice older man who greeted her whenever she arrived or left her new home and helped carry her shopping bags to the elevator. Yes, there was even an elevator, and she no longer had to trudge up and down a staircase that smelled of soiled diapers intermingled with pot.

She wasn't ready to reveal this yet. She wanted to enjoy the high that came with having money, without worrying about her next meal or how to make rent. Never again would she sell her soul by writing another vapid article on women's fashion or beauty tips. She no longer had to rely on pen names, the ones she'd used because there was no fucking way she would attach her real name to that kind of drivel. It was beneath her. Beneath her skills as a writer who had sworn to tell the truth no matter how much it hurt or who it betrayed.

Now she could write whatever she wanted. In her voice. The voice of a renegade, a bullshit revealer. No one would survive her truth. No one could hide from her, from the secrets they had told her, the abuses she had suffered at the hands of the foster system designed to fuck children over until they turned out to be just like ... like what? Like her?

She was fucked up. She knew it. She never hid it or lied about it. And this was one of the many reasons she loved her friends. They saw her fucked-upped-ness and took her in, anyway. They didn't throw her back into the dregs of her lonely existence where she had been flailing about like one of those inflated balloons that whizzed through the air and then slipped to the ground, empty and discarded.

So she owed them that. But she didn't owe them an explanation of why she had spent all her money. Cashing the checks made out in her name. And they didn't need to know that she had moved to a new, beautifully furnished, clean apartment that felt more like home than any other place she had lived in.

She would tell them soon enough. But not yet.

She smiled, sinking her head into the fluffy new pillow she had bought at Bloomingdale's. She stretched her legs along the silk cream sheets, the smell and taste of luxury filling the pores of her skin with delight. Unadulterated and sublime. And she gripped the edge of her mattress, full and bouncy as it rested on her brand-new rustic, cherry-colored sleigh bed, its headboard thick and dark, strong enough to cradle the weight of her body, the weight of her dreams and nightmares as they played against each other in her head while she slept.

And the crazy thing was, she had not brought any men to her new place. She didn't feel the urge to hunt them down in bars, bring them back, and screw them until she fell asleep. This place, with its ample space, high ceilings, secure walls, was enough. She was safe here, cocooned as if inside a womb that had all the nutrients she needed to thrive. To breathe.

Yawning widely in the space that belonged only to her, unmarred by outsiders and outliers, she kicked off the covers and trudged to the bathroom in search of drugs that would relegate her migraine to the numbness she needed it to go into before she met with Talia for their writing session.

Popping four aspirin into her system, she hopped into the shower, not a bathtub with rusted faucets, but an actual walk-in tiled shower with a variety of high-powered body jets and sprays that spewed generously from a showerhead that covered every inch of her head, face, and body with gentle, massaging water.

She was in heaven. A heaven only money could provide. And it didn't matter to her if that money had not come from an ethical place. A place of truth and integrity. She deserved it. Deserved to be wealthy and happy. It was her time. She felt powerful. And money made it possible. Possible for her to use her words, her work to level the playing field, usurp the power denied to people like her. People without family. Without roots.

Money was all she needed, and now that she had it, everything she'd ever wanted seemed possible.

An hour later, Max sat opposite Talia at a small table in the coffee shop they had been frequenting every Sunday morning since they started making money. Their newfound wealth allowed them these small luxuries that made all the difference to struggling writers. Armed with laptops, frothy cappuccinos, and a tray of warm croissants—butter for her, chocolate for Talia—they pounded their fingers along the keys as words spilled out of them.

"What are you working on this week, Max?"

Max looked up and laughed as Talia licked the remaining milk chocolate from her fingertips, slid her tongue over her rounded lips, and shifted her eyes and eyebrows toward the ceiling with an exaggerated expression of contentment.

"If I told you," Max replied, "then I'd have to kill you." She winked and tossed her a playful grin.

"I'll tell you what I'm writing." Talia grinned back.

"Oh, yeah?" Max stopped typing. "What? Another short story about Sasquatch and his toe-licking fetish?"

Talia's cheeks grew pink. Maybe she did tease her too much. "Aw, come on. You know I'm just playing with you."

"Making fun of me is more like it." Talia stared at her, pursing her lips into a rounded, childlike pout.

"What's a friend for if we can't joke with each other?" She reached out to pat Talia's fingers, and when she didn't move them away, Max squeezed them slightly before returning to her keyboard.

"Okay," Max said absentmindedly. "What are you writing?"

"You'll be proud of me." Talia offered her a smile that told her all was forgiven. "I'm writing micro-essays."

"No shit." Max gave her a look of appreciation.

"I took an online class, and they are *wonderful*. Short, punchy essays that read and sound like poetry. I just love them."

"That's amazing." Max smiled at her. "I am proud of you, but

I'm more excited for you. No one gets how empowering writing nonfiction is. I'd love to read some of them when you're ready."

"Of course." Talia blushed. "Just not yet. They're not polished right now, and I'm still trying to find my prose footing. But it's so much fun. I can't even describe the rush it gives me to write them. And I have so many of them already. Like eleven!"

Max smiled at her friend. Their gazes met, and Max hoped that Talia felt her affection.

After a few quiet moments, Talia's voice brought Max's fingers to a sudden halt. "So now that I told you, you have to tell me."

"I don't know. You're not going to like it."

"Well, now you have to tell me." Talia inched closer to her over the table.

Max paused and looked at Talia for a long moment before sighing heavily at the weight of her plan. She would be taking a chance, a chance that her friend would be loyal to her, loyal enough not to betray her.

"If I tell you, you can't tell anyone. And by anyone, I mean Chelsea and Sophia. You have to swear." Her words rushed out of her mouth before she could take them back.

"Max, what are you planning?"

She took a breath. What the hell, she thought to herself. She was dying to tell someone, so it might as well be Talia.

"I'm writing an exposé," Max said, watching Talia's expression carefully. She was easy to read, and Max didn't have to try too hard.

"About what?" Talia sat back in her seat, her features wrought with dread.

Max hesitated before pushing out the words. "About writers using AI to draft novels and poems and stories that they submit for publication as their own work. About how easy it is to use AI. About how editors and readers laud anything, even drivel composed by cheaters who use AI to make cash. About the publishing industry and how full of shit it is."

"Max," Talia said, her mouth grim, her fingers nervously picking at the leftover crumbs from her croissant. "Why?"

"Because it's the right thing to do. Because it's a scam that validates crap while real writers, creatives like us, are buried in bureaucratic processes and unrelenting rules that some asshole made up to keep us from having our day, from being read, from gaining membership to the industry that says it discovers new voices but only wants voices that already come with readership—like Paris Hilton and Matthew McConaughey."

Max took a breath and let out a snort full of mockery and loathing. "They don't even write their own shit. They have ghost-writers who don't get paid nearly as much as they should." She sat back in her seat and challenged Talia with a look, daring her to say something. Anything. She knew Talia agreed with her.

"So you're exposing us?" Talia pushed her chest against the table, closer to Max. She cupped her hands around her mouth and whispered, "How we used AI to write our novel?"

"Yes." Max's voice fell flat.

"That's not fair! You're putting us all on the line here."

"The publishing industry isn't fair. It's a rigged system, and we're all like hamsters in a wheel trying to earn our way into it while others—the rich and famous and those with connections—all get a free ride while we drown in oblivion. I'm exposing it for what it is. Just another corrupt system that's only concerned with making money—not making art."

Max almost felt sorry for Talia. She was no match for her. She was too soft. Too nice. Max's niceness had been snuffed out ages ago, when her parents died and she had been surrendered to the foster care system—also hungry to make money from abandoned children, rewarding abusers and sacrificing the lambs it was designed to protect. That's the next system she was going to bring down. She was going to burn it down and dance in its ashes.

"I agree with you. But you're willing to bring us down—your best friends—just to make a point," Talia hissed. "I thought we were in this together and agreed to wait."

"I'm tired of waiting." Max spit the words out, not realizing how angry she was with all of them until she felt her heart thrum against her ribcage and her pulse quicken beneath the soft skin of her throat. "I'm sick of Chelsea and Sophia acting like they own this show, patting me on the back like I'm some kind of domesticated dog that needs placating."

"We're all with you, Max. We all want to do the same thing, and we will when it's time. Chelsea said we could expose the system right after we make a shitload of money from the film rights of the book. Just like you want, Max." Talia paused, opened her mouth to say something more, but closed it again.

"I don't buy it." Max shook her head, disappointed that Talia didn't see the big picture. She hated the way people lied to themselves. Chelsea and Sophia. And even Talia, weaving this story of "after this" and "just wait and then we'll be happy. Promise."

"There will always be an after." Max tried to explain. "Don't you see?"

Talia shook her head. "See what?"

"First it was when the book made a splash. Now it's when the book becomes a movie and makes an even bigger splash. Afterwards, it will be something else. Chelsea and Sophia—maybe even you—don't want this to come out. You're getting too much money from it. I don't think anyone will ever want to reveal that AI wrote this book. There's too much riding on it."

"What about you, Max? You're reaping the benefits. You'll lose that nice car of yours. What about your reputation? You'll be in the same sinking boat as the rest of us. Why can't you let this play out a little while longer? It won't be forever."

Talia's pleading grated on Max's nerves, and she was trying very hard not to lash out. She knew Talia hated conflict, and a small part of Max felt bad, knowing that if she went ahead with her plan, it would prevent Talia from earning the respect and gratitude of her family that she so desperately wanted.

Relying on people to love you, to respect you, to validate you was futile. Max hoped her actions would teach Talia to stop begging for other people's validation. To love herself. To rely on no one for anything. Not even her.

Max thought of her Mustang and the freedom she felt driving it on the highway at a hundred miles an hour, as if death itself was at her heels, chasing her home. She thought of her apartment and the warmth it provided her. She thought of all that money sitting in her bank account.

Having money was amazing, but she knew something none of them did. Not Chelsea. Not Sophia. And not Talia. All this material stuff was bullshit, too. Transient. It wouldn't last. They would still want more, even after they had it all. That was human nature. They were all made of holes that were impossible to fill, consumed by hungers no one and nothing could satisfy.

And that's why she had to do it. For all of them. And for herself. She had nothing to lose, and the fact that the women she loved and respected were manipulating her with empty promises so they could get what they needed out of it—sacrificing her for their own desires—reminded her she would always be on her own.

"Can't you just wait until we talk to Chelsea and Sophia? Please?" Talia's words reached Max from the fog of her depression. Her disappointment. It came in waves, and it was overwhelming her now, clouding her thoughts and focus. She heard the desperation in Talia's voice and understood that she needed the other two women to help her talk Max down from what they saw as her self-righteous pulpit of destruction.

"No." Max's voice came out colder than she intended.

When Talia didn't respond, Max leaned over the table, her nose inches from Talia's, close enough to make herself clear and heard, to feel Talia's warm breath against her cheek.

"I'm not asking for permission. I'm not waiting for someone else to tell me what I can write about and when. I have never let myself be led by anyone else, and I am not starting now."

Max sat back in her seat and crossed her arms against her

chest, giddy with indignation. She was going to burn this mother-fucker down, and she didn't care who got buried in the rubble.

Not even if it was her.

eighteen
chelsea

Dorian Dimwitty's rage is palpable even though she really had no reason to be so pissed. I mean, seriously, Ascher gave her every opportunity to fix her sh*t and she didn't. Such a great mindf*ck of a character study.
– Wuthering Heights 4 Life

Chelsea worried the whole train ride to Talia's in Harlem, especially since her friend had insisted that the four gather in person, even rescheduling twice to make sure they'd all be there. She chewed some Tums to beat back the acid flaring in her stomach.

On the walk from the train, she distracted herself from whatever this emergency meeting was about by rehashing how her Revenge Story had advanced. They had signed the movie contract four weeks earlier. Pre-production was in full swing, Alec reported when he called a few hours ago. He was about to embark on a round of interviews on behalf of MF Ascher and needed an additional retainer until the advance from the movie deal paid out. Chelsea wired him the money from the second offshore account she'd set up, creating another degree of distance between her and what she sent him.

Alec broached the subject of entertaining offers from the Big Five to take it even wider, but Chelsea shot it down without letting him mount another argument. Why should they share with the same publishers that rejected them all these years? The book royalties showed no signs of slowing, infusing the four friends with over half a million each the previous week.

She took another Tums at the foot of the dilapidated stoop of Talia's building, converging simultaneously with Sophia and Max. Storm clouds thundered above with the promise of a late April shower.

"We still don't know what this is about?" Sophia said.

Chelsea couldn't help but note that Sophia's clothes no longer carried the slight tinge of overuse, and that the soles of her shoes were relatively unscuffed. All signs pointed to the fact that Sophia, too, was spending some of the money.

"No idea," Chelsea said. "Max, do you know?"

Max shrugged and plunged her hands into her pockets, her silence causing even more alarm to flood Chelsea's nervous system.

"No clue," Max finally answered, her casual and reserved demeanor in total opposition to her norm.

"Great," Chelsea muttered as they waited for Talia to buzz them in. The obnoxious blare bounced around in her head an extra beat before they stepped inside and made the trek up to the apartment.

Talia stood waving from her doorway down the hall. The light outside her tiny studio had been replaced with a soft white LED bulb, which cast a glow over the springy hair bouncing across her shoulders. Chelsea gripped the strap on her messenger bag, because the closer they got, the easier it was to read the uncertainty cast over Talia's face.

Shit.

"Hi," Talia said, waving them inside.

"What's wrong?" Sophia asked, hints of worry seeping into her measured tone.

Talia and Max exchanged glances.

Shit, shit, SHIT.

"Does something have to be wrong for us all to get together? Really, Sophia, you're such a worrywart." Talia's fake chuckle didn't ease Chelsea's nerves. She noted a wheelie bag and travel tote propped next to the door. A white tag wrapped around the handle with the letters TUS hung down the side.

"You went to Tucson?" Chelsea said.

"Just a quick trip to a spa. I wanted to get a bit of pampering in before—"

"Before what?" Chelsea asked. Her heart sank as Talia dragged her gaze to Max.

"What is she talking about, Max?" Sophia asked.

Chelsea's uncertainty raked across her ribcage, waking up the anger she tried so hard to keep walled up.

Max remained still, except for the shit-eating grin spreading across her hardened face, daring Chelsea to echo Sophia's question. Chelsea stared at Max, the frustration threatening to burn through her skin. She couldn't let this get to her, couldn't let *Max* get to her.

Falling back into the meditative breath work she'd been relying on to keep herself in check since the divorce, Chelsea conjured up the memory of La Fortuna waterfall spilling from the side of the Chato volcano in Costa Rica. Anytime she needed to calm herself and think of a happy place, that was where she went. With each inhalation, the sound, sight, and smell memories aided in calming her.

Talia's voice pulled Chelsea back from the banks of the waterfall. "Let's have a drink!"

Sophia stood next to Chelsea as Talia placed a bottle of wine alongside four glasses and a bowl of popcorn on the counter.

Max lunged for the wine and poured an equal amount in each glass, emptying the bottle.

"To Talia. You deserve to pamper yourself. Good for you,

taking off to some spa." Max lifted her glass and took a heavy sip before settling into a chair.

Talia shifted her unsteady eyes from Max to Sophia.

"Come on, girls," Max continued. "We have all this money, and saving it isn't doing a damn bit of good. Look at these two." She jutted her head towards Chelsea and Sophia. The motion and the intent behind it ignited that ember of indignation snuffed out by Chelsea's breathwork.

"What's actually going on?" Chelsea could feel the heat rise with each second that ticked by.

"I thought we could get together and talk. About ..." Talia again turned her attention to Max. "Your plans, Max."

The air remained seeped in tension as Chelsea fought to keep the edge from her voice. "What plans?"

Max drained her glass and wiped the back of her hand across her lips. "I wrote an essay about AI and how fucked the publishing industry is."

"You did what?" Chelsea felt the sting of the betrayal rise up. Max had promised to keep herself in check, and though Chelsea kept her true motive under wraps, that wouldn't hurt her friends. Not like Max's article would.

"I did what I wanted. Which is what I always do."

"But you didn't send it to the *Times* or anyplace else, right?" Talia asked. If they were in a court of law, she would be chastised for leading the witness.

"Holy shit." Chelsea pinched another Tums between her teeth.

"Max ... Talia," Sophia started, leaning forward. "If something happens and word gets out that MF Ascher is us, and that we wrote the book using AI, we might all be sued and responsible for paying fines or judgements."

"Then they can take all our stuff back. Except my Mustang. That bitch and I will ride across the border together."

Sophia released a shaky breath. "If you do that, you leave the rest of us on the hook for your portion, too. It's called joint and several liability, and Alec said—"

"Alec? See, this is the problem. You two"—Max pointed between Sophia and Chelsea—"keep going behind our backs. What did you tell him this time?"

"I didn't tell him anything." Sophia closed her eyes. "If you listened before jumping to conclusions, I could explain."

"The only people jumping to anything are you two. Talia and I have been on the outside of this while you both call the shots. I'm not doing it anymore. No one is getting sued or paying anything back, so stop with your bullshit."

Chelsea turned to Max, who met her stare without a beat. "Did you do anything with the essay, yes or no?"

"What if I did?" Max's eyes darted down for a quick moment, and Chelsea knew she hadn't. Yet. But she was close. Too close.

"We agreed you could blow up the publishing industry, but not yet. And not without telling us," Chelsea reminded her.

"You do plenty without telling *us*."

Her hands begged to be balled at her sides, but Chelsea kept her palms flat against her thighs. "The only thing I, or we, did without telling you was talk to Alec. That's it. And we did that to protect all of us."

"Bullshit. You're out for yourself and the money. You're no better than the publishing scumbags we hate."

Talia gasped. Even Sophia widened her stare.

Chelsea took a step closer to Max, which wasn't difficult in the tight space of Talia's apartment. "That's not true."

"The hell it isn't."

"Ironic coming from a woman who bought a new car and god knows what else after we decided to take it easy with the spending." The ire hissed from Chelsea's clenched teeth.

"No, *we* didn't decide. *You* decided. You don't get to make decisions for me, Chelsea. I don't give a shit if it is your name on the line with Amazon."

"This is bigger than that, Max. You don't have a damn clue."

"You're right, it is! Bigger than the money. Bigger than Talia's sister's stupid wedding. Bigger than Sophia's MFA cohort drama. And bigger than ..." Max stepped forward and pointed at Chelsea. "Whatever it is you aren't telling us."

Max was never going to stop. Not for any of them. Not even if Chelsea told her about her intent to burn Rick to the ground.

"You want me to wait for one reason or another," Max continued. "Well, I'm done waiting for permission that will never come. My exposé is finished and everyone will find out what we did soon enough."

"You think *I'm* controlling things. Come off your high horse, Max."

"Fuck you, Chels. You don't know everything about me."

"Don't I? You've written about all of it enough times. You're a victim of everything and everyone. But you aren't the only one in this room with a shitty origin story. We've all been victims."

Max's face softened ever so slightly as her gaze roved around to where the others sat. It was a moment when Chelsea knew she could stop, back down, and Max might do the same. But Chelsea couldn't bring herself to do it, fueled by the toxic memories of all the other times she backed down to save someone else's peace at the expense of her own. So, she did something different—she doubled down.

"Do you want the money, or do you want to burn down the publishing industry? Because you can't have it both ways, Max." Chelsea took one more step towards her, looking straight into her hard brown eyes. "And the fact that you're willing to go down in flames and take the only three people you purport to love with you shows me exactly who you are and what you're all about. Yourself."

Her bottled rage finally erupted. Was it fair to aim it all at Max when it was really meant for far more deserving targets like her parents who berated her, her brothers who abandoned her, her professors who belittled her, and her editors who believed Rick over her? Probably not, but it didn't matter. Chelsea had spent her whole life putting a lid on the anger that came to defend her, opting instead to wear her calm exterior while it gutted her insides.

It was out, and no measure of Talia's sobbing or Sophia's calming whispers would put the lid back on that box. For the first time, Chelsea took a stand for herself against someone who was trying to hurt her—someone who was so fucking wrong about her.

Max didn't speak, moisture rimming in her eyes, defiantly refusing to fall. Any apology that might have been dusting her lips was swallowed up in the wake of Chelsea's words. Instead, Max placed her glass on the table and walked out, leaving the door open behind her like a hole that would prove difficult to fill.

nineteen
talia

My reader group selected this book. Half gave it Five stars and the other half DNF. I actually loved it. It has something for everyone, checks every box, stirs every emotion. The relationships are both believable and unbelievable.
*   –Reader-Gamer12*

Talia begged her friend, the one she idolized, to run after Max and take back her cruel words.

"No fucking way." Chelsea snatched her messenger bag off a chair and left without a backwards glance.

"I guess your little party didn't go the way you'd hoped." Sophia said dryly, standing by the door.

Talia wiped her cheeks with a handful of tissues. "I thought we could work it out. We need to all make up."

"I'm not sure we ever will. Not anymore." Sophia drifted into the hallway, closing the door behind her.

One by one, Talia's friends had walked out on her. Her plan to make Max change her mind and end with everyone in a big hug-fest failed. Now Max probably thought she was against her, too.

Talia grabbed her phone to call her. She had to reassure Max that she was on her side. At least, more than the others were.

"Dammit!" she shouted when it went to voicemail. She paced her tiny apartment, waiting for the beep. "Max, it's me. I'm so sorry about what happened. I didn't mean for any of it to go that way. Call me back, please. I love you." She threw her phone onto the bed.

A minute later, a text message buzzed and lit up the screen. Talia grabbed it, praying Max was sending a message that all was forgiven. No such luck. It was Alec. Shit, that guy was relentless.

He'd been texting Talia every week or so over the last few months. Most of his texts were friendly, bordering on flirtatious. But Talia had ignored them—until now.

ALEC

Hey, you up?

Talia was reeling with emotion from the evening's events. The fight had left her raw and vulnerable. She responded.

I am

Whoa, you answered! How are you?

How am I? Terrible.

Fine. You?

Good. I need to see you.

Why?

Some business stuff. I don't know why Chelsea's in charge of everything. The four of you wrote the book. You should be able to speak to your lawyer and the very handsome face of MF Ascher.

It was impossible to know in a text if he was being smug. No emoji or anything. Talia took his comment at face value and considered it sincere.

> Okay, when?

How about now?

> Now?

Yeah, it's only nine-thirty. I'll send my car service to pick you up.

> You have a car service?

Don't you? You sure as hell can afford one.

Talia had never thought of that. Old habits were hard to break. She loved the ease with which she traveled around the city with her MetroCard on public transport. Occasionally, she'd hail a cab. Even more occasionally, an Uber.

A ping interrupted her thoughts.

Are you still there?

Talia couldn't stand the quiet in her empty apartment. The fight between Chelsea and Max haunted her. A fight she'd caused by insisting everyone gather.

> Yeah. Okay, send a car.

REALLY?? Great! Driver will be there in fifteen ... good?

> Fine.

She didn't bother to change out of sneakers and jeans, just swapped her sweatshirt for a blue V-neck sweater. Tears had left her with panda eyes. She cleaned up the smudged mascara with a Q-tip and swept her hair into a high ponytail. Good enough.

The car service arrived on time to the minute. The driver wore a dark suit and acted more like he was working for the secret service than a limo company. Talia sank into the back seat. At least the long drive to lower Manhattan would be in comfort.

Just as she began to relax, they pulled up to a high-rise on the Upper West Side. A doorman jogged over and opened Talia's door as the driver came around to extend a formal hand.

Talia turned to the driver. "Are you sure this is the right place?"

"It is, ma'am," he said. "Mr. Pendergrass is waiting upstairs."

"Holy shit." She accepted the doorman's outstretched hand and exited the limo.

Talia followed the doorman to the elevator, where he scanned a key card and then pressed the button for the thirty-sixth floor.

Alec was waiting for her in the doorway of an apartment. "Welcome."

Talia entered, momentarily wondering if she'd made a huge mistake coming to see him. But now that she was here, she couldn't wait to see what was inside. The foyer opened into a huge great room with a sliding glass door overlooking the park.

"So, you moved recently."

"I did. Thanks to MF Ascher." Alec had cleaned himself up in a big way. No more scruffy beard and flip-flops. He looked exactly like the person he'd been hired to be, a successful Manhattan attorney representing the hottest new author on the literary circuit.

"Finally, I live in a place befitting a man of my stature. Mind taking off your shoes? I'm fastidious about keeping my floors clean, and those runners you have on are probably filthy."

"Oh, right." Talia pried them off, grateful she'd worn thick white cotton socks. No way she wanted Alec taking notice of her feet.

"Would you like some wine?"

"I suppose one glass won't hurt." A framed photo of a young Alec in a cap and gown caught her eye. "May I look around?"

"Be my guest."

As Alec uncorked a bottle at the bar, Talia wandered from room to room and peered out the windows. Two bedrooms, two and a half bathrooms, hardwood floors, a brand-new kitchen with stainless steel appliances, and a great room that could hold twenty people. "This place must cost a fortune."

"Oh, it does." Alec handed her a long-stemmed glass with a generous pour of red wine. "Thanks for coming over, Talia. You know you've always been my favorite."

Talia sipped the wine. She was no connoisseur—all she could tell was that it tasted like money. "Favorite what?"

Alec studied her face, his eyes fixed on hers. "Favorite of your foursome. We had a little fun, back in the beginning. Not as much as I'd have liked, but, well ..." His gaze slithered downward but turned back up as if he'd changed his mind. "Look at you now. You've written a bestseller, made a shitload of money, changed your life."

"And yours, evidently." Talia pulled her focus away from him. "Why am I here, Alec? And if you were expecting we might, you know, that's never going to happen."

A flash of disappointment darkened his face, but only for a moment. "I won't claim it hadn't occurred to me. I mean, I've carried a torch for you for years. But I'm seeing someone new right now."

"That's nice." Talia doubted it was true. She lowered her face into the oversized wine glass and took a long sip. It was tasting better and better. "Do you have any cheese and crackers or something?"

"I'm sure I do." He opened a few cabinets as if he didn't know where he kept his own snacks. "Wheat Thins okay?"

Talia loved Wheat Thins. "They'll do."

Alec shook crackers onto a plate alongside some slices of cheddar as he rambled about the amenities in his new apartment building. Then, he launched into a new topic. "You know, I've been thinking about something. Let's sit."

What a segue. "Okay." Talia followed him to the enormous white sectional in the great room. The buttery leather practically swallowed her.

"It's about the way you're all hiding behind this MF Ascher name. Chelsea is adamant that the truth about MF Ascher can never be revealed. Sophia, too. And Max, well, she's a wildcard in all this. But you're a little more—how do I say this? Reasonable?"

Reasonable. Talia mulled that one over. She spoke with caution. "I think keeping the mystery going is part of the allure."

"For now, but that's going to wear off soon. MF Ascher has to do something new—launch another book or come out from behind the proverbial curtain. If you guys are working on another novel, that's fabulous. We can start dropping hints."

Talia stuffed a cheese and cracker sandwich into her mouth and washed it down, barely tasting the ridiculously expensive wine. "Maybe. Um, we've talked about it. But you know how long it takes to write a good book. I mean—"

"How long did the first one take? With four of you working on it, I can't imagine it would take more than a few months."

Talia's anxiety ticked upward. "Actually, it takes longer than you'd think. Four writers, four opinions, right?" Her laugh was scraggly. "Plus, we don't even have a concept for a second book." The only concept she could think about at the moment was a scenario in which four friends have a huge fight and never speak to each other again.

"Then consider revealing who MF Ascher is." Alec threw two crackers into his mouth. "It would be like rocket fuel on a dying fire."

"Our book is dying? Is that what you're saying?" Talia's nerves were definitely on fire. There was no way any of them would admit to being MF Ascher. And a second book? Not happening now, especially not with Max on the verge of releasing her exposé.

Alec stroked one of Talia's trembling hands as he scooted closer to her on the sectional.

"Not exactly dying," he said. "But you know how fickle the industry is. The truth is, if you all come out as a piece of MF Ascher, each of you will be famous in your own right. And we all get even richer."

What did he mean by *we all* get richer?

"My point is, Talia, one-hit wonders don't stick around long. And who knows how the movie will do."

"Right, the movie." Talia's thoughts returned to the book. She couldn't imagine how anyone could ever take that jumbled mess and turn it into a cohesive script.

Alec took her wine glass and set it on the marble coffee table. "So that's where we are. Something new has to happen."

"Right, something new." Was she just repeating his words now? She'd had too much to drink. Her ability to think coherently was fading. "Can I have some water?"

"Jesus, Talia, are you even listening?"

"I am listening. I'm thinking." What was it Chelsea had said about them being victims? Well, they weren't victims now. When the money started rolling in, they'd jumped on board with no serious regard for what *might* happen. But in their wildest imaginations, they never could've predicted the impact on their friendship.

Talia went to get her own water, since Alec made no move to accommodate her request. She took a large bottle of Voss from his fancy sub-zero refrigerator, guzzled half of it, then wiped the dribble on her chin with her sleeve. "If you think I can talk them into revealing that we are MF Ascher, you are sorely mistaken. Although, if Max's exposé gets published, it'll probably—"

"Max wrote an exposé?" Alec jumped to his feet, snickering like a cartoon villain. "She's outing MF Ascher, isn't she? Fantastic! When? I need to get a PR blitz going ASAP!"

Now she'd done it. Talia considered jumping from his balcony. "No! It's not fantastic at all. We don't want our names connected to the book. It would ruin our chances of getting agents and traditional publishing deals!"

"You are so goddam naïve, Talia," Alec said, reaching for a bottle on a high glass shelf above his bar. He poured himself a shot of some amber liquid and knocked it back.

"Why is that naïve? You know what? Forget it. I don't care anymore. We've all made a shitload of money out of this. So what if the fire is dying? I don't mind being a one-hit-wonder, especially when it's not even me!" The idea that they could walk away from it all gave Talia a momentary thrill. She'd get Max back, and all would be right with the world.

Alec took another shot of whiskey or scotch. Talia couldn't tell what it was, only that it was fueling his anger. "No way are you girls quitting. There needs to be more MF Ascher. The fire must be stoked!"

"What's the matter with you?" Talia stood firm. "You sound like a lunatic."

"I will not let the flames die." He spoke with emphasis on every word, seething. And his fire references were getting on her nerves. He always did write the worst metaphors. "I need MF Ascher to stay on everybody's mind. I need interviews and appearances and podcasts. I need to be on TV! And once the world knows that you four are the infamous MF Ascher, there will be a flurry of excitement. You'll have book deals thrown at you like candy! Demand for me will skyrocket!"

"Why you? If we reveal ourselves, the media will want *us*."

"Because I'll be repping all four of you. Fuck, this is fantastic!"

"Wait. Wait, wait, wait." Talia gripped the edge of the counter. "What do you mean, you'll be repping all four of us? Your contract is for one book, the one written by MF Ascher." As soon as Talia asserted that belief, she doubted its veracity. The contract was pages long. She couldn't remember any of it.

"Hasn't anyone ever told you to read the fine print? I have exclusive rights to represent all of you and everything you write going forward," he said with an air of professional authority. "We'll make a fortune, all of us!"

Talia thought through Alec's words. Did it mean that as long as she kept writing, he would get a piece of every dollar she made? The only way to detach from him was to sink her own ship. Her mind was whirling with freeing herself. The more she thought about it, the more she wanted to quit. "And what if I stop writing? What if we all do? We've talked about it."

They hadn't actually talked about it, but surely they'd thought about it. Every struggling writer thinks about quitting from time to time.

"I don't believe you."

"Believe me or not, I couldn't care less. But I'm going to tell them I want us to walk away, let it all fade until nobody even remembers the name MF Ascher."

Her calm tone, fake as it was, seemed to unnerve him.

Alec slammed his glass on the bar and grabbed her shoulders. "You will do no such thing!"

Talia tried to twist herself out of his grasp. "Let go of me. That hurts."

He released her, but moved in on her until her back hit the wall. His breath smelled of liquor and a hint of garlic. She pushed against his chest, but it was like trying to shove a refrigerator.

"You do not want to mess with me. Don't forget, I'm the one who went to law school. I know all kinds of shit. And we are at a crossroads. One way or the other, we are taking the next step together. So, you girls have to make a choice. Either reveal the truth about who MF Ascher is or start writing another goddamn book."

"There will never be another book!" Talia spat the words at him. Anger supplanted fear and, evidently, her good sense. "We're barely even talking to each other as it is. This whole charade is the worst thing that's ever happened. All because the industry only cares about money and nobody can tell a real book from one written by a fucking robot!"

Alec stepped back as if punched in the jaw. "A what?"

Talia froze. Oh god, what had she done? "I gotta go."

She pushed past him, grabbed her purse, and ran to the door. But Alec was too fast for her. He yanked her back and shoved her toward the couch.

"Sit the fuck down and tell me what you're talking about." His face was crimson with rage. "Are you telling me you used AI to write the book?"

Now she'd done it. Max wasn't the one who would destroy them.

She was.

twenty
almost everyone

I hate this book, but it's on my nightstand forevermore. No more melatonin or pot gummies or Xanax for me! A few pages of Dimwitty and I am dead asleep. One star for quality of writing, plot development, and character arc. Five stars for curing my insomnia.
    –Sleepy Girl, Tyler Texas

MAX

Max couldn't get out of bed. And it was not because she was drunk. She hadn't had a drink after leaving Talia's apartment. She only had regret, a foreign feeling to her. She never regretted anything. Ever. She was decisive, and when she chose to take action, she committed to it and didn't look back. And because she didn't look back, she never had to stay and watch how her actions impacted others. She didn't care enough to. People didn't matter to her much. Only the truth. And people, she realized early on, would do anything not to face the truth. They were inherently cowards. Like her.

But this was different. In one instant, she had come face to face with Chelsea's anger. Her hurt, really. It was all there in her eyes, in the way she fought so hard not to clench her fists. The way she lashed out at Max, tossing her cool, unaffected mannerisms out the window. It was the hurt she saw in Chelsea that made Max tear up, made her leave without defending herself—not the accusations.

Max had heard them all before. She was selfish. She was a bitch. A whore. And she was all those things. But she was not a liar. No one could have accused her of that. Until now. This book made her a liar, and the exposé would redeem her.

But Chelsea's reaction changed everything. Max felt the change, and it was the depth of Chelsea's desperation that made her realize this was not just about the book, or the exposé, or the promise they had made to each other.

Chelsea was hiding something. She needed this thing with the book to happen. But why? Why couldn't she just tell them? Max would understand. Maybe that's what hurt more, that Chelsea didn't trust her with her secret. The real reason she needed the book not to be exposed as a sham. To wait, as they had all agreed.

But Max was impatient. She wasn't used to waiting around for other people to make decisions that impacted her. She never had family. Never had to think about others, their feelings, their motives. It was the consequence of being all alone in this world. And this, having to wait to tell the truth, was painful for her.

She punched the pillow with frustration and rose from the bed, still in last night's clothes. She sat at her desk and opened her laptop. Her exposé was front and center, along with her pitch, ready to be sent to the *New York Times* via Brad, the man she had slept with all those months ago. The one who stole her copy of the book and left his business card behind. He was her only connection, and she was not embarrassed to use that connection to get this piece published. It would go viral. Anything about the publishing industry and AI's impact on it did. She would finally get her revenge.

She sat back in her chair and released a long sigh that left her empty and resigned.

Having these three women in her life was a burden. "And a gift," she said aloud, reminding herself of the light their friendship had brought into her small, dark world.

She began rereading her warring words on the page, clashing with the soft memories of s'mores at the lake house, drunken laughter over wine, endless discussions on writing and dreams that were supported and encouraged.

She never had that before. She never had friends before. They cared about her. She knew that. She felt it. And they were right. This exposé would ruin them.

Max let out a short, ironic laugh and brushed the loose curls away from her forehead with thoughtful determination. Somehow, the need to protect them had become more important to her than her need to burn the publishing industry to the ground.

She closed the document and moved it to the trash icon. She paused only for a fraction of a second before deleting all the files in her trash. There was no going back. Not to that version.

She opened a new document, and her fingers danced over the keys with a fresh take on an old injustice.

TALIA

If Talia had a nickel for every "if only" wish she'd uttered in her life, she'd be a millionaire ten times over. But this "if only" would haunt her forever. If only she'd kept her mouth in check, drank less, never gone to Alec's place, not let Max run off, hadn't insisted the girls meet. All the way back to if only the book hadn't gone viral, hadn't fallen into the wrong hands, hadn't been published, hadn't been written. If only they'd never fooled around with Artificial Intelligence. Even the moniker sounded evil.

Talia had no doubts that AI would end up being far more

destructive than not. Too many people would use it to destroy others or commit crimes or cheat. *Cheat.* That's what she and her friends had done, and they were good people. Imagine AI in the hands of those who were cruel, depraved, psychotic.

After revealing the ultimate secret to Alec, Talia ran. She ignored the car service driver calling after her and jogged a few blocks until she was out of breath. Then she waved down a cab.

Her hatred for Alec burned her throat. The minute she walked inside her apartment, nausea struck. She barely made it to the bathroom before throwing up the red wine he'd given her. It tasted vile, like a punishment. One she deserved.

In the shower, hot water pounded against Talia's shoulders and back. She scrubbed every inch of her skin and shampooed her hair three times. But washing her outside parts did nothing to cleanse the tainted parts that lived inside her.

Sleep eluded her. The luxurious new sheets were now itchy. The bathtub faucet dripped with rhythmic irritation. Then her neighbors started their sexual routine even though it wasn't their regular day.

Talia gave up trying to sleep. She made herself a cup of tea and scrolled social media. Not a good way to relax, that was for sure. Finally, the couple next door wrapped things up. Talia returned to bed and snuggled into the cocoon of her comforter. Just as she nestled her face into her cushy pillow, her cell vibrated. And then it vibrated again.

"Shit." She read the texts, all from Alec, demanding she call him *this instant* and *right now* and *before she regrets it.*

Talia threw off her covers, let out a shriek that would wake her amorous neighbors, and hurled her phone against the wall.

CHELSEA

The phone sat on the counter next to Chelsea's messenger bag, which she'd tossed aside as soon as she got home from Talia's the night before. She hadn't even bothered to charge it, and now, in the soft rays of a new day, it taunted her from across the room.

The light rain fanned across the window, the spray bringing her back to the waterfall in Costa Rica. It was the summer before ninth grade, on the only family vacation that wasn't interrupted, delayed, or canceled because of her parents' hospital or patient obligations.

The waterfall hike was the one activity Chelsea had wanted to do, and the only thing that was forgotten, until her father stopped on the way to the airport. Chelsea fell back into the scene of that waterfall appearing through the parting rainforest flora. The sound drummed through her ears as the refreshing spray washed over her body. The mossy scent twisted with wet wood and sweet fruit wafted through her nose. Her father, so stoic and hard, wrapped his arm around her shoulder, a fleeting moment of affection punctuated by a kiss on the top of her head.

Chelsea closed her eyes. She wasn't wrong to be angry with her parents or Rick, but she shouldn't be so mad at Max. Chelsea understood more than anyone how hurtful words could be and how those deep wounds could fester. She went across the room to grab her phone. Pushed aside the pride that kept her from texting Max. She gathered her thoughts. She needed to do the right thing and be the bigger person.

> Max, I'm so sorry. I didn't mean to come across as controlling. You're right about there being more to this. For the first time in three years, I have a chance to get back at Rick, and if I can, maybe …

She paused, her thumbs hovering over the screen. What would it mean if her plan worked? The concept of destroying Rick fed her in a way she couldn't quite put into words. And she was afraid to think about it too much, in case it unraveled and she was left hanging at the end of the frayed threads.

Her phone vibrated with a new message from Alec. Chelsea canceled the message to Max to see what he wanted.

> I need to see you and Sophia in my office
> ASAP. It's an emergency. Something has
> come up that can't wait.

Fuck. What else could possibly go wrong now?

twenty-one
sophia

In a world where everyone is concerned about the impact of AI on the creative arts, MF Ascher is a shining beacon of hope. No machine can replicate this brilliance. It takes not only a human, but one who has truly lived and experienced deep emotional loss, to write such a poignant story. Cold computer logic can never compete.

-Dr. J. Saint Pierre, New Hampshire Journal of the Literary Arts

Alec had upgraded his office since Sophia and Chelsea's last visit. He'd moved to the Carnegie Tower in Manhattan, into a forty-seventh floor suite with a partial view of Central Park.

"We know *he's* spending money," Chelsea muttered as they seated themselves in his reception area while Alec's young, beautiful receptionist—wearing peep-toe shoes, Sophia couldn't help but notice—called to notify him of their arrival.

"Did he tell you why he wanted us to come here?" Sophia asked. Her palms were sweaty. Something seemed off about this. The series of texts to Chelsea, the demands that they meet right away. The "don't-tell-Max" addendum.

"I'm sure he just needs signatures," Chelsea said, but she didn't look certain. The way she kept glancing out the window showed she was just as on edge as Sophia. They'd both been like this since Max's threat. She intended to bring the whole house of cards down, her zealous self-righteous need to punish the publishing industry for years of rejection overshadowing what Sophia considered more important: self-preservation. Their reputations. Sophia didn't want to be part of the exposure of an industry gone wrong. She'd never get an agent, a real agent, if she were part of such a scandal. There'd be no publishing deal, no interviews for *Sophia Aldren, best-selling novelist*. She'd forever be linked to a scam, a farce.

"Mr. Pendergrass will see you now." An assistant emerged and led them to Alec's office, where floor-to-ceiling windows allowed natural light to fall upon the numerous framed pictures on the opposite wall. Alec on *The View*. Alec shaking hands with producers. A full-page article about Alec, the public face of the reclusive MF Ascher. Alec's smug smile everywhere, proud of ... what, exactly? What was his accomplishment besides having met the ladies at an overpriced, underwhelming writing workshop?

He offered them scotch, pulling a bottle from his desk drawer and pouring some into the coffee mug on his desk. "Or my assistant can fetch you bottled water, tea. Anything for the great MF Ascher. Or half of her, at least."

Sophia and Chelsea exchanged a glance. Alec drinking before lunch was definitely a bad sign.

"What do you need from us, Alec?" Chelsea jumped straight to the point. Sophia, feeling like a sidekick, was happy to let her friend take the lead.

"I need a sequel. That's what I need. Another book by MF Ascher."

Sophia's stomach dropped. This was the other concern, the other fear. What happened when there was no sequel?

"We didn't write it yet," Sophia told him. "The first one was ... for fun. We didn't expect it to get this big."

"Right. But it can't be that hard to write another. One book divided by four people can't possibly take that long. You can probably do it … oh, I don't know, maybe in one weekend. Go back to your lake house with a couple of bottles of wine. I'm sure you can come up with something."

"We're working on our own projects now," Chelsea said. Her voice sounded firm, but Sophia picked up on a slight tremor in her friend's hands as she reached into her bag for her roll of Tums.

"Don't you want another movie deal? Millions of dollars are on the line."

"We have enough money to shift our focus onto other projects," Sophia said. She channeled her grandmother's energy and was pleased that she was able to speak calmly. *Never let them see you sweat,* Grandma always said. *Ladies always present a calm exterior.*

"Really? Like your convenient legal thriller about liability in civil cases? Those don't sell; believe me, I know."

"As I said, the four of us are working on our own writing," Chelsea repeated, but her voice was less firm than a moment ago. "I think I will take that scotch now."

"You and me both." Alec topped off his coffee mug before filling one for Chelsea. For all the trappings of his fancy office, he lacked glassware. In any other situation, Sophia would have been amused to see Chelsea drinking twenty-five-year-old scotch from a chipped blue mug with "I Put the Lit in Litigate" written in script across the side.

"So, how about it?" Alec continued. "A sequel? I've drawn up the contract already. I'll take the same percentage. What do you say, get it to me next week?"

"Next week?" Sophia knew it. She fucking knew it. He'd figured it out.

"Or sooner? Maybe you can get it to me tomorrow." Alec's smile didn't meet his eyes, and, for the first time, Sophia felt threatened by him. He wasn't the casual, awkward, somewhat earnest failed writer he used to be. He'd become a shark in an expensive suit, and he smelled blood. "After all, it's just AI."

"We don't know what you're talking about," Chelsea said, her fingers tightening on the mug. For a brief moment, Sophia thought that Chelsea might fling the contents in Alec's face, or perhaps smash the mug on the side of his head. Too bad it was just wishful thinking.

"Don't give me that shit. Talia, your little chatterbox, let it slip."

"That's not true," Sophia said. There was no way Talia would betray them now. Max, sure, her exposé was ready to go. But Talia? When would she have even talked to Alec? All he ever did was text her late-night booty calls, and Talia always claimed disinterest.

"She told me last night. She also told me about Max. Do you have any idea what a fucking mess you've created? People believe I know MF Ascher personally, but it's a fucking AI. How am I supposed to get ahead of this bad press? Everything I've said is a lie. Everything you told me was a lie."

Sophia looked at the window, assessing the glass. That was something Gage had always said: make sure you're in a safe place. Identify your exits. Obviously, the windows on the forty-seventh floor weren't exits, unless you were a Russian oligarch who displeased your leader. But she had a momentary fear that Alec might be willing to give her and Chelsea a shove, based on the way he was seething. Anger, though, was something that could be controlled. Anger was better than desperation. Anger could be resolved with words, maybe money. Desperation might only be resolved when bodies hit the ground.

"Alec, we can handle this. It won't get out," Sophia said, using a soothing voice to calm him.

"How?" he asked, his fury radiating almost tangibly outward. His fingers were white as they gripped his whiskey mug, partially obscuring the text proclaiming himself the World's Best Lawyer. "Max is going to tell everyone and bring us all down. We're going to lose everything! You have to stop her."

"How?" Chelsea swallowed whatever was left in her mug.

"There's no way to control that woman. She's on a mission, and she won't stop until she's dead."

Her words made the room feel darker, like a heavy malevolence had descended upon them. It made Sophia shiver, even though she knew Chelsea was kidding.

"Of course," Sophia said, trying to lighten the mood. "Murder is always the answer. We just kill her, and then we're free." It was meant to be a joke, like Chelsea's, but she immediately felt ill. The idea of murder, even in jest, made her think of Gage, Gage in his federal prison khakis, cuffed to a table, utterly remorseless. *Only the first time is hard,* he'd told her. *After that, it just becomes fun.*

"That might be the only way," Alec agreed. "Silence her forever. Then we can keep the MF Ascher money train rolling."

"That's not even funny. Nobody's going to die," Sophia said, feeling the need to clarify, to say it out loud, to get that awful idea out of the air. Alec wouldn't have a security camera in here, would he?

"Of course not." Alec said, but Sophia thought she detected a hint of sarcasm. He filled his mug yet again. "But we need to do something."

"She might listen to reason," Sophia suggested, though Max wasn't known for compromising her principles.

"She might listen to Talia," Chelsea corrected. "She clearly doesn't give a fuck about the rest of us."

"What if ... what if we went back to my lake house? We'll have another retreat weekend. Call it a chance to reconnect or something. We get Max there and have a talk with her? Try to convince her?" Sophia unlocked her phone to check her calendar. She hadn't been approving as many bookings lately, since she no longer relied on the rental income. "Next weekend, the house is empty."

"Good, yes, get her there and have a *talk*." Alec drained his whiskey again. "That'll work. And write another book while you're at it."

twenty-two
chelsea

Just when you think this story is going one way, it goes the opposite. The author reaches out of the page and jolts the reader with clarity and wisdom. MF Ascher has created a true work of art that will be hard-pressed to be duplicated.
–Publishing Monthly

There weren't enough antacids in the state to placate the chaos that ravaged Chelsea's gut. The respite of the lake house did little to take the edge off the burning. Even the salted caramel chocolate truffles Talia waved before her nose failed to stir her appetite. She hadn't eaten much since they left Alec's office last week, and she'd slept even less. Food and sleep were luxuries Chelsea couldn't allow herself to indulge in these days.

At first, it was the fight with Max that battered her mind, but later her anxiety got a further boost by Talia's inadvertent disclosure to Alec, something she and Sophia agreed not to talk about with Talia or Max until this trip. The suspense was eating Chelsea from the inside out.

"I'm going to call Max again." Talia licked the chocolate from her fingertips before picking up her phone. "I hope she's not backing out after she promised she'd come."

Chelsea chugged a glass of water, deciding that the last thing her inflamed stomach needed was alcohol. And while there wasn't much that scared or intimidated her these days, the anger pouring from the scab that Max's actions tore away came close.

It wasn't all Max's fault. Much of that anger was directed inward at Chelsea's own actions and inactions through the years. If she had stood up to her parents when she left medical school, perhaps she wouldn't have fallen for Rick. But then again, being raised by narcissists made it harder to avoid them.

"She's still not answering," Talia said, unwrapping another shiny red candy wrapper.

"What are we going to do if she doesn't come?" Sophia asked Chelsea, nudging her back to the present.

"I guess we can at least start with Talia," Chelsea said.

Talia's wide gaze moved from her chocolate to Chelsea's face. "Me? What did I do?"

"Alec. That's what you did," Sophia shot back.

Talia remained unblinking, sucking her lips between her teeth, the chocolate no doubt melting inside her wordless mouth. The rosiness of her cheeks faded with each second of silence.

"It was an accident!" she cried.

"How do you accidentally tell someone a secret like that?" Sophia asked, her ponytail flapping with each emphasized nod of her head.

"I was so upset after Chelsea's fight with Max that I wasn't thinking straight. I didn't mean to tell him. It slipped out. Please don't be mad at me."

Words intended to placate only salted that open wound of betrayal. She steeled her anger with a hefty breath. "Now that Alec knows we used AI to write the book, he's got something to hold over our heads. It makes the situation with Max even trickier."

"You need to fix this, Talia," Sophia added.

"Me? How?"

"You need to convince Max to put the brakes on that article,"

Chelsea said, her words coming out in a much more stable tone than the one roaring in her head.

"For how long?"

"Indefinitely." Chelsea knew this was a tall order, a task that was almost impossible. And that if Talia went through with it, it might sever the last strings of her frail friendship with Max.

"I can't do that. We can't do that. We promised."

"We'll keep the promise," Chelsea continued, her stomach unseizing for a moment as Talia's defenses crumbled. "But we can't put a date on it."

"What if she refuses?" Talia swiped the hair from her face.

"Then *make* her." This time the voice that breathed out was much more like the one jabbering in Chelsea's head.

Talia darted a glance at Sophia, who remained steadfast alongside Chelsea. They were aligned, the two of them on one side leaving Talia alone, her usual ally still a no-show.

The roar of the Mustang growling up the driveway dissipated the tension, offering a brief reprieve. Chelsea drew in a breath, willed it down into her belly to break the bind and readied herself to face a person who could ruin everything she had worked so hard to put together.

The dance between two people in the aftermath of a fight was a delicate one, especially when so much was at stake. From the second Max knocked—something she'd never done before—Chelsea prepared herself. She would have to employ every tactic she'd learned to keep her cool. She would take several steps back, even though she didn't want to. The only sin she'd committed was losing control of the fury she'd bottled up for so long.

"Hey, ladies," Max said, dropping her backpack by the door and waltzing past them into the kitchen.

Sophia caught Chelsea's eye and wordlessly implored her to hold it together.

Chelsea followed the others and remained on the outskirts of the conversation between her three friends. Max was making it a point to laugh at everything Sophia or Talia said. But Chelsea didn't detect a hint of malice in Max, which struck her as both comforting and troubling. Still, she allowed her thoughts to fixate on her waterfall while her physical self remained in the kitchen, where copious amounts of wine and vodka were being poured and consumed.

Little by little, her composure returned. There were several pieces missing, collateral damage of unleashing that compressed fury at Max. Chelsea again wrestled with letting her friends in on her Revenge Story, but something held her back, clapped a hand across her mouth, forced down the truth with each swallow.

Why didn't she tell them? She trusted them to support her, no matter what. It was more about the end result. If things didn't work out, she didn't want to have to explain or deal with the embarrassment of another disappointment.

But she did need to do the right thing and apologize to Max. She would take whatever anger Max threw at her as penance for saying such horrible things to one of her best friends. Even though Chelsea still believed what she said ... to a point.

She cleared her throat. "Hey, so I think we need to clear the air."

The chatter stopped, the space so silent she thought she could hear her own heartbeat. All attention turned to Max, who took her time sipping from her cup, drawing out the moment. It made Chelsea wonder if there was something else prompting Max's deliberate stalling.

"Alright, let's get to it." Max reached to refill her glass, never breaking eye contact with Chelsea. "But before you say anything, I need to tell you—"

A loud knock startled them. Chelsea turned to Sophia, who shrugged and strode to open the door. It didn't take long for the mystery visitor to make his way into the house and shatter Chelsea's plans.

Alec Pendergrass grinned. "You ladies didn't think you could have *this* party without me, did you?"

"You invited him, too?" Max said, disgust flowing freely from her mouth.

"No, that's not what happened," Sophia said. "We didn't tell him to come."

Max tilted her head and moved her suspicious gaze from Sophia to Chelsea.

"Another secret meeting with *him*. Why am I not surprised?" Max scoffed and drained her glass in record time.

"The only surprising thing is that you actually showed, Max." Alec turned to Chelsea. "I didn't think this plan of yours was going to work." His gaze stayed on her a beat too long.

The urge to take the now empty wine bottle and smash it over his thick skull thrummed through Chelsea. She shook her head at him, but if he noticed her ire, he ignored it and focused his attention on Talia.

"I tried calling after you left my place. Did you get my messages?"

Talia blanched, and Max's head snapped in her direction. "YOU, too?"

"No, it's not what you think." Talia's eyes teared up.

"So, what was the plan? Get me here and do what—guilt me into shutting up? Please. You should've known bringing this motherfucking asshole wasn't going to work."

"Whoa, whoa, Max. No need to get so nasty. We're all friends here," Alec said.

Max swirled around and jabbed at the air between them. "*You* are not my friend. Not now. Not ever." She turned her back on him, and Chelsea thought she could see the anger rippling beneath Max's skin.

"How could you bring him here?" Max hissed. "This is *our* place. I can't believe you would do this to me. All of you." She turned her gaze on the three women, a look of betrayal lodged in her eyes.

Chelsea opened her mouth to explain. Apologize. Say something, anything, to get Max to back down, but nothing came out. She had no explanation for Alec's appearance. She and Sophia hadn't invited him, not directly or otherwise. But Max wasn't going to believe any of that. All she would take away was that they hatched a plan with Alec behind her back.

"I need air." Max yanked the bottle of vodka from the counter and walked out the door.

Chelsea's chest burned, not at Max or even at Alec, but at herself. She let this get too far. She never should have lost control last week. She never should have put off apologizing to Max.

"You got anything else to drink in this place?" Alec said.

Her heart slammed against her chest.

"You need to go, Alec," she said. "Now."

Chelsea was surprised by the lack of defiance in his eyes. She expected a fight; instead, he put his arms up as if resigned.

"If you say so." He sauntered towards the door and left.

Something about his quick compliance didn't sit quite right with her. She walked over and opened the door, certain he would be standing out there, but to her relief, all that met her was an empty porch.

"That was odd," Sophia said, peering out into the darkness beside her.

"I'll go find Max," Talia said, wringing her hands.

Chelsea shook her head and shut them back inside. "Let's give her some time to cool off."

twenty-three
max

*Based on the description, I thought this was going to be a romance.
It's not. If you're looking for the next Colleen Hoover, this is not the
book for you. Can't recommend in my newsletter.*
–TheRomanticRomperReview

Max lay on one of the Adirondack chairs by the dock, observing
the way the moon's light reflected off the lake's surface, the half-
empty bottle of vodka dangling from her fingertips.

She thought of the last time they had been at the lake house.
It seemed so long ago, when everything between them was easy
and fun and light. It was the night they played with AI, the night
they made a computer program draft a book for them, laughing at
the absurdity of it all.

But this time, sitting there with a yawning space of fear and
fragility stranded between her and the girls, everything was different. It all shifted the night Chelsea took their fun and put it
online. There was money now. And power. It had changed them.

Not just her friends, Max quietly acknowledged. Money had
changed her, too. It gave her safety. Security. All the things men
could never give her. She fell asleep easily now. Alone. She had the

power to navigate her life—to stay or to leave—whenever she wanted. She was not stuck. She was free.

Her friends were the only ones who sustained her, preventing her from ending a life that still bled from the wounds of a miserable childhood. She stayed for them. But now, she wasn't even sure how long that would last. Max was teetering, all because Alec had shown up uninvited to their safe space. No men were welcome there, especially not him.

She sighed and let her face fall into the familiar grim expression she saw in the mirror every day—her gaunt eyes, her mouth turned downward in dismay.

The alcohol had already turned her insides into jelly, her head heavy and dull. Only a few minutes outside, and she missed her friends. She imagined Talia's squeaky giggle. Sophia's controlled speech, as if she were afraid that if she said too much, she would reveal the deeper layers of herself none of them had ever encountered. And Chelsea's eyes, ice-blue oceanic depths that spoke of a woman who played life like a chess player. Her brain, mining for vengeance with hypervigilance.

The last time they had seen each other, during their fight at Talia's apartment, Max almost acknowledged Chelsea's hurt, the reason behind her outburst. But something had held her back.

What was it?

Max couldn't put her finger on it. Maybe it was pride. Jealousy. Hurt that the three of them had gone back on their word, excluded her, maybe even lied to her. Wasn't this impromptu weekend at the lake house, after all, just a ruse to pacify her? To talk her into holding off on her exposé?

Did they really think that little of her? That she would hurt them?

That's what bothered her the most. They didn't trust her.

Her thoughts turned to Alec. There were thousands of lawyers Sophia and Chelsea could have chosen to represent them. Why did they pick him, of all people? He was despicable, and his fake smile, his aggressive masculinity, his pretentious entitlement were enough to make her want to gouge out his eyes.

The last thing Chelsea had said before Alec showed up was something about clearing the air. Yes, that's what they needed to do. Lay it all out on the line, tell the fucking truth! The thought of reconciling with her friends gave her a glimmer of hope and she considered returning to the house, silently praying to gods she didn't believe in that he would be gone.

She tried to get up, but her body wouldn't obey. She felt like a slug whose slimy secretions glued her in place. She sighed with exasperation and cursed herself for drinking so much. Again. She would have to wait it out or wait until one of them came to get her. Or maybe she would just sleep here by the water. It was nice. Quiet. Peaceful.

"Hey, there. I was looking for you."

Alec's voice made her cringe. Her skin pricked with agitation, and she ran her partly bitten nails down the length of one arm to subdue the shivers running through her.

"Fuck," was all she could muster, her eyes remaining closed. She felt nausea rising to her throat and tried to swallow it. She wasn't sure if it was the alcohol or the idea of being forced to interact with him that made her want to vomit.

"What's the matter, Max? Don't you like me?" he drawled, and she could feel the smirk on his face. It was as if it had hands, its fingers sliding clumsily over her body.

When she didn't respond, Alec let out a thick laugh that made her bones feel cold and exposed.

She struggled to open her eyes, but they remained shut, as if someone was pressing her lids over her eyes so she couldn't see what would come next. She trembled against her will, cursing her body for betraying her.

"Your friends like me. Don't you want to like me, too? I can be a good friend to you."

Max tried to sit up in her chair, but her body resisted the sudden movement.

"What the fuck does that mean?" She heard her voice from a distance, its vibrations echoing back to her. She sounded like a little girl, the force of her defiance gone when she needed it most to combat this asshole, this tool who thought he was deserving of her time ... of their time.

Max felt him move beside her, but she couldn't pinpoint his exact location. Her head was thick and fuzzy. A shadow fell over her, standing there, then leaning over her—the way her "daddies" used to lean over her in the middle of the night, waking her up from a deep sleep. There was a heavy weight on her stomach, pinning her in place. She struggled to push him off, to knock his knee off her midriff, but he wouldn't budge. She wasn't strong enough.

"It's okay, Max. Just relax. It's better this way." His voice was soothing. She felt his fingers push her hair away from her face. She shook her head and tried to bite him, but he had a strong grip on her jaw.

Max felt his fingers cover her mouth and pinch her nose. She couldn't breathe. She tried to fight back. To flail her arms. To kick. But he was on top of her, pushing her down with his weight.

A blackness overtook her, and the last thing she saw was her and Talia and Chelsea and Sophia on the night they laughed and drank and threw commands at Chelsea's computer—as a joke.

The memory grew faint, and a sudden thought collided with her inability to breathe. Her friends. Still inside the house. And Alec, going back to them. Without her to protect them.

She tried to scream their names, to call for them, but she felt herself moving backwards, being pulled into a void without sounds or words, their faces fading into nothingness as her lungs struggled for oxygen and then gave up.

twenty-four
chelsea

I was on the edge of my seat one minute and balled up crying the next. I'm going back to therapy so I can process the unresolved anger and grief this book brought out in me. All this time I thought it was just gas.
—FictionFiend

It had been three days since Max stomped outside for air at Lake George and didn't return. That night, Chelsea had taken a step to go after her, but thought better of it. Max was pissed *and* drunk. Nothing good would have come from that exchange. Not long after, they heard the roar of the Mustang and ran outside in time to catch it kicking up the gravel as it sped away.

Since then, Chelsea couldn't work, eat, sleep, or think about anything but Max and what she might be doing. She hadn't answered any texts or voicemails. Talia couldn't reach Max, either.

Chelsea found herself writing stream-of-consciousness, the angst pouring over page after page. How could Max disappear and, once again, leave the three of them behind to worry? All that bullshit Max spun about how she wouldn't hurt them was just that—an elaborate fucked-up story.

When Chelsea let the unadulterated anger come out of her

and onto the page, she lost hours. And while it started out directed at Max, at some point, her ire shifted to Rick. By the time the spell broke, Chelsea was breathless, staring at words aimed at her parents. The ones who heaped their admiration and joy on her brothers because they were walking the path their parents paved in gold, while she hobbled behind like a stray animal, unloved, unwanted, and begging for scraps.

She shook her head to clear the clouds of her childhood clinging to the deepest recesses of her mind. Her stomach burned with acid. She reached for her Tums, but there was only one left. She slammed her laptop shut, slipped on a light jacket, and went out to the bodega down the street.

The cashier, who was busy watching the eleven p.m. news, barely acknowledged her entry. Chelsea went towards the section she'd come to know well over the past few months and grabbed a couple of bottles of antacids.

She paused at the liquor fridge. How odd that a bodega had Grey Goose stocked among the Pabst Blue Ribbon and Hamm's. She took the vodka, interpreting it as a sign that she should go see Max tomorrow and extend the proverbial olive branch.

She got up to the register and tossed back four Tums right away, the pastel tablets cracking between her teeth. The TV screen behind the cash register brightened with the red breaking news banner.

"Police in Lake George made a gruesome discovery today when a boater reported he'd seen what appeared to be a car in the water," the newscaster said.

Chelsea focused on the image as the footage cut to the banks of the lake near Sophia's house.

"The police pulled out the vehicle, a red Mustang, earlier this evening."

"Forty-six dollars," the cashier said.

Chelsea ignored him, shocked by the sight of Max's car being towed out of the water. Every bone in her body shook as the reporter kept going on about a single car accident. No survivors.

The remains of a Caucasian female inside. The police had identified the woman by the registration but wouldn't release her name pending notification to the family.

The bodega began to spin. Max. That was her car, the one she bought as a fuck-you to the world and to her friends. The one she loved and drove away in three days ago. The one that she lived for and apparently died in.

"Hey, lady. You got to pay for that stuff."

She threw all the cash from her pocket onto the counter and stepped away, her trembling knees making it almost impossible to walk. The cashier called after her to take the bag, but Chelsea didn't stop. She rounded the corner outside the bodega and her knees buckled, hitting the wet pavement with a crack that echoed through the alley.

Max. She was gone. She was *dead*. And there, in the middle of a piss-soaked alley, Chelsea curled up into a ball and did the one thing she hadn't done in years—she cried.

———

Chelsea rebuffed the police officer's attempt to calm her. Between the hysterics and the blood streaming from her knees, the paramedics wanted to transport her to the hospital, but she refused. As the EMTs tended to her wounds, she told the cops that her friend was the person in that car up in Lake George.

The officers took her to the station to give a statement. They offered to call someone, but she shook her head. She needed to be the one to call her friends and give them the news.

Sophia got to the station first, her quick gait and swollen eyes meeting Chelsea's. Sophia's brow crumpled; her mouth opened without sound. Before she could speak, Talia staggered in and fell into Chelsea.

They talked to the police, who were in touch with their counterparts handling the case in Lake George. The cops concluded that Max had passed out behind the wheel after drinking too much and drove into the lake. There were no skid marks or any indications of foul play, just an empty bottle of vodka under the seat. Another drunk driving fatality.

The three took an Uber to Sophia's in Queens and spent what was left of the night in varying stages of disbelief, until one by one, they fell asleep, exhausted by grief.

Now it was morning, or afternoon—time didn't really seem to exist at the moment. The hot water pelted Chelsea's tender skin, the pressure in Sophia's shower far better than the trickle from her own. She relished the tingling, the numbness that spread, the steam soaking her nostrils. The bruises on her knees ached under the pressure, but instead of avoiding the pain, Chelsea leaned in.

She stepped out of the shower and into an old pair of sweatpants Sophia had left for her. Even the soft fabric caused the black skin spreading across her knees to throb. She peeled her wet hair from her face and tossed back a few ibuprofen and Tylenol on her way out of the bathroom.

Talia and Sophia sat on the couch, sipping coffee and picking at doughnuts Talia had delivered. Chelsea bypassed the food and went to the coffee.

"We should plan a funeral." Talia twisted a huge chunk of hair around her finger.

"Even though it'll just be us?" Sophia said.

"I think that's the way Max would have wanted it." Talia sniffed. Out of the four—three—of them, Talia would have the hardest time getting through this. Chelsea needed to keep herself together, for Talia's sake, more than anything.

They hadn't talked about the hard stuff yet. The house was rife with guilt and regret, but none of them had enough heart now to dive down that rabbit hole. The events before Max died, their motivations for bringing her there, no longer mattered.

Talia's phone dinged. She cleared her throat, blotting her swollen eyes. "Alec is outside."

"What the hell is he doing here?" Sophia asked before Chelsea could get the words out.

Talia shrugged. "He's been texting me nonstop since they announced Max's name on the news. He wanted to know where we were. I told him we were here and completely devastated."

"You *invited* him?" Sophia said, the anger in her voice unmistakable.

"No, I didn't," she answered, shaking her head emphatically. "I told him to stay away, but apparently he doesn't listen."

Chelsea didn't want to see Alec, but when the knock came at the door, she had no choice.

"He doesn't stay longer than five minutes," she hissed back at Talia, who nodded and blotted again.

She opened the door and walked away without acknowledging him.

"Depressing in here." He drifted toward Talia on the couch. Sophia leaned closer to her, blocking his access to a seat.

"What did you expect?" Talia asked.

Alec said nothing and shifted from one leg to the other.

"We're all in shock," she continued. So far, Talia was the only one willing to talk to him.

"It was the logical conclusion to her tragic life. Maybe you can use it as inspiration for the next book," he said.

"There isn't going to be a next book." Chelsea seethed.

"Of course there will be. There's a movie de—"

She took a step forward. "No, there won't. We're done."

"No, no, no. You aren't bailing on me now. Not after everything I've done for you."

"You haven't done anything for us," Sophia corrected. "It's more like the other way around."

He ignored them and moved over to the dining room table to check out the doughnuts. "Do these have honey? I have a deadly allergy and would hate to give you girls anything more to deal with."

The pounding in Chelsea's head was nothing compared to the

uptick in her heartbeat. It jolted and kicked against her chest with every second he lingered.

"Alec, please. You should probably go. We're not in any state to talk about this," Talia, the eternal peacemaker, implored him before things devolved even further.

"I'm not going anywhere until we all get on the same page about what happened at the lake." He bypassed the doughnuts and helped himself to a glass of wine, the dregs of last night.

"We know what happened at the lake," Sophia said.

"Max stormed out after you showed up." Talia finished the thought. "We told the police—"

Alec reeled around. "You talked to the cops?" He turned his slovenly gaze to Chelsea. "It's like you want to get caught."

Talia huffed. "I don't think anyone here cares about our AI book anymore."

Sophia shot Chelsea a look. There was a definite disconnect rippling through the room.

"Are you dense? I'm talking about the *accident*." His fingers punctuated the word with air quotes.

Alarm spread through Chelsea like a red wine stain on a white carpet. The room stilled, the words palpitating in the air.

Alec continued. "You came to my office and said the only way Max would stay quiet is if she was dead. So ..." He twirled his hand in a fast-forward circle before folding his arms over his chest.

The air went out of Chelsea's lungs as the conversation about Max and her exposé replayed through her head. Her throat tightened.

"Alec," she whispered. "What did you do?"

Sophia's jaw tightened, and Chelsea wondered if she was having the same realization: they'd been in the office together that day. Had joked that the only way to shut Max up was if she was dead.

"I took care of it, like you said. And besides, it's not like it's totally my fault. She was alive when she went into the water. If she hadn't been such a raging drunk, she would have woken up when I put her behind the wheel."

Talia's face drained of what little color remained. "Oh my god," she whispered before doubling over.

"Alec," Sophia started, her voice strained. "We didn't want Max dead. We never would ... she was our friend."

"She was going to ruin all of us. I'm not losing my law license because some drunk bitch couldn't keep her fucking mouth shut."

"Oh my god," Talia wailed.

"I did it for you, too, Talia. For all of you. It's what you wanted—"

"No, we didn't! We never told you to kill Max." Chelsea's body rippled with rage. Once again, someone she believed was on her side turned out not to be. He wasn't a friend, but he was hired to represent their interests.

"We were fixing it," Talia whimpered. "At the lake house. Max would have listened to us if you hadn't barged in."

Alec scoffed. "It sure didn't seem that way to me. That's why I stopped by. I had to protect myself ... *us* ... by any means necessary."

"You did what you wanted to do. That isn't our fault," Sophia said, her voice colder than Chelsea had ever heard it.

But Alec shook his head. "It was all of us. We're in this together, ladies, whether you like it or not. You said the words, I carried them out. It makes you complicit in her death." He leveled a finger at each of them, stopping inches from Chelsea's chest. "I own you in more ways than one. If I go down, I'm taking you with me."

Not again. Chelsea's whole life had been marked by people who either used her and threw her away or pretended she didn't exist. And now, this piece of shit leveled accusations and threats at her and the only two people left in this world she trusted. All of that guilt and shame over Max's death would need to be set aside, put away in that box she had become so adept at fortifying and burying inside.

She needed to come up with a way to get them out of this. She owed it to Sophia and Talia to undo the wrong her need for vengeance against Rick had brought down upon them—and Max.

"Get out." Chelsea knew the words came from her, their presence still burning in her mouth. But they didn't sound like her. "Leave before I say or do something you'll regret."

Sophia sat back down next to Talia, her arm around their most delicate friend, the one who would likely now bear the burden of guilt more because she had outed them for using AI to Alec in the first place. But Chelsea had made the comment about Max needing to be dead. *She* was the one who had published the damn book.

"Fine. But stop talking to the cops." Alec stormed toward the door, flinging it open and pausing. "I'll check back in a few days when you all come to your senses and calm the fuck down."

That wasn't going to happen. The anger from a lifetime of being fucked over was fully uncaged and ran rampant through Chelsea's body.

She closed her eyes. The characters had somehow diverted her original Revenge Story, and she needed to course-correct.

"What the hell are we going to do?" Sophia asked as Chelsea stared out the window, silently working through plotlines. She landed on the one that made the most sense and the one that would give the three of them closure and the freedom to ensure they'd remain safe.

The one she didn't dare speak about until she was sure it was the only way. She wouldn't breathe life into it quite yet.

twenty-five
sophia

Does anyone else read books for enjoyment anymore? It seems like everyone wants to psychoanalyze everything. Ascher's book is an entertaining story. That's all it is. There's no deep philosophy behind it. Stop pretending Ascher is some literary genius. Four stars.

Sophia made a pot of coffee, the thousandth since they'd begun their mourning period. She still used her grandmother's ancient Mr. Coffee, the yellowing plastic making her think of happier times, breakfasts back when she still had a family. Now she was using it to make coffee for the closest people she had to a family, something to help them get through one of their last days of freedom, before Talia cracked and confessed and they all went to jail for the rest of their natural lives.

Trusting Alec had been a mistake. She'd read him wrong, thinking he was like them, a desperate author, a writer seeking adoration, one who understood the industry and its vagaries. But there was something darker inside him. His presence had brought a miasma to Sophia's house, an almost tangible evil. If she squinted, she thought, maybe she could see it, a vile green gas, or perhaps red, like Max's blood. Not that Max had been bloody, presumably. Alec wasn't like Gage, willing to get his hands dirty.

The cruel casualness struck her the most. *I took care of it. I did what you wanted. She was alive when she went in the water.*

And then worse, *I own you.*

Her eyes darted toward the stairs leading to her sanctuary. Her writing room, with the vintage typewriter she pretended she used, and the modern desktop that she did use. And on the table between them, the contract. The real one, the meaningful one. Not the one that Alec had, the one with fine print turning the four of them into his property. No, it was the one she'd been waiting for her whole life: an offer of representation.

It had still been too fragile to share, until now. When it was just an email, *Sophia, I love it!* Followed by another: *Dear Ms. Aldren, I am pleased to offer you representation. We at Florilegium Literary are so excited about your manuscript!*

And finally, the contract, her signature already affixed. She'd scanned it and sent it in just last week. She finally had an agent, one who would sell her novel—number four, that was the magic number—and if that sold, maybe they'd like another. Maybe novel number two could come out of the drawer, get dusted off, and one day grace the *New York Times* bestseller list.

How could Alec claim rights to her work, past, present, and future?

And why was that what she fixated on when Alec had just admitted to killing Max? She didn't like to think of herself as selfish. Perhaps this was just her way of coping. She looked at her friends, Chelsea's face grim and angry, Talia still shocked.

"What did he mean you told him to do it?" Talia's soft voice broke Sophia's trance. "You told him to kill Max?"

We were joking, Sophia wanted to explain. Just a joke to lighten the mood. *We were all staring down a future where our reputations were destroyed and we made a dark joke.* But she couldn't tell Talia any of that, couldn't admit they may have been complicit in a murder. Saying it out loud would make it real.

"It wasn't like that," Chelsea finally said.

"Max is dead. Alec ... may have killed her." Talia seemed stuck in processing mode.

"May have? He did kill her. He admitted it, and it's because he found out that we wrote the book with AI and knew Max was going to expose us all," Sophia said.

It wasn't a great explanation. It wouldn't sound right in court, at their sentencing hearings. Conspiracy to commit murder in order to cover up fraud? They'd serve years, decades maybe. If they were lucky, maybe she and Chelsea and Talia would be assigned to the same prison, start their own gang. *We've killed before, we'll do it again*, they'd warn the other ladies. And then they'd all get shanked. Sophia understood prison hierarchies. None of them would survive, especially not Talia. She was too flighty, too desperate to please. She'd fall in with the wrong crowd. She'd accept a gift, not knowing the strings attached. *Never accept gifts in prison*, that was Gage's sage advice. He'd had stories about debt, about what he'd extracted from his fellow inmates, though he always phrased it in a way it sounded like he was talking about someone else on the recorded calls. Sophia's mind was spiraling, imagining them in federal prison khaki, or county jail orange, both an offense to her fashion sensibilities, a triviality she had to focus on to keep from spiraling deeper.

"It's my fault. *I* told him about the AI," Talia whispered. "I didn't mean to. It slipped out."

"Come have some coffee." Sophia pointed to the kitchen table, the ancient white Formica top currently covered in the detritus of their night of mourning. "We'll figure this out, won't we, Chelsea?" She didn't want to seem needy, but Chelsea had all the answers. She was their ringleader, the one who'd uploaded the book in the first place, the one who controlled the money, the one who joked about killing Max. If anything, this was all Chelsea's fault. Maybe if Sophia testified against her ... maybe she could keep herself free. No, that wouldn't matter, anyway. Her name was sullied. Her book would never sell. Nobody would want to read anything from her unless it was a true crime work of nonfiction outlining their sordid exploits.

"Wait." Sophia nearly dropped the coffee pot. "The exposé!"

"What about it?" Chelsea was staring into her mug, looking like she wanted to climb inside and drown herself.

"That's what this was all about, right? Stopping Max before she submitted it anywhere? Maybe it's not too late."

"Max is dead! It is too late." Talia shoved the takeout boxes aside and dropped her head onto the table with a thump.

"It's too late to save her, but maybe we can save ourselves," Chelsea said. "If we can get rid of Max's article, no one ever has to find out that there is no MF Ascher or that the book was written by a machine."

"We could go to her apartment, find her computer, and delete the file. We could destroy her computer if we have to. Drop it in the Hudson or throw it in front of a bus or burn it behind the lake house." Sophia's mind spun with possibilities.

"Is this what we've come to? First you practically put a hit out on Max, now you're talking about breaking into her apartment and trashing her stuff?" Talia raised her head to glare at them.

"We might not have to break in." Sophia ran upstairs and retrieved Max's backpack, the one she'd left at the lake house the night she died. Sophia had brought it home and stashed it in a closet. She liked to avoid clutter, keeping to her grandmother's tradition of always having the downstairs ready for visitors, no matter what. *What if the pope stops by*, Grandma would say, yelling at Grandpa for leaving his pipe and newspaper on the table. She wasn't Catholic, nor was she important enough for a papal visit, but the cleanliness lessons had stuck.

"Where did you get that?" Chelsea asked when Sophia brought them the bag.

"She left it behind at the lake house. I assumed when she sobered up she'd come over and ask for it." Sophia couldn't help but wonder if the abandoned bag should have been a clue that Max hadn't left on her own. She had noticed it but viewed it as a promise that Max would return. What if she hadn't seen the bag, and truly thought Max was leaving for good? Would she have followed the sound of the Mustang tearing away? Chased her down to confiscate her keys, keep her from drunk driving, settle her into a hotel if she didn't want to stay at the lake house? If that bag hadn't suggested a return, would they have followed? Alec said she was alive when she'd hit the water. If they'd witnessed it, if they'd followed, if they'd cared, they could have gotten her out. Sophia was a strong swimmer, and Chelsea had some medical training. Between the two of them—with Talia on the dock wringing her hands and shouting encouraging but probably wrong advice—they could have saved Max.

Talia unzipped the bag carefully, treating it as though it was a religious relic deserving of caution and respect. Maybe they'd be lucky, and the laptop would be inside.

"No computer," she said, "but here are the keys to her apartment."

Max was one of those people who kept her house and car keys separate, the Mustang key always hidden in the car, a lack of precaution that made Sophia nervous. *Making yourself a target*, Gage would have said, and in this case, he was right. Alec was so easily able to start Max's car and drive her toward her cold, dark death.

Talia dropped Max's keys into her purse. "Hopefully her laptop's at her apartment and not in her car."

"Let's go." Chelsea, resuming her role as ringleader, led them out the door. "We've got to find out what she did with that exposé."

talia

WHAT'S THE POINT? I swear I read it (at least most of it) because my book club can be snippy. TBH, my book club is mostly tired mothers who want to get out of the house, and we usually read cozy mysteries and cowboy romance. But one of our members is an adjunct professor at a junior college and she said "Dimwitty" is brilliant. So, I guess it is.

—Wishy-Washy in Colorado

Max's landlord, a crusty man with a scruffy gray beard, blew cigarette smoke to the side. "First of all, these keys won't open no apartment in this building. And second, she moved out."

Talia gripped the counter separating them. "When?"

"Couple months ago," he said.

Impossible, Talia thought. No way would her best friend keep such big news from her.

Chelsea smacked Talia's arm. "You had no idea? I thought you and Max were tied at the hip. I can't believe she didn't tell you."

"I can't either," Talia said. It felt like yet another betrayal.

"Do you know where she moved to?" Sophia asked.

The landlord dropped his cigarette into a plastic cup. "Who's asking?"

"Me. Us, her best friends." Talia sniffled. "Please, we're trying to find her."

"Her best friends, huh? How is it you don't know where she lives then? I can't release that information to just anyone. Maybe she doesn't want you to know where she moved to."

"You don't understand." Talia grew desperate. "Max is—"

"Missing." Chelsea cut her off. She pushed her way in front of Talia and slid a twenty across the scratched wood counter. "Did she leave a forwarding address?"

"Twenty bucks? You shittin' me?" He grinned, showing off crooked tobacco-stained teeth.

"For fuck's sake." Chelsea withdrew a Benjamin from her bag and held it up. "What's the address? And you'd better be right, or I'll have the health department here by morning."

Talia admired Chelsea's authority, her ability to make a demand with righteous indignation.

"The health department?" The landlord sat back. "What the hell for?"

"Mold. This building is riddled with it." Chelsea waved the hundred-dollar bill. "I can smell it."

The old man's eyes flicked over the three of them. He reached up to pluck the money out of Chelsea's hand, but between her height and the length of her arm, he had no chance.

"I might have it." He thumbed through a box of index cards. "Here we go, Max DeLeon." He turned the card and showed it to them. The sight of the handwriting made Talia's stomach curdle. She knew Max's barely legible penmanship as if it were her own.

Chelsea snapped a photo of it, tossed the money at the landlord, and ushered Sophia and Talia out to the car.

Sophia drove, Chelsea sat shotgun, and Talia wallowed in the back seat like a forgotten child. As they headed across Queens to the exclusive suburb of Forest Hills, Talia's knees bounced. Her thighs stuck together beneath her skirt. How could this be happening? She closed her eyes and leaned her head back, wondering what would have happened if she'd never met her three best friends. Sure, her life would be empty and pathetic, but at least she wouldn't be suffering. At least Max would still be alive —maybe. But if she were dead, Talia wouldn't have ever known. The pain in her gut wouldn't exist. It was a selfish thought, and it shamed her.

Silence filled the car, and Talia couldn't imagine what Chelsea and Sophia were thinking. Most likely, they were not having the same dark thoughts. Sophia was too practical, a "what's done is done" kind of thinker. And Chelsea was hyper-focused on moving forward and making sure Max's article never got published.

A nursery rhyme, the one about monkeys jumping on the bed, came to mind: *Four failed writers played with AI ... one went rogue and had to die—*

"You gotta be kidding me," Sophia said as she pulled up to the curb and hit the brakes hard.

Talia lowered her window. The apartment building was a classic brownstone with an arched wooden double-door entrance at the center. She counted four stories. Each apartment had a curved balcony hanging over the quiet, tree-lined street.

"Fuck me," Chelsea said.

Talia didn't say a word, agonizing over what other secrets Max might have kept from her.

They rode the elevator to the fourth floor and stepped into a hallway. Talia's breaths came in fits and starts. She felt like the damsel in a horror movie, the kind when everybody in the audience is whispering *don't go in, don't open the door.*

Talia's hand shook so hard she couldn't insert the key into the lock.

"Gimme that." Chelsea snatched the keys from her. The dead bolt clicked as the lock disengaged. The door swung open. For a split second, Talia was sure she'd see Max standing there.

"Fuck me," Chelsea said again.

It was beautiful, elegant, sparsely furnished. At the center of the room was a plush white couch with one matching chair. The hardwood floor gleamed. Sheer curtains hung loosely over the windows. It was as if Max had decorated her new home with lightness in mind, a stark contrast to her dark clothing and the heaviness that encapsulated her life.

The living room flowed into an open kitchen with sleek appliances, white cabinets, and pale gray and white granite counters.

"Look at this," Sophia said, standing in front of the open refrigerator. "A bottle of Dom Perignon."

"Maybe she was planning to have us over for a little housewarming in her new apartment," Talia said, a suggestion that only made sense to her. She opened a cabinet and found a set of twelve glasses—four water, four wine, and four champagne flutes. "We should open it now, in honor of Max."

"No. We're here to find that damn laptop," Chelsea said. "Put it back."

Chelsea's reprimand made Talia feel even smaller. "You're right. I'm sorry."

Talia bet Max had the champagne on hand for them. She imagined her filling the flutes, toasting their success, and then showing off her new apartment. If it hadn't been for fucking Alec Pendergrass, that's exactly what they'd be doing right now. Her hatred of him grew deeper and more intense, like a fire hit with a spurt of gasoline. Fucking fire metaphors—she wished they'd stop entering her mind—just one more reason to hate Alec.

Talia's thoughts switched to the task at hand. "Her laptop's probably in her bedroom." She halted at the sight of Max's neatly made bed. The creamy duvet and throw pillows were eerily similar to Talia's. Did it mean anything? Had Max been channeling her in some way? Talia pushed the crazy thoughts aside. Max probably just liked the same colors she did.

The computer was on the bed as if waiting for Max to return.

"Found it." She brought it to the living room and handed it to Chelsea.

"Excellent." Chelsea sat on the sofa and opened it. "We need a charger. Tal, do you know her password?"

"No, but I could probably guess."

"Here's my charger." Sophia pulled one out of her bag. "You start guessing passwords, and I'll search for a notebook or paper where she might have written them down."

Talia suggested dates, places they'd been to, and variations of *fuck, fucking, and motherfucking.*

Chelsea slammed the lid. "Sophia, have you found anything?"

"Not yet." Sophia had a stack of folders and spiral notebooks and loose papers spread across Max's small desk.

"I'll look in the bedroom again," Talia said, despondency weighing on her. Max would never have wanted anybody rifling through her stuff. It would have made her feel violated, the way she had been as a little girl.

Talia opened the window in the bedroom to let in some fresh air. The breeze carried the scent of green grass and spring flowers. She turned and took a moment to look in Max's closet. In contrast to the uncluttered bedroom, the walk-in was an explosion of clothes and shoes and boxes not yet unpacked. She picked up a familiar black hoodie and sank her face into the fabric. The scent of a lost friend. No doubt, she'd be the one to go through Max's belongings. Maybe Chelsea and Sophia would offer to help. Either way, Talia would take care of it. She owed her best friend that much, at least.

Talia put the oversized sweatshirt on and zipped it up before going in search of something, anything, that would uncover Max's passwords. She'd hardly gotten through one drawer when Sophia's shout made her jump.

"Oh, my god!"

Talia ran into the other room, practically careening into Chelsea. Sophia sat at Max's desk, holding a thin stack of papers.

"You won't believe this," Sophia said.

Max had printed her exposé. It was dated only two days before she died. Sophia read it aloud. The writing was brilliant. Max had thoroughly eviscerated the publishing industry, as she promised. But there was hardly any mention of AI, only one innocuous reference, and absolutely nothing about MF Ascher, the book, or them.

"She didn't write about us at all," Chelsea said, her voice barely above a whisper. "This could've been published and it wouldn't have mattered one bit. Why didn't she just tell us?"

Talia dissolved into tears. Guilt consumed her. "This is all my fault. I opened my big mouth and told Alec about the AI. Max wouldn't be dead if it hadn't been for me."

"Stop." Chelsea pulled Talia into her arms. "Every one of us can claim responsibility for something that led to Max's death, even Max herself. So don't let—"

"There's more." Sophia's voice was unsteady, breathless. Her eyes filled with tears. "It's from three years ago. And it changes everything."

My dear sisters,

I write to you to let you know that this is the last time you will hear from me. If you're reading this letter, it's because I'm dead.

But before I go, I need for each of you to know what your friendship has meant to me these past few years. I don't believe in god, but if there is one, I thank HER for bringing you into my life. I will forever be grateful to the stars that aligned and brought us together during that super dull writer's workshop. I learned nothing that weekend about writing, but meeting you three taught me that when I open myself up to the universe, there is goodness out there to be gathered and held in the palm of my hands.

I don't own much. Just my crappy car, a few clothes none of you will wear because they're all dark and drab—like the secrets I keep to myself—and the rights to all my creative work, published and unpublished, like my articles, manuscripts, personal essays, and books. Take anything you want from my shitty apartment, maybe something that will remind you of me if you choose. This is my last will and testament, if anyone asks. Just make sure that fuck-face landlord doesn't get his hands on anything. Donate whatever, sell off whatever you can for extra cash. I've done a lot of that lately, so there's not much left—at least nothing of monetary value. Everything left in this small room is mine, my treasures, and I want you to have them.

Lastly, NO.

There is nothing you could have done to stop this. To keep me from killing myself. This has been my destiny. I had no say in being brought into this life and I never had a say in what was done to me. You don't know the half of it, but it's not because I didn't trust you. I just didn't want my dark to overshadow your light, the light that you have shared with me—but in the end, no amount of light is enough to make me want to stay in this place.

Dying is my choice. I've spent my life trying to escape one way or the other, and if you're reading this, it means I've succeeded. So don't weep over me. Don't grieve. Know that I am happy, finally. And know that you three have been the only chinks of light to ever come my way. You took me in as your friend and entrusted me with your stories and your lives, and I hope that I have, somehow, in some small way, let you know how much you mean to me.

Go raise hell, scream, and rail against the fucking machine, and laugh when you think of me. Talia, Chelsea, and Sophia—you are the only family I have ever had. I love you.

Max

twenty-seven
chelsea

What the actual f*ck did I just read? And why do I have the inexplicable urge to read it again?
  —booksarebetterthanpeople

A preternatural silence descended on the apartment and settled into Chelsea's heart. The letter was equal parts terrifying and beautiful—just like Max. Her talent and larger-than-life passion for hating the world and all those who wronged her undercut every swipe of her pen across the page.

Then there was the second thing that accompanied the suicide note: a will, also handwritten, probably simultaneous pages ripped from a spiral notebook. The most surprising thing was the notarized signature and stamp beneath Max's scrawled name, making the document and its directives legal.

This was all too much to run through Chelsea's internal *what if* and *if only* and *what about* story simulators. The essay. The suicide note. The will. She paced, feet sinking into the wool area rug, head spinning, bruises aching. She reached into her messenger bag and pulled out the bottle of Tylenol, swallowing a few before chasing them with a handful of Tums.

Chelsea needed every bit of mental reserve to figure this shit out.

"She left it all ..." Talia choked and sobbed at the same time. "To us. Even when she didn't have anything."

Chelsea scraped her hand across her forehead. How did someone like Max have the foresight to leave a legally binding will when she had nothing?

"She didn't want anyone she didn't like getting her things," Sophia muttered, still searching the two sheets of paper for answers she would never find.

"Like the state," Chelsea said. Not after all the government had taken from Max as a child in the foster care system.

"I don't know what to do with all this," Talia whispered before blowing her already raw nose. "Does this mean she actually tried to die by suicide?"

Sophia nodded. "Max wanted to die before; we knew that. She told us about the depression when she was younger and that she planned to do it."

Slitting her wrists, taking pills, even hanging herself. And while Max had not previously succeeded in ending her life, Chelsea recognized she was still trying to do it every day from the time they met—by slowly drinking herself to death.

"This was three years ago!" Talia plucked the pages from Sophia and waved them around. "Why didn't she ask us for help?"

They resumed their silence, the lingering questions about that time in Max's life going unasked and unanswered. Chelsea's medical school psych rotation had taught her when someone wanted to die by suicide, they did it. They planned in secret, appearing normal to the world at large, while they were plotting to leave it.

"Maybe we changed her mind without knowing it," Chelsea mumbled. Though Max planned to do it, wrote the letter and a will, she hadn't followed through with it.

Talia sighed and swiped at the tears careening down her cheek.

The air hummed with so many silent questions that, for a moment, Chelsea heard the whispers. She cast her gaze about Max's place, her secret sanctuary that remained as she had left it before taking off in the Mustang for the lake house.

There was nothing here that made it Max, except for the combat boots kicked off by the couch. Did this place give Max some measure of peace? Chelsea hoped so.

—

They opened the champagne and spent some time in Max's apartment, swapping stories about her, things she'd said or done that made it feel more like she was here. The writing workshop she stormed out of because the instructor was a "fucking hack" when he claimed Gloria Steinem wasn't a real writer. How she teased the hell out of Talia but still was there to pick her up when Talia's family made her feel bad. And she loved celebrating their wins no matter how minor.

Sophia cleared her throat. "I need to talk to you about something." Her usual flawless presentation had been marred by worry and grief. "I didn't want to bring it up with everything going on."

"Please tell me this is good news because I can't take anything else," Talia said.

Before Sophia said the words, Chelsea knew what they would be. Once upon a time, she had worn the same expression. The same triumph.

"I signed with an agent." Sophia punctuated her statement with a rush of breath fitting for someone burdening the world with good news when everything else was burning.

Talia opened her eyes and arms wide, but before she could complete a hug, she pulled up and opted for clapping. Chelsea joined her and the three took some time to soak up all the joy that accompanied the news.

"But there's a huge problem," Sophia said after giving them details.

"Please don't tell me you used AI." Talia's shoulders slumped.

Sophia rolled her eyes. "The problem is, I signed with the agent before I knew about the fine print with Alec. That's why I'm so worried. If Alec starts throwing it around that he has me under contract—"

"The agent will pull the offer." Chelsea nodded, understanding immediately that her screw-up would put a friend in the crosshairs for humiliation. "And that might taint the pool for anyone ever repping you again."

"Exactly."

Talia threw her head back and groaned to the ceiling. "Alec! That motherfucker."

"Correction," Chelsea said. "That motherfucking asshole."

The three exchanged glances, which eventually led to a round of laughter at the homage to Max.

"She should be here." Talia said. "I miss her so much."

Yes, she should be here. If it wasn't for Chelsea's linchpin comment. If it wasn't for Alec taking things too far. If it wasn't for Chelsea trusting him in the first place, Max would be here. Once again, she trusted the wrong person. Alec and Rick were one and the same, as if they'd morphed into one evil monster set on destroying her.

"She died for nothing." Talia smothered her face with her hands.

That, too, was something that stoked the rage searing through Chelsea. If Max died *for* something, maybe the whole thing could someday make sense. Maybe they could grow to accept it at some point. "Wait a minute," Sophia said, drawing Chelsea back. "If Max left us everything she had, that means her share of the book, too."

"Yeah, so?" Talia squinted and moved her gaze between Sophia and Chelsea.

And then a sudden realization burst through Chelsea's head. It could work. It could serve two purposes.

"What if ..." Chelsea paused before uttering the idea that

could spin them in a new direction. Was it insane or brilliant? Or both? "What if we made Max the one and only MF Ascher?"

Sophia's eyes darted around the room as she considered it. "That could work, and it would protect us from any future scandal if the AI is discovered."

"And it means there won't be another book ... or movie." Chelsea thought of this as the Revenge Story plot branched off, the characters rewriting, and in the process, re-righting themselves along a new path. One where Max could do a lot of good for the story, even though she would be absent from its pages.

"And maybe it'll give Max the recognition she deserved but never got," Talia said, jumping in. "Right?"

There was something else that this new channel opened up inside Chelsea's brain. She moved to Max's desk, grabbed all the notebooks and writing samples, and stuffed them into her bag.

"What are you doing?" Talia asked, glancing over her shoulder.

"Just looking and thinking." Chelsea half responded as she pulled out a stack of business cards and started sifting through them. She stopped when she came to the one from the *New York Times* reporter, Brad Harrison. The one Max hooked up with back in October. The one who scrawled the note about borrowing her book along the bottom. The one who later wrote one of the most insightful reviews that, no doubt, had a lot to do with raising the book's profile and sales.

Chelsea's brain buzzed. This could fix everything and bring Max peace.

"Making Max MF Ascher still won't solve the problem of Alec and the contract." Sophia dropped the will into her vintage Valentino tote.

"That's right," Talia said. "According to Alec, he owns us."

Chelsea tucked the business card into her bag. "I know how we can do it, but we have to all agree or it won't work."

Talia perked up, and Sophia tilted her head, leaning a little closer. Chelsea had to pitch this just right because if she didn't, not only would they reject it, but they might also figure out how dark she could be.

"I think the only way we can end this, all of it, is to get rid of Alec." She tracked her friends' reactions. The slight narrowing of Talia's eyes. The faint crease furrowing between Sophia's eyebrows.

"You mean fire him, right?" Talia blinked rapidly. "Can we do that?"

The trio remained affixed to their respective spots, Talia and Sophia exchanging a subtle what-the-fuck-is-she-talking-about glance before pointing their stares back at Chelsea.

"What do you mean?" Sophia asked.

She cleared her throat, ready to reveal the Revenge Story plot twist that had screeched through her head since Alec not only confessed, but tried to gaslight her into believing she wanted Max dead. If they could do things *just right,* they would all walk away free and clear. Sophia would get her big publishing contract. Talia could write her romances.

And of course, if this all went as planned, Chelsea would get what she wanted, too: the unraveling of her greatest foe.

"He needs to die. It's the only way to get everything we want."

Talia's face, chafed with grief, drained from blush to gray.

"You want to kill him?" Sophia asked, leaning in closer.

Chelsea pressed her lips together. "I want *us* to kill him. The three of us. It's all or none."

"You can't be serious," Talia blurted. "Sure, we all hate him, but murder?" Talia moved to the end of the couch, where Max's imprint remained on the blanket crumpled in the corner. She moved her hand along the soft fleece, like she didn't dare disturb the fabric for fear of making that slight curve disappear, taking Max with it.

Chelsea turned to Sophia and silently pleaded her case. Sophia, perhaps more than any of them, needed this to happen. If Alec didn't die, her chance of publishing might, and that was something Sophia was unwilling to sacrifice.

"Sophia?" Chelsea said.

Sophia, hands resting in her lap, swallowed hard. "I'm in."

Chelsea turned to Talia. She was the weak link. But as long as they stuck together, they could accomplish anything. For seven years, it had been the four of them against the world. And though Max was no longer there, her spirit lingered in the air around them. If it worked, they would be free to live without the burden of Alec hanging over their head.

"Tal," Chelsea said softly. "It's all or none. If you can't do this, we won't. We'll figure something else out." Though there was no other way.

Talia closed her eyes and stroked Max's blanket. Chelsea hoped her timid friend would come around and agree. She had to be on board. They couldn't do it without her. If they did, Talia would be prosecution witness number one.

"Okay," Talia opened her eyes. "I'm in. All in."

Chelsea exhaled, relieved that they all agreed. But timing was everything—and it had to be perfect. Alec needed to live long enough for the final plot twist to work.

twenty-eight
sophia

It's impossible to judge a book without knowing the gender of the author. Is this an illustrious work by a gentleman who truly understands the human condition? Or is it a poor attempt at literary fiction created by an emotionally frail woman who is parroting what she thinks she understands? My book club is divided. Personally, I loved the book, and I have a crush on the author. FWIW, I'm bisexual. Four Stars.

Sophia was the obvious choice to deal with Alec. Chelsea was too hot-headed, and Talia was … a little too soft. She'd break down and ruin everything. Sophia could hold it together through anything. She wouldn't lose her temper, she wouldn't cry, and, most importantly, she'd stay on script. There was a delicate balance to their plan, and it depended on this meeting.

She sat in his office, hair smoothed into a ponytail, back perfectly straight, legs crossed at the ankles, the very picture of decorum. Grandma would be proud. Grandma would also be proud of Sophia's choice to wear peep-toe shoes. In general, her grandmother had found that sort of footwear vulgar, but she also encouraged Sophia to use whatever it took when dealing with men. *Men are a terrible combination of fragile and volatile*, she'd said. *You must handle them firmly, but carefully. Like a bomb. A bomb with an ego.*

"So you've decided to do it?" Alec asked. She could sense his smugness, the way he felt he had all the power in this situation. He thought he was in complete control.

"Yes. We're going to write another MF Ascher book. But we have some conditions." This was the important thing, the conditions. They were the key to everything.

"I don't know that you're in a position to set any conditions," Alec said. And there it was, the smirk. The ego. The delicate-to-manage bomb.

"I rather think we are. We own the MF Ascher name. Are you going to go public with the truth about how we wrote the book? That reflects poorly on you, especially when we tell everyone you were in on the secret all along. So we're in this together, the four of us." That hurt, that was a knife to her heart, the way the four of us now included Alec instead of Max, a soul-friend exchanged for a killer. But she kept her face impassive.

"That's right, we are. So why aren't the others here?"

Sophia waved her hand dismissively. "We thought it best that I come alone. Chelsea, she's feeling a little guilty about, well, you know. And Talia, she's been overly emotional and confused about everything. And me, I have something extra, something I don't want them to know about." The bait was supposed to be that last part, the idea that Sophia had a secret, that she might be on his side. She'd miscalculated, though.

"What's Talia confused about?" Alec latched on to the wrong part. He actually looked concerned, like his feelings for—and obsession with—Talia were real. "Is she okay? Is she mad at me?"

Okay, Sophia, different tactic. "She's not mad at you. Not exactly. More like she's mad at herself. It's weird, the relief we all felt when we heard what happened to Max. I mean, she was our friend and all, but she was an outsider, too. And she was super controlling of Talia. Talia used to complain about her, wanted to get away. She thought Max might have a crush on her or something, and Talia's not like that. She likes men, real men." Every word she said made her sick. Good thing Sophia didn't believe in ghosts. Max would haunt her for sure if she heard this.

Alec preened. "Real men. Yeah, we've hooked up a few times."

"And that's why she's conflicted." Sophia ignored his obvious lie. "She's ... you know how Talia writes sweet rom-coms? Everyone always thinks that's who she really is. But she's not her writing. She's a dark romance kind of girl. Likes the bad boys, the dangerous ones. The killers." She was afraid she might have gone too far with that. It was too over the top, too ridiculous. But so was Alec's ego.

"I knew it," Alec said, more to himself than to her. "And you want, what? You're keeping secrets from your friends now?"

"I want you to release me from the part of the contract that says you have the rights to my individual future work. I'm trying to separate myself from MF Ascher. I don't mind continuing the trilogy"—that got his attention, *a trilogy*—"but I want to be able to publish under my own name separately. You're not the kind of agent I need."

"Why not? I represent all kinds of artists."

That was another lie. He'd only been an entertainment attorney for a few short months, and that was completely different from working as a literary agent, anyway. God, why hadn't they read that contract more closely?

"I want to sell my literary fiction. That's not your forte. Besides, we all know literary fiction doesn't sell well. You wouldn't make much off me, whereas you would if we wrote another MF Ascher novel."

"What's to stop your friends from writing without you? All they have to do is spin a little AI magic." Alec got up from behind his desk and crossed to the front of it, leaning against it casually, far too close to Sophia. She remained sitting in his visitor's chair. He was looming over her as a power play, showing that he looked down upon her. Too bad for him that she saw herself as a queen on a throne who made the peasants stand. That image made her mouth quirk with a smile, but she quickly got herself under control. Must remain calm.

"Even if they did, I'd still get my share. We own the name together."

"You lost Max. What if they lost you, too?" Alec's grin showed all his teeth, like he was trying to appear threatening.

"What are you saying? That you'd get rid of another liability? Here's a fun fact for you; I'm untouchable. Max was easy; she didn't have a family. She had no one to avenge her. I do."

"Yeah, right. You're alone, Sophia. You always have been." Typical man, thinking a single woman was alone, as though the lack of a husband or boyfriend meant the lack of any protection.

"I'm not alone. I have an older brother who loves me very much. His name is Gage Williams. You might know of him."

Alec had been smirking, but his face slowly turned to a mix of confusion and horror. "*The* Gage Williams? The ... oh my god, I've read about him. He's ... he's your brother?" He looked at her the way everyone always did when they found out: with fear, suspicion, and a definite wondering if psychopathy ran in families. There was a reason she never told anyone, not even her best friends, the truth about her big brother.

"He is. And he'd do anything for me."

Alec rallied, gathering his dignity. "Isn't he serving several life sentences? It's cute you think using his name could protect you."

"Do you know what it's like in prison? You don't practice criminal law, so I doubt you have any idea. There are men whose favor you want to curry. Men who can make your prison experience safer, or, alternatively, make it hell. There are a lot of people who want to stay on my brother's good side. If you were to ever harm me, you'd never be safe again. There'd be a bounty on your head."

"That only would matter if I were in the same prison as him." Alec's tone was not as confident as it had been just a moment ago.

"No, it wouldn't. Because everyone on the inside has friends on the *outside*, people who care about them and want to keep them safe. Friends they did time with, maybe? Killers who were released? Besides, if anything happened to me, Gage is my sole heir. He can't use the money on much in prison, but he can use it on revenge. You'd never be safe, Alec. And you'd always be wondering if the one who gets to you first is going to do it quick, or if he's going to try and impress my brother and see how long he can make it last."

She watched as Alec crossed to the window to stare out at the New York skyline. "You know, Sophia," he said, without turning around. "You're right, I'm not the best representative for your literary work. Let's stay together on the MF Ascher project, but I'll whip up a release of rights for you so you can go out on your own with your other writings. Sound good?"

Sophia smiled at his back, noting that he was slightly shaking. "Perfect. Now let's talk about the movie. As I said, I'm here on behalf of my co-authors. And we want to utilize the termination clause in our movie deal. We can't work with Rick Stafford."

That got Alec to not only turn back around, but to make him do so in a whirl so fast he stumbled, nearly crashing into the corner of his own desk. Sophia bit her lip to keep from laughing at him. Men didn't like to be laughed at. It would destroy these delicate negotiations.

"You want to terminate that contract? Forget it. There has been too much invested, too much time and money."

"No, we want the contract. We just don't want Rick Stafford to be a part of it. We've heard some unsavory things. Isn't there a morality clause? It's our understanding that Rick may be involved in a plagiarism scandal."

"Fuck off, Sophia. You didn't write your own book!"

"Yes, but that's our secret. We heard Rick's plagiarism story is going to break soon, and we want to get ahead of it. We don't want anyone looking too closely into MF Ascher, and we're afraid of the association. I'm sure there are other companies salivating to take their place." She hoped that last part was true.

"There's something you're not telling me. What's the real reason?"

"If I tell you, I'm betraying Chelsea's confidence."

"I'm releasing you from your individual contract. I think you owe me."

Sophia let out a long sigh. She had to appear reluctant, let him think he was winning. "Well, I suppose you should know. Don't tell anyone, though. Lawyer-client confidentiality, right?"

"It's called privilege," he corrected, which she did know, she just wanted to appear unsure. That was a way to hook Alec in, let him think he was the smart one.

"A long time ago, Chelsea was married to Rick. I don't really know what happened, but he left her and broke her heart. She hasn't been able to have another relationship since then. I guess she thought that if she delivered the Ascher book to him, he'd start to have feelings again. She ... well, let's just say she served her heart to him on a platter, and he put a knife in it again. Since the plan failed, and we know there are other options, she wants to end it. Break up with him, like he broke up with her."

"That's the problem with women," Alec snorted. "We should have used a different production company to begin with. That would have shown Rick what he was missing. He might have come back to her to get the next book. It's called planning. Maybe you girls should learn how to do it."

twenty-nine
chelsea

I did not see that coming. I need to go pray for Ascher's immortal soul.
–Psalmy In Ohio

Chelsea turned the business card in her hand, smoothing the pads of her fingers over the writing. She'd spent the last week planning how to handle Brad Harrison. She conducted copious amounts of research, and read every piece, editorial, and review he'd written in the last three years.

She also went down the rabbit hole of social media, something she avoided unless she was being paid by a client. Most of Brad's was wildly uninteresting. He usually posted about current events and news stories, most of which weren't his. Some were even lighthearted and sweet. What kind of reporter didn't toot their own horn every chance they got? He rarely posted pictures of himself, and even those few did nothing to provide any insight into the sandy-haired man beyond the fact that he liked dogs and had an affinity for Macallan.

Chelsea stepped out of the Uber in front of the Hotel Fresco. Its mixture of noir and art deco inspired countless writers to ponder the world from inside its famed doors and made it the perfect spot to meet a reporter.

Brad sat at the end of the bar. Chelsea arrived a calculated six minutes late and did her best to shorten her normal long stride so as not to appear like she was marching into battle, which Talia often likened her walk to.

Brad's gaze lifted from his phone, and wow. Max had not done this man justice. She quickly diverted her attention away and smoothed down the wrap dress she'd dug out of her closet. While she initially planned on wearing jeans and a T-shirt, Talia encouraged her to dress for the occasion. Chelsea balked at first, but then acquiesced. She wasn't comfortable, but there was a power play at work that might go in her favor.

Brad stood as she approached, his seafoam eyes burrowing into hers. The way his hair curled around his ear was quite distracting. What the hell was going on? She felt like Talia had taken over her body and was making this into one of her meet-cutes. *The two met over drinks while she took a break from planning a murder…*

"Are you here to meet Brad, by any chance?" he said. If Chelsea didn't know any better, she'd say he looked hopeful. Maybe that was her wishful thinking. She had promised him an exclusive, after all. That's what that was.

She cleared her throat and put on her best neutral face, trying to scrub the details of Max's sexcapade with him from her brain.

"What if I am?" she asked.

"Thank god I don't have to come up with a line to get you to join me." He waited until she claimed the stool next to his and offered his large, smooth hand. "Brad Harrison."

She moved her gaze down his face to the hand and then took it. "Chelsea Specter. Thanks for meeting with me on such short notice."

"Of course. I'm a sucker for a possible exclusive. That, and a drink with a beautiful woman." He summoned the bartender with a wave and waited for her to order her Grey Goose and cranberry before ordering his Macallan.

"Have I seen you around this hotel bar?" he asked.

"I've never been here before today."

His eyes narrowed a beat before his left eyebrow popped up. "What made you pick it?"

Because this is where you're sitting in the one selfie you posted on your Instagram page.

She shrugged. "I'd heard it was a cool place." She took a sip of her drink immediately after it appeared and willed it to wash down the nerves. She had a job to do and if she didn't get it done, her plan to take Rick down might be fucked.

"We have a mutual friend. Well, had," she continued. "Max DeLeon."

The sparkle dimmed in Brad's eyes for a moment. "Yeah. I heard about that. I only met her once, but she was interesting and smart."

"She was. And an amazing writer." Chelsea shifted in her seat, reached under the counter, and withdrew the package from her bag.

His gaze moved to the envelope on the bar, and then to the business card she set on top, the one he'd left for Max.

"Ah." He grinned and dipped his head. "You know, she never did call me to get that book back. Even after I gave it a five-star review."

She withdrew a copy of their book, her fingertips dotting the cover. "What if I told you I know who MF Ascher is?"

He leaned closer, his eyes shifting ever-so-slightly between hers, trying to gauge her sincerity. "I'd be very interested in that."

She nodded, tracing the rim of her glass. "This envelope contains some of Max's work. A brilliant exposé on the current tumultuous state of the publishing industry and how AI is going to gut it. There are also a few pieces she finished, started and stopped, some notes." Including a few Chelsea manufactured to pique his interest about a certain asshole Hollywood producer.

Brad squinted. "What does this all have to do with MF Ascher?"

"I want you to print the exposé, and at least look at the other things. Publish or chase anything that interests you." Which Chelsea really needed him to do, or the Revenge Story would fall apart.

He leaned back, ran his thumb down the ridge of his jaw before crossing his arms across his chest. "If I do what you're asking, you'll tell me who Ascher is?"

"Yes."

"Can I get an exclusive with her?"

She took the last sip of her drink, letting the ice clink against her teeth. "That can't happen."

"Can't or won't?"

Chelsea leveled a gaze at Brad, searched his face for any hint that he wasn't going to bite. She wouldn't really know until she started reeling in the lure.

"Look, if you can't agree to the terms, I'll move down the list to Hunter James at the *Post*." It was line-in-the-sand time.

"You drive a hard bargain," he said, his chest swelling with a deep inhale. "Can I get you another drink?"

"I know, and no." Chelsea held fast to his gaze, even as it continued to calculate and recalculate whether or not she was bluffing. Time to double down. "You've got five seconds, or I'll walk and take MF Ascher with me." Every good writer knew that a ticking clock raised the stakes of any story.

He chuckled and rubbed his head. "Okay. Fine. Assuming the writing's as good as you say it is, I'll print Max's piece on publishing and look at whatever else she has." He slid the envelope into his jacket.

Chelsea stood and pulled a twenty out of her bag, setting it under her empty glass.

"You don't need to rush off," Brad said, sliding from the stool.

"I've got somewhere to be."

"Wait a sec," he said, standing alongside her. "How do I know you'll keep your end of the deal?"

The scotch drifting from his breath mingled with the citrus scent wafting around him. He was taller than her, another surprising thing about him. It all made her head swim, or maybe it was the vodka.

"Because I'm telling you I will. Run the article and I'll give you the biggest literary sensation to hit the scene in decades." She stepped toward him, pushing herself into his personal space. His jaw pulsed as his eyes dipped to her lips and back up.

"I'll be in touch after I see it in print. Don't let me down ... Brad."

She walked away, fighting to keep her heartbeat steady, even as the satisfaction with what she had set in motion filled her with an intoxicating sense of power. It was a big risk, putting any trust in Brad. But she was counting on the fact that as a reporter he operated under another set of rules entirely—unlike Rick and Alec and all the others who came before.

thirty
talia

Ascher is funny and brilliant in a way I've never seen before in a work of fiction. The voice, although mechanical at times, touched my soul. The only reason I gave four stars instead of five was that I felt it needed a character list, a family tree, and a map.
–Confused in Connecticut

"Mini honey jars? Seriously?" Talia could not believe how pedestrian her younger sister could be. It was amusing.

"What? They're so cute," Jenna said. "And they come with the little wooden round thing you use instead of a spoon. I went to a shower a month ago, and everyone loved the honey favor."

They were sitting at their mother's dining room table with scissors, cellophane, ribbons, and little name tags that would designate each person's place at the table.

"And honey symbolizes the sweetness of a perfect union. That's what my marriage to Lawrence is. Perfect."

Right, Talia thought. The accountant and his secretary. The woman he cheated with and left his wife and kids for. The dirty little secret the Goldstein family had swept under the rug. As it was, their mother had to hide her disappointment that her prettier daughter was marrying an accountant. Not a doctor (first choice) and not a lawyer (second choice). It was like earning a "C" on an exam. Talia hated to admit it, but a little piece of her looked forward to seeing her mother squirm as Jenna walked down the aisle toward a man who wasn't good enough for her—one who would saddle her with angsty stepchildren. Of course, they would think it was Jenna's fault their parents divorced. Why did the other woman always get blamed when it was the man who had broken his vows?

Talia softened. She felt a little sorry for her sister. Jenna had been in a panic over finding a husband. Now, at thirty-four, she was finally getting one. At least he was Jewish.

"You know what? You're right. And who doesn't love honey?" Talia punched a hole into a card and threaded a silky ribbon through it. "And favors are a good place to cut corners, anyway."

"Talia! How can you say that? We are not cutting corners!"

"I'm kidding," Talia said, although she wasn't. Her parents were dropping at least a hundred thousand on a single day to celebrate a marriage that would most likely end in divorce. Jenna, a stepmother? Talia pitied those kids already. Not that Jenna was evil, not at all. She was just too weak to tolerate the inevitable conflict. It would play out like a bad movie. The only one she didn't sympathize with was Lawrence, her future brother-in-law and the lying philanderer who left his wife for a younger woman. What a cliché.

Talia tied a perfect bow and held up the cellophane-wrapped honey jar. "Very cute." She shoved her aversion to honey out of her mind. How many times had she slathered the sticky goo on her toes so that some fetish-fueled creep could lick it off? Thank god she'd never have to do that again. With all the money accumulating in her account, she was free. But she'd give back every penny to have Max alive and by her side.

"Hey, Tal," Jenna said. "I know all this maid-of-honor stuff is costing a fortune, but I hate that you're missing my bachelorette party this weekend. I bet Mom will cover your flight to Nashville if I ask her to."

Talia drew in her lips and told herself to at least feign appreciation. If only her sister knew. She had enough money to put all eight bridesmaids into first-class seats, cover the Airbnb, and host the spa day without missing a penny.

"I wish I could go, Jen, but I—I have a funeral to go to."

Even though there was no actual funeral, Talia was too heartbroken to pretend to be happy for her sister for an entire weekend. She was struggling just to get through a few hours of favor prep.

Jenna tilted her head. "Who died?"

"An old friend—from one of my writing groups." She couldn't say Max's name. If she did, she'd surely break into sobs. Although, she thought, Max would've been delighted that Talia had used her death as an excuse for ditching Jenna's bachelorette party.

"Oh, well, I guess I understand then. But are you sure? I mean, my bachelorette party's going to be so much fun. And everyone says Nashville is a blast." Jenna pouted. "And you're not only my maid of honor, you're my big sister. Everyone will be asking why you're not there."

"So tell them, I don't care."

"Well, that would really put a damper on everyone's fun." Jenna's pout grew poutier. "My maid of honor, *my sister*, not with us because her friend died. I'll tell them you're, I don't know, at one of your other friend's weddings."

Talia couldn't believe how childish her sister sounded. "Tell them whatever you want, but a bit of advice, Jenna—you're about to become the stepmother in a complicated family. You'd better learn to put your own needs second."

"I know that. But can't I at least have this one last hurrah? Finally, be the bridezilla all my friends have been? I've waited a long time for this and have the rest of my life to be stepmom to three bratty kids."

"I suppose so," Talia said, pleased that Jenna had a realistic take on her future. "I still can't go to Nashville. But I'll be the best maid of honor at the wedding. I will tend to your every need, I promise."

That seemed to satisfy her little sister for the moment. Talia sped up wrapping and tagging the favors, hoping to escape before her mother returned.

Twenty minutes later, they were done.

"Well," Talia said as she stood and gathered her purse. "I gotta run. Those honey jar name tags really are lovely. I'm sure the guests will love them."

Jenna trailed after her. "Do you have to go already? Lawrence should be here soon, and Dad is picking up Chinese food from that place we loved as kids. We can have a family dinner."

Family dinner. Two words that brought back some of Talia's most unpleasant memories.

"Sorry, Jen, I have to get back to the city."

"Fine." Jenna hugged her. "Oh, and one more thing."

"Yeah?" Talia was inches from the doorknob, her fingers itching to grab it.

"I've had a few last-minute cancellations, so if you'd like to bring a plus-one to the wedding, there's room."

"That's okay. I'm sure I'll be occupied enough looking after you." Talia was counting the days. In less than two weeks, her sister's wedding would be in the rearview and she wouldn't have to return to New Jersey until Thanksgiving.

"Oh, come on, please. It's better if you have a plus-one, even if it's just a friend. You know, so that Mom's girlfriends don't pounce on you and try to set you up with their sons."

Why would Jenna care about that? And who among their mother's friends would want to fix up their sons with her, an overweight struggling writer with eggs quickly approaching their expiration date?

"I'm not worried about that," Talia said.

"What about your girlfriends, the ones you go to the lake with every year? There's three of them, right?"

"Two. One died, remember? And no, I'm not asking my friends. Why would you want me to? You've never even met them." Talia opened the door, but then turned back. "Wait, I know. You have a table with holes in it, don't you?"

Jenna's fair skin turned pink. "It's the cousins' table. And the family from California canceled. I don't know why they said yes in the first place. And now it's a seating disaster. Please help me fill those spots. I can't have a half-filled table. It'll look awful."

Talia had no wish to argue and delay her departure. Riva would be showing up any minute. "I'll ask them, but no promises."

thirty-one
chelsea

I think these reviews are fake or written by bots. 'Dorian Dimwitty' should've been my first clue that this book was gonna suck. Lesson learned.

–Truck and Run

Replying to Truck and Run: *YES! Finally, someone with the balls to say it. This book is a piece of shit. Nothing made sense. I plowed through it because I don't like throwing away fifteen bucks.*

–Page Daddy

"I'm working on it," Chelsea said into the phone to one of her ghostwriting clients. It was a fairly big name in thrillers, and at the moment, the man wasn't happy she wasn't ahead of schedule like she'd been with his previous three books.

She leaned back in her chair and rolled her eyes at the ceiling. Why was she still torturing herself when *her* Revenge Story was so much more compelling than the same old cookie-cutter bullshit she wrote for others? It wasn't hard to pull together a simple plot like the one this guy had written. But Chelsea's story was working itself out in real time, and *that* took talent this guy couldn't comprehend.

She'd kept up the appearance that she was still a struggling writer. Although she could have paid off her student loans and the publisher advance months ago, she continued the charade of sending monthly checks in the agreed-upon amounts. All to continue the illusion that she was broke and keep attention off her.

An incessant banging on the door forced her to extricate herself from the phone conversation. "You'll have it by the weekend." She hung up before the client could counter with another list of whiny demands. Chelsea had too much going on to listen to that shit another second.

She opened the door to find Rick staring down at her. "What do you want?"

"You've been dodging my calls. Again."

"That's the beauty of being an ex-wife. I don't have to talk to you anymore." Chelsea pushed the door closed, but he forced it back open. She lurched back, surprised by his audacity. "What the hell—"

"I don't know what game your buddy MF Ascher is playing, but this shit's gotta stop." He moved past her and into the apartment like he owned the place. She closed the door softly, taking extra time to gather her insides and ready herself for the inevitable next step.

She crossed her arms and waited while he walked back and forth along the same faded groove she'd worn all the days and nights she spent trying to solve problems he caused.

He ceased his journey and squared himself off against her. "You need to call him," Rick said.

"Who?"

"MF fucking Ascher. You need to call him and give me the phone."

Chelsea inhaled, inched her shoulders up a bit towards her ears. "I can't do that. Alec does all the talking for *her*. You should know that."

Rick's head shook like a bobblehead. "I'm not talking to that asshat boyfriend of yours another damn second." Rick reached into his pocket and pulled his phone out, holding it up. "He's starting something he won't be able to finish. You know how I can be, Chels."

"You mean a piece of shit? I'm well aware." She crossed her arms to fortify her position.

"Don't fuck with me. That asshole attorney got me kicked off my own movie. Said Ascher had a change of heart over some bullshit story that was coming out." He dropped the phone down and resumed his pacing. "And then you know what happened?"

"No, but I'm sure you're going to tell m—"

"I got a call from a reporter at the *Times*. Going on about new information that's come to light about some med-school student who died outside of Boston a decade ago." Rick ran his hand through the already thinning hair on his head. His hair loss was a sore subject for him. Chelsea stared at it long after Rick stopped rubbing it, just to make sure he noticed. He smoothed his hair over to cover his scalp. Satisfaction poured over her like rain on a hot summer day.

She cleared her throat. "Rick, I don't know what you're going on about, but I have work to do."

"There are a lot of similarities between this girl's death and *Murder and Other Secrets*. It was ruled an accident, but now this reporter wants to talk to the police because there's a theory that only the murderer would know some of the details in the movie." Rick resumed his path, Chelsea tracking every step, the way his hands shook at his sides, the skin puckered around his jaw and eyes.

"What does this have to do with me, exactly?" she asked on his sixth pass.

He halted, turning his vein-riddled neck and pointing his pinched gaze toward her. "First, you're going to get Ascher on the phone and get me back on my movie." Rick leaned toward her. "Then, you're going to tell me where you got the idea for that book."

This was the moment Chelsea had been waiting for since she

slipped Brad the envelope. A rush of adrenaline flooded her body, making her heartbeat wild and untenable. She had to proceed carefully here, or else she might screw things up for herself.

"I'm not doing anything," she said without a hint of nerves. "I'm not calling anyone, and I'm sure as hell not explaining *my* book to you."

"Chelsea," he rasped. "Did you know her? You were in med school at the same time as ..."

The way his face twisted, the red veins streaking through his eyes, the dark circles deepening underneath. Rick wasn't mad; he was scared. She had the upper hand, for the first time ever, and that warmth blossomed like the excitement she had felt when she sold her book all those years ago.

"I'm not telling you a damn thing. Besides, it's not my ass on the line," she said, allowing a slight sneer to spark at the corners of her mouth.

"What did you do?" He stepped back and edged around her, glancing at the door, ensuring there was a clear space between him and it. God, this felt good, seeing him squirm like a trapped animal.

She shrugged. "Med school was hard, and that girl did everything possible to make my life miserable. So I did what I had to do to make sure I got what I wanted. You should know better than anyone how that goes."

"You're bluffing."

Each one of his steps backwards emboldened her. She was the master storyteller in this relationship, not him. She understood what it took to weave the threads together, build suspense, and make sure the story satisfied, and that included taking down the bad guy before he ever saw it coming.

"Believe what you want, Rick. But you put your name on that story when you stole it. I guess you'll find out if any of it was true when the cops show up."

thirty-two
sophia

Ascher's prose flows like honey, ensweetening all they reach. Would that I could sup upon his words, alas, they offer no sustenance for the body, only for the soul.
  –Oxford Reviews

When given a choice between looks and comfort, Sophia had always chosen looks. MF Ascher money meant she didn't have to make that choice anymore. She sprawled on her cozy new curved gray leather sofa, the handcrafted one that took six weeks from order to delivery. She had her cashmere throw—a delicate pink that Grandma would have loved—on her lap, and a glass of red wine in her hand. She twirled the glass, another new purchase, a Versace Medusa Lumiere. The extravagance of the moment didn't bring her the joy it should have. There was a void this weekend, and it hung over them.

It was the first time they'd been back to the lake house as a group since Max died. The grief caused by her palpable absence struck each of them differently. Chelsea had taken a long walk, saying she was going down by the lake. Sophia suspected that she'd be visiting Max's death spot, just a quarter of a mile away. The tow truck had left divots in the grass there, a tangible reminder of the tragedy. Talia was dealing with it in a different way. She was upstairs, soaking in the clawfoot tub. "I never feel clean anymore," she'd said before heading up an hour ago with her bottles of bath salts and oils. She probably didn't feel clean because she'd taken to wearing Max's old sweatshirt everywhere, and, in Sophia's opinion, it was getting rather rank. As a subtle hint, she'd stocked the room Talia always stayed in with a brand-new fluffy robe. Maybe if Talia snuggled up in that, Sophia could get her hands on the sweatshirt and throw it into the washing machine.

Sophia heard the back door open with a whine. It gave her a start, triggering an irrational fear that Alec had come to finish them off. No, that wouldn't happen. She was protected, she reminded herself. She'd already given his name to Gage, in passing, but her brother could read between the lines. If Alec harmed her before they could get their revenge, he wouldn't have much time to celebrate. But of course, it wasn't Alec. It was Chelsea, her heavy footsteps stopping in the kitchen as she poured herself a glass from the decanter.

Chelsea entered the living room, swigging from her glass as though it was one of the old cheap ones purchased by the box from the local convenience store, from the back corner with the novelty bottle openers and the *It's Wine O'Clock* T-shirts. But Sophia refrained from shouting out in horror, begging her friend to pause and appreciate the clarity of the crystal, the way it elevated the sensory experience.

"How was your walk?" she said instead.

"I didn't go too far, just down to your dock. And it was strange; the air was thick and I felt like I was breathing in a cloud of anger."

"Max," Sophia breathed. She'd felt it down there too, this fury, as though the wood of the dock had absorbed Max's emotions when she went out there on her last night.

"Max," Chelsea confirmed. "It's so weird being here without her. She'll never be here again."

"Max?" Talia's voice asked. Sophia hadn't heard her come down, but she should have smelled her. Rose and lavender from the bath, and thankfully not body odor from the sweatshirt. Her flowery scent was still overpowering, but much more pleasant. The robe was a good strategy. Talia looked comfy and warm. "I wish ..." she waved her arm in a gesture they all understood.

"We wish she was here, too. To Max," Chelsea held up her glass in a toast.

"Wait, I don't have one yet." Talia rushed into the kitchen for her own glass and the decanter. "To Max."

"Are you ladies ready for some food?" Sophia finally uncurled from beneath her cashmere blanket to resume the role of hostess. She'd picked up a fabulous charcuterie board on her way to the lake house. It didn't look quite as beautiful as it had in the specialty market, losing some of the artistry when she transferred it from the plastic it came on to a slab of teak wood specially purchased for the occasion. She didn't have the same styling skills, and some of the meats had uncurled from their crafted rosette shapes. Nobody cared about the flaws though, as they took their seats at the dining table and helped themselves.

"You can afford the good stuff with a little bit of money, can't you?" Chelsea said as she piled an array of nuts and cheeses on Sophia's new platinum edged L'Objet appetizer plates. It felt like a barb directed at her. Funny that she'd be the judgmental one, Sophia thought; Chelsea was still in her terrible apartment, wearing the same thrift-store jeans. She had all this money now, but hadn't bothered to update her life. It was like she refused to allow herself any pleasure.

Talia picked up the tiny jar of honey to drizzle over her Brie. "My sister is using honey as wedding favors. Can you believe it? So tacky."

"All wedding favors are tacky," Chelsea said. "Rick and I had shot glasses with our names engraved on them. They said, *Take a shot, they've tied the knot*. His idea, by the way, not mine."

"Those are tacky," Sophia agreed. "But food isn't. The best

favors are the ones you use up. I don't see a problem with honey if the jars are cute."

"Are they cute?" Chelsea asked, but her tone implied that no jars were cute, ever.

"You should come see for yourself. Jenna asked me to fill three seats. Apparently, some cousins aren't coming, and she doesn't want empty chairs. She said to bring my friends."

"Oh, god, no," Chelsea groaned. "Count me out. I'm not sitting through a wedding."

Sophia tipped her head and thought about it for a moment. "I'll go."

"What? Why?" Talia almost choked on her pistachios. "You hate love and romance."

"No, I choose not to participate. That doesn't mean I hate romance. I enjoy the pageantry of weddings, tuxedos, gowns, champagne. Drunk relatives making fools of themselves on the dance floor. It's fun." On a selfish note, she needed inspiration for a wedding scene in her current work in progress.

Chelsea snorted. "I never thought of you as a wedding person."

"I guess you don't know me as well as you thought. We should both go, so we can see Talia in her bridesmaid's dress and meet the sister we've heard so much about. Besides, it's formal, right? I've had a vintage floor-length Alexander McQueen hanging in my closet for years. It deserves a night out." She was fortunate to be the same size as Grandma and that she had a grandmother with exquisite taste. Her family had been well off, before spending it all on wasted rehab for Sophia's mother, and later, bad investments Grandpa made with some business associates. They met a suspicious and untimely end, but it was too late to get the money back.

"I wish Max were here," Talia said. "Could you imagine her at a wedding?"

"Absolutely. She'd show up in all black and pull the bride aside to tell her what an outdated institution marriage is." Chelsea frowned. "Anyway, I have no interest in going. And besides that, I don't have anything to wear."

"You can afford to shop," Talia reminded her. "Please do me this favor, Chels. If I fill two of the three empty seats, I'm done. We can spread the chairs out a little to make the table look right."

"*Or* you could"—Sophia made eye contact with Chelsea and they both nodded. They were on the same page—"bring a date."

"Ha!" Talia finished her wine and poured some more. "A date? You know I haven't had a boyfriend since Mark, that awful waiter. Remember him, the one with the poorly drawn tattoos and the eyebrow ring?"

"The one who was always chewing gum with his mouth open and dumped you for a chef who puts cilantro on everything? He didn't deserve you," Chelsea said.

"I'll drink to that." Talia downed a large gulp. "Screw Mark and his cilantro-ho."

"But Sophia is right," Chelsea continued. "You could take a date."

"Yeah, right. Let me just hop on the dating apps. Maybe I should post a picture of my feet. That always brings me winners." She still seemed bitter about how she attracted men, even though the fetishists had paid her bills for years.

"Talia," Sophia said, trying to sound encouraging. "I think what Chelsea and I are trying to suggest is, what if you took someone else? Someone we all know."

"Stop hinting, Sophia. She's not getting it. Talia, take Alec. It's perfect. That gets the four of us together at a neutral location. And it gives us a reason to interact with him."

Talia was so surprised she dropped a cracker, getting tiny crumbs on Sophia's pale gray hand-tufted rug. "Bring Alec? He's a murderer! I'm not taking him as my date anywhere. Especially if we're going to go through with, well, you know. The thing. That we talked about. Before. The plan. The idea. The ..."

"Stop!" Sophia and Chelsea shouted simultaneously. Talia was the worst co-conspirator ever.

"We should put our phones outside," Sophia said. She might not have personal criminal experience, but this was something she knew: phones were always listening. They didn't need any of what they were about to discuss recorded anywhere, even by the AI adbots in their phones. Although the shopping suggestions might be amusing.

"Why?" Talia asked.

"Because if we all turn them off, it looks suspicious." Sophia held out her hand, and her friends relinquished their phones, Talia with reluctance. She took them outside and put them on the table, so any GPS location bots would think they were having dinner. Maybe she was overly paranoid, but she was finally at a good place in her life, and she wasn't about to let plotting a murder derail her. She wasn't Gage. She was smarter than he was.

When the potentially spying phones were safely away and all the glasses were refilled, Chelsea spoke up. "So ... the wedding. We can lure Alec there as your date. We can't do it at one of our apartments or in his office."

Talia's mouth dropped open in shock. "You think we should ... take care of him at my sister's wedding?"

"Why not?" Chelsea asked. "Don't you think it's the perfect opportunity?"

"No!"

"I told him you like bad boys. It wouldn't be out of character for you to invite him," Sophia said. "Besides, he's a lawyer. Doesn't that trump your sister's accountant? Two birds, one stone."

"No! It's my sister's wedding!"

"What if ..." Chelsea leaned forward and whispered, even though there was no one to overhear, "... we poison the wedding cake? Just his slice, not all of it."

"It's my sister's wedding!" Talia repeated, as though they couldn't understand. "Nobody is dying at my sister's wedding! Can you imagine what the New Jersey gossip blogs would say about it? I can see the headline now—*shyster lawyer dies at Riva Goldstein's daughter's wedding to—*"

"Talia," Chelsea said. "I mean this gently and with respect. Nobody gives a fuck about your sister's wedding. Your family isn't that important. Nobody in New Jersey cares what happens to some random woman marrying her ... he was her boss, right? Didn't they have an affair?"

"Right?" Sophia jumped in. "It's already scandalous. Everyone going to the wedding already knows what they did; a death won't make it worse. If anything, it will make it more interesting. And Chelsea is right. Nobody outside of your family cares. It's not like they're getting a wedding announcement in the *New York Times*. At most, they'll get a one-line mention in the synagogue newsletter, if there is such a thing."

"Of course there is," Talia said. "Every temple has one. My mother reads it religiously."

"Are there stairs?" Sophia asked. "A fall down the stairs is plausible. He could slip, especially if he's drunk."

"No," Chelsea said. "There are probably cameras. We can't physically touch him. It needs to be more subtle."

"Where's the wedding? A hotel? An event center?" Sophia asked. "Can either of you shoot a gun?"

"Ooh, a sniper rifle from across the street." Chelsea considered it briefly. "No, we can't shoot him like that."

"What if the gun is disguised? Never mind, that's ridiculous. We'd have to buy a gun, and there are registries. It would be linked back to us." Sophia didn't like the gun idea, anyway. It was too loud, too attention getting.

"I have one," Chelsea said, and shrugged when they both gasped. "What? You know where I live. It's for self-defense."

"We're not shooting anybody at my sister's wedding! It's insane! I'm the maid of honor! My mother would blame me if my date got shot. She'd say I did it for attention."

"What if we make it look like your sister killed him?" Chelsea asked, only half kidding.

"You are out of your mind. Both of you!" Talia marched into the kitchen, where she apparently decided that the best way to take out her frustration was by uncorking another bottle of wine.

"She's never going to agree." Sophia helped herself to apple slices from the charcuterie board and dabbed some honey on her plate, the golden syrup spreading slowly to the edge. She glanced up and noticed Chelsea staring down at it, too.

"Wait," Chelsea said. "Didn't Alec say he's deathly allergic to honey? What if he accidentally ingests some honey from the tacky favors? Like if it got in his glass somehow and he drank it?"

"That would never work. Do you know how many doctors there will be in the room?" Talia dismissed the idea outright as she topped off their glasses. "At least a dozen! My second cousin won the husband competition four years ago, and she matched up many of his co-workers with family members. Though I don't know if proctologists usually deal with allergic reactions."

"What if ... he ingested the allergens ... elsewhere?" Chelsea asked, a glint coming into her eyes.

"Like where?" Talia said.

Chelsea and Sophia made eye contact, passing another silent message. They both looked down at Talia's perfect, beautiful feet.

thirty-three
talia

Haters gonna hate, but Dimwitty is the sh*t! Keep writing MF. You've made a fan for life. Anyone in the Richmond area wanna meet up for a book talk?
–MF Ascher Fan Club

Talia went to bed furious and horrified. How on earth could her friends even suggest they kill Alec at Jenna's wedding? Not to mention using her feet to lure him—she hadn't sold her toes in ages.

She wished she'd never mentioned her sister's plea that Talia bring her friends. What a disaster. She couldn't wait for Alec to be done away with, but they'd have to come up with a more appropriate time and place.

At two a.m. she woke up to pee. Once Talia was back in bed, the quiet disturbed her. She was used to her neighborhood, where traffic and sirens and shouting never stopped. She lay on her back and stared at a ribbon of moonlight that cut through the ceiling, ruminating on her friends' insane ideas. Yes, she had agreed they would do away with Alec, but she didn't think she'd be told to do it—and with her feet no less! Chelsea was the most capable, and Sophia was emotionally detached—at least enough to pull it off.

Talia kicked her covers off and groaned like a sick walrus. Ever since that horrible excuse for a human entered the picture, everything had gone wrong. She hated him more every day, a hatred she nursed and nurtured the way Max had done.

Alec Pendergrass had shackled them. He'd stolen their freedom to create, to write the stories they needed to tell. Max would have tossed him off the roof of his high-rise if she could. She never wanted to involve him in the first place, and she had been right. Talia owed her best friend. Alec had killed her. And Max still was not free.

Talia sat bolt upright, struck by a thought so powerful it was as if Max had reached down and smacked her on the head. Once Alec was out of the picture, there'd be nobody to represent MF Ascher. The spokesperson would be gone, and *that* meant (she could hardly believe how the idea thrilled her) Talia could take over and carry Max's torch. She, Talia Goldstein, would release Max's ghost and allow her to rest. She'd never had the drive or desire to blow up the industry the way Max did, but maybe she could split the difference—blow it up as Max's proxy. The sooner Alec died, the better, and if her sister's wedding presented the first opportunity, so be it.

"I'll do it," Talia announced at breakfast. "I'll invite him."

Sophia raised an eyebrow. "You're sure?"

Talia nodded. "Positive. And I know just how to do it."

Chelsea gave her a look of approval as Talia dialed his number and put the call on speaker.

"Talia? It's early—did you have a sexy dream about me?"

Talia took a beat. She needed to play it close to the vest, to be herself, but a little flirtier with the slightest tinge of urgency.

"Actually, no. But I do have a favor to ask."

Alec cleared his throat of early morning phlegm. "Let's hear it," he said.

Talia knew Alec liked directness, so she got right to the point. "My sister's getting married, and I need a date."

Chelsea shook her head and moved her hands in a motion that looked like kneading bread. Sophia scribbled a note on the back of an envelope: *Ease him into it! Be needy!!*

"Actually, I *want* a date. And, at the moment, I'm not seeing anyone. So I'm wondering if you'd go with me."

"Escort you to your sister's wedding? I'm intrigued." The sound of Alec urinating came through loud and clear.

Talia nearly gagged. Sophia stuck her tongue out and pointed into her throat. Chelsea stifled laughter.

"When and where?" The toilet flushed.

"A week from tonight in Teaneck."

"Yeah, no. I'd love to be with you, but I don't do New Jersey. No fuckin' way am I going into the Lincoln Tunnel. Besides, I'll be golfing in Florida next week."

Talia gritted her teeth. If this plan didn't work, how would they get to him? She forced herself to sound coy. "There are other ways to get to New Jersey, Alec. Come on, you can afford to charter a plane from LaGuardia."

Chelsea gave Talia an encouraging thumbs up.

"Right, well. As much as a rubber chicken dinner sounds like a rip-roaring good time, I'm still going to be in Florida all week."

Chelsea mouthed the words: *Keep trying!*

"All week?" Talia faked a whine as she sat on the couch, propped her feet on the coffee table, and crossed her ankles. "You don't really want to be golfing all week, do you?"

"Yeah, I do. I love golf."

She snapped photos of her freshly manicured toes. "I know what else you love," she said, quickly editing the pictures and blurring the background.

"Yeah, what's that?" Alec's tone turned salacious. Goodness, he was an easy target.

"These." She sent two photos and waited.

A slight grunt was his response. "Nice."

"You like?"

"You know I do. Send more."

"Ah-ah. Your turn." Talia did her best to sound flirtatious.

"Oh, yeah? Gimme a minute."

Talia grinned at her compatriots. Sophia scurried from the kitchen with a can of whipped cream and drew curlicues around Talia's toes with it.

"Maybe this will help move things along." Talia sent the new photo, her feet chilled by the cream. It made her sick to be faking foot phone sex with him. But if that's what it took, she'd just have to suck it up.

"Oh, Talia," Alec said, his phone clicking. "Take a look at this."

His dick pic was, well, impressive. Talia held up her phone to share the image. Chelsea's lips formed a perfect 'O,' while Sophia grimaced.

"Alec, wow," Talia said. "I had no idea."

He said nothing; all she could hear was the rhythmic sound of him jerking off.

Talia sweetened the seduction. "You really are a stud, aren't you?"

More groans, grunts, and moans.

Talia continued, playing along, pretending she was participating. "Sometimes I can hear my neighbors fucking through the wall. It is so titillating I can hardly contain myself. The girl squeals like a kitten, and when she comes, it's like—"

"Oh, god! Oh, god! Yeah, baby!"

Then nothing.

"You know," she started. "It's too bad you'll be golfing because my sister's wedding would be the *perfect* place for us to finish what we started all those years ago."

Talia waited.

Finally, Alec spoke. "Text me the place. I'll be there."

"See you then." Talia disconnected the call with a shit-eating grin.

thirty-four
chelsea

I wanted to put this book down at least a dozen times because it made no sense. And then just like that, BOOM. Shellshocked is not a strong enough word. There aren't enough stars in the sky to rate this book as high as it needs to be. Blown away.
–D. Raymond

There are moments when a writer doesn't exactly know what's going to happen next in the story. Sometimes, there are too many possible courses of action the characters could take, and any one of them might send the plot careening in multiple directions. But this wasn't a story Chelsea could control. It was real life. And as much as she wanted to predict and orchestrate every move her characters made, she couldn't.

Case in point: she would have preferred for Brad to have waited to publish Max's exposé, instead of running it the day after she returned from the lake house. Planning a murder was one thing. But doing so with a *New York Times* reporter breathing down her neck was another. She agreed to meet Friday, the day before the wedding, because it was the only shot she had of wrapping up her Revenge Story.

She sipped her water and glanced out the window of

Montague's. The view from the back corner table hadn't changed much since the last time she'd been there over three years ago. The dilapidated bike rack was rustier. The lamp post remained filled with curling flyers and stickers. She shook off the past and concentrated on the present. The cortisol coursing through her body over the past few days left her skin feeling bruised.

It was risky, and while everything about this day and all the others before it was plotted and planned, Chelsea understood how shit could happen and bring it all crashing down around her.

Her phone buzzed, but before she could reach it, Brad was striding over from the hostess stand, smiling widely and turning heads. Her stomach fluttered, but she chalked it up to nervous anticipation and not the fact that he could wear a pair of jeans better than any man she'd ever met.

"I wasn't sure if you'd show." His blue-eyed gaze moved across her face, heating her skin.

"Do sources usually stand you up?" She kept her attention on his eyes and not on the cute band of freckles that trickled across his cheeks.

"Just the beautiful ones." A faint circle of pink flushed his cheeks as he grinned and pushed his phone into the middle of the table with his sizable hand. Chelsea didn't appreciate that Brad managed to spark that long-ago buried part of her life she had locked away after Rick.

"And here I felt special," she said.

He cocked his left eyebrow, curiosity edging the corners of his eyes. "Beautiful and brilliant makes for a very dangerous combination. Especially for a man like me."

Chelsea nodded, remaining back in her seat, not allowing Brad's gravity to pull her toward him. "Whatever do you mean?"

Brad chuckled as the waitress set down the scotch Chelsea ordered him. "You knew what was in the envelope when you handed it to me, including the story Max was writing about the kid who died at Harvard. She put together one hell of a case."

"What makes you think I have any idea what you're talking about?"

He grinned, the satisfaction and *gotcha* spreading over his face. "Because it's eerily similar to the movie plot that launched Rick Stafford's career." He took a draw from his glass before continuing. "Considering he's your ex-husband, it wasn't hard to figure out that *you* wanted me to find it. But don't worry, I won't print that part."

Her heart thrummed through her head. She needed to remain at arm's length for what she hoped might come next—any minute, in fact.

"You aren't correcting me, which means I'm right," he continued.

The sincerity of his smile made him more attractive. But there was still one thing he hadn't figured out yet.

"I thought we were here to talk about MF Ascher," she said, diverting the conversation back where she needed it to go for now. "If you'd rather tell campfire stories—"

Brad waved his hand. "No, we're here for the same thing. Mostly. We can talk about Rick Stafford off the record another time." He leaned back, the definite blush in his cheeks deepened as he cleared his throat. "I mean, if you want to."

As hard as it was, she ignored his proposition and folded her hands on the table to keep them from shaking. "You should probably hit 'record.'"

"Right, of course." He pushed the red icon in the middle of his phone screen and sat back. "For the record, it is Friday, June thirteenth at 12:06 p.m. I'm here at Montague's interviewing Chelsea Specter about the identity of MF Ascher."

A cacophony of sounds grabbed everyone's attention. Brad turned as Rick rushed towards them. Her chest threatened to split when he slid a chair over to their table. He arranged himself like a king on a throne of thorns and drained her glass of water.

"Chels," he said, his lips wet. "Sorry to interrupt your little date, but we need to talk." Rick turned his attention to Brad and jerked his chin towards the door. "You should go, buddy. You don't want to be a part of this. Trust me."

"Actually, I do." Brad thrust his hand out. "Brad Harrison from the *Times*. I left you a message a few days ago, Mr. Stafford."

Chelsea couldn't look away as Rick made the connection. The widening of his eyes. The catch of his Adam's apple as he gripped Brad's outstretched hand. The two men locked onto each other like prizefighters sizing up the other before the bell rang.

Rick donned his important-Hollywood-producer mask. "I'm a busy man, *Brad*. I can't answer every ridiculous message about *Murder and Other Secrets*."

"So you did get it. Good." Brad seemed immune to Rick's act, which made Chelsea's stomach flutter even more. "Since you wrote the movie, I thought you'd want to respond to a source's assertion that some of the details in your film were too close to a student's actual death to be a coincidence."

"How, exactly?" Rick asked. Chelsea wondered if Brad could hear the slight rise in his voice.

"The death was ruled accidental, but according to the same source, a detective who saw the movie is considering reopening the investigation to make sure they didn't miss something."

Chelsea remained in the grandstands at Wimbledon thus far. Until Rick turned his arrogant gaze to her.

"You wanna tell us what happened to that girl, Chels?"

She cleared the dust from her throat and batted her lids over dry eyes. Had she even blinked since he walked in? "I don't know what you're talking about."

His shoulders lurched, and he rolled his neck in time with his eyes. "She's the one you need to talk to, *Brad*, not me. Whatever she told you so far is a lie, that I promise."

Intrigue sharpened Brad's face. "I don't quite follow. Please enlighten me. If you don't mind." Brad crossed his arms across his impressive chest.

"Rick, this isn't what you think. Don't." Chelsea added a bit of desperation to her voice.

Opportunity sparked in Rick's eyes. He leaned to her ear and whispered, "You should have given me Ascher when you had the chance."

He sat back into king mode, devoting his attention to Brad. "I'm sure that's why she called you. To make up some bullshit about me."

Brad lifted his brow. "Actually, this doesn't have anything to do with—"

"I don't know about killing anyone, but she does. She was at Harvard at the same time as that girl. And soon after she died, Chelsea inexplicably dropped out to become a writer. Or so she claimed." He scoffed.

"Rick, please." Chelsea waited for him to turn his gaze to hers. When he did, she tried her hardest to ensure she appeared as scared and pleading as she could. She willed her eyes to get teary.

He ignored her faux pleas and charged ahead. "You got the idea for the book after you murdered that girl, didn't you?"

Brad sat forward, leaned his forearms on the table, narrowed his stunning blue eyes toward Rick. "What book are you talking about?"

"The one she wrote. It was called *The Secrets We Keep*. She had a big publishing contract, too, before they killed it. I'm sure you can figure out a way to verify it."

"I'm sure I can. So why'd they kill it, exactly?"

"It was too close to *Murder and Other Secrets*. But that's only because I used it to write the screenplay. Changed the title though. Made it more punchy." Rick grinned. "Anyway, I'm not the one who should be under suspicion for murder. It's her."

Every bit of breath rushed from Chelsea's lungs as the vice that had squeezed her relentlessly for the past three years broke away. She gripped the table with both hands to keep herself upright as the relief turned her muscles to jelly.

"Hang on," Brad said, touching his forehead for a brief moment. "Did you just admit that you stole *her* book for the movie?"

Chelsea was afraid to move. Afraid to breathe. Afraid that this moment, the one she'd planned and replanned and re-replanned would slip away before she could enjoy it. If this was a dream, she didn't want to wake up.

"Well, yeah, but you're missing the point," Rick said. "I can't be the killer because I didn't write it. She did."

Brad cocked his head. "And you're a plagiarizer."

"Okay, but she's worse! And she thought she was smarter than everyone. But not me. She never has been, and she never will be." Rick leaned back and crossed his arms, arrogance wafting from him.

Chelsea let her head sink to the table, the black tablecloth absorbing the tears surging from her eyes. Her body racked with waves of emotion rolling over her. She needed to commit every second of this to memory. From the rosemary garlic butter dipping sauce infusing the air, to the sizzle and pop of the skillets of cod being delivered to patrons, to the scratch of the fabric across her forehead.

Montague's. Fucking Montague's and its Friday fish fry special, the only thing Rick had remained committed to since they met. And he really believed he had outsmarted her.

She lifted her head, and the sobs morphed into laughter. Cackles that only ever escaped when she was with her best friends. Joy unlocked a whole other layer she'd numbed so long ago.

"She's hysterical. Further proof of her guilt." The bravado in Rick's voice fueled her triumph.

She gulped in a breath, and wiped away the moisture from her face.

"I've pictured this moment but never believed it would actually happen."

"You killed someone and you're laughing. You're sick, Chels," Rick said.

A new wave of laughter bubbled up. "You are such a fucking idiot, Rick. No one murdered that girl. Tracey MacMillan walked off campus one winter night to chase her cat. The problem with that was her cat had been dead for ten years. She was delusional after studying for finals. Too much Adderall, caffeine, and seventy-two hours without sleep. She died of a heart attack."

The victorious blush that warmed Rick's face a moment ago washed away.

She leaned toward him. "The story Brad's talking about, the research, the detective statements, the police reports are all fake. I made them up and slipped them in with some other things, hoping they would get his attention."

Chelsea moved her gaze to Brad's wrinkled brow. "I'm really sorry I used you like that. But I couldn't figure out any other way to get him to admit that he stole my book."

Understanding danced across Brad's features, clearing the way for a wide grin. "Like I said. Brilliant and beautiful. Well done."

They both turned to Rick, who blanched. Chelsea could see the stages of his realization. The denial. The anger. The fear. All of it cycling across his face and body as he pushed back violently from the table and pulled his polo shirt away from his skin.

He cleared his throat. "You can't prove any of this. It's my word against yours."

"This time, I have a witness." Chelsea believed for a split second that Rick might wrap his hands around her throat. It was an end she could accept now that she'd exposed him.

"Actually, way more than that," Brad said, raising his phone and flashing the screen towards Rick. Once the pieces fell into place and he realized it was recording, Rick knew he'd been beaten. And that she'd done it. He tried to avert his eyes, but the tears were already glimmering at the corners. He stormed out, shouting threats back at them the whole way.

"Wow, and here I thought I was just getting the goods on MF Ascher. I don't know what's the bigger story."

Chelsea eased herself up, the weight of her past remaining behind in the chair. "I'm sure you'll figure it out." Vengeance and vindication lightened her in a way she never dared to believe was possible. But she wasn't done yet.

"Max DeLeon was MF Ascher. She didn't want anyone to think of her as a sellout for writing a commercial success. But she deserves better than the end she got. Please give her the dedication and credit she deserves. She was a survivor. A talented writer. A brave woman. And the best kind of friend."

Brad nodded and pushed the stop button on the phone recorder, a broad smile affixed across his handsome face. "I will. And if I can do anything else for you, let me know."

She took a step away, but stopped. "Actually, there is one more thing."

"Name it," he said.

"Send me a copy of that recording."

Chelsea smiled before floating away from the longest act in her story, ready for whatever the next one held.

thirty-five
talia

Who the hell is MF Ascher anyway? And by the way, every author knows not to use Deus ex Machina! You don't need an MFA to know that. Hmm, MFA—MFAscher? Coincidence?

There was nothing in the world Talia loved more than a long, hot bath in an oversized tub. She'd woken up extra early to indulge in one before hair and makeup began in the bridal suite at nine o'clock sharp.

The previous night at the rehearsal dinner, Talia had performed her duties as maid of honor. She tended to Jenna's every need, made sure she didn't get too drunk, and looked after the other bridesmaids.

When the best man, one of Lawrence's old college buddies who'd been knocking back tequila shots all night, started to tell a story about wife number one, Talia interrupted him with a playful laugh, guided him away from the microphone, and took over with a sweet story of what an adorable little sister Jenna was. It was exhausting.

As steam rose from the surface of the water, Talia lowered her body into the bath. "Ahhh." The tub was extra deep and long, allowing her to sink all the way to her chin. She leaned her head back and closed her eyes. By tomorrow at this time, it would all be over. She'd go from bridesmaid to murderer in one night. A part of her had turned numb, as if their plan to kill Alec was outside her consciousness. Disassociation—don't think, just do. There would be no memory of premeditation. It would be chalked up to a tragic accident. A man with a severe allergy unknowingly ingested the allergen.

Fuck yeah!

"Max?" Talia scrambled to sit up, splashing water over the edge of the tub. Great, now she was hearing voices.

She took a deep breath and opened the drain, feeling foolish. Max's ghost was not in the room. Her mind was playing tricks on her. Standing in the empty tub, she doused her body in fancy oil (a lovely amenity provided by the hotel), drizzling it over her shoulders, back and buttocks, along her legs and onto her feet. After massaging the oil into her skin, she wrapped herself in the plushy white towel and stepped out of the tub, careful not to slip. If nothing else, she appreciated that her sister and mother had selected a high-end hotel.

The alarm kicked her into gear. She needed to be in her sister's suite in fifteen minutes. She packed her undergarments, including a body shaper that felt like a straitjacket, into a pink satchel with her name and *maid of honor* embroidered on the front, and headed upstairs to begin what would no doubt be a very long day.

By three in the afternoon, Talia couldn't take any more drama. Her mother and the photographer got into a fight over the arrangement of Jenna's veil for the mother/daughter photos; room service brought hamburgers and beer instead of tea sandwiches and champagne; and one of the bridesmaids was furious because her pregnant belly had grown since her last fitting (duh!), so her dress didn't hang right. Worst of all, in the midst of the chaos, Jenna's soon-to-be stepdaughter got her first period. She grew hysterical and needed tampon insertion instructions. That little chore fell to "Auntie" Talia.

Once the menstruating teenager was taken care of, Talia slipped away, praying she wouldn't run into the bridal party on her way upstairs. In her suite, the door to the adjoining room was open, and her friends were settling in.

"You're here," Talia said. "Thank god. I need a dose of some normal people."

"I'd hardly call us normal," Sophia said, studying Talia with a discerning eye. "Makeup looks good. Killer fake lashes. And the dress isn't as bad as I thought it would be."

"Thanks." The cobalt blue off-the-shoulder A-line gown with ruffles around the skirt was not entirely unflattering. "I kinda like it, even though my body is stuffed into a level ten compression stocking. I can hardly breathe. I can't stand this hideous updo, though."

"Take it down then." Sophia opened the minibar and selected a snack-sized bag of chips that cost twelve dollars, a luxury she could afford.

"I can't do that. I'll get into all kinds of trouble defying the hairdresser's vision."

Chelsea chuckled. "With what we have planned for later, you're worried about pissing off a hairdresser?"

"That is ridiculous, isn't it?" Talia stood in front of the mirror. Her hair had more swirls in it than a soft serve ice cream. She pulled out one bobby pin and let out a ringlet. Then another and a few more. By the time she finished, dozens of bobby pins littered the table. She shook her head, and her wavy brown hair fell around her shoulders. "Better?"

"Much," Chelsea said.

"Feels better, too." Talia sat in one of the swivel chairs, her dress billowing.

"Aren't you supposed to be tending to the bride?" Sophia asked.

"I had to escape for a few minutes. Way too much drama up

there." She glanced at her phone. "Photos begin at four, so I have until then."

Chelsea stood between her two friends with a bottle of Veuve Clicquot and three champagne flutes. "Let's have a toast."

"I'm in." Sophia sat on the love seat and propped up her feet. "What are we celebrating?"

"Not my sister, please. I've already toasted her a million times."

"We're toasting—" Chelsea paused and a relaxed smile spread over her lips. "My successful meeting with Brad yesterday. It was ... interesting."

"Interesting?" Sophia asked. "What does that mean?"

Chelsea glanced between them. "We'll know more soon. So let's just toast to moving on, to setting things right, and, most of all, to Max."

Talia nodded, shivering at the memory of hearing Max's voice earlier. She was still with her, if ephemeral. She could feel Max's presence, smell her body wash.

POP!

The champagne cork flew across the room, breaking Talia's trance.

Chelsea filled the flutes to the point of overflowing. They laughed and clinked their glasses. Talia thanked god for the two friends she had left in the world. Without Max, they were her cornerstone, the foundation upon which everything rested. As terrified as she was of what she had to do later that night, she would not give in to fear.

The time had come. Tomorrow at this time, Alec Pendergrass would be dead.

thirty-six
sophia

Five Fabulous Stars!!!!! This is the most amazing book I've ever read, and I've read dozens of books!!!!! This book is the perfect marriage between pretension and commercialism, drama and humor, dynamic characters and enigmatic plot!!!!! My debut, launching next month, will also touch on these same things!!!!! Sign up for my newsletter to learn more!!!!!

Sophia's grandfather's best friend was a Jewish man with twelve children and, at Sophia's last count, over thirty grandchildren. This meant she was somewhat of an expert on Jewish weddings, having attended probably more than even Talia. As a child she'd loved them, wearing shiny patent leather Mary Janes and a pretty dress while older ladies cooed over her and admired how well-behaved and adorable she was. She was a useful distraction while Gage raided the cash envelopes on the gift table, careful to only steal in increments of $18. He wanted their money, not their luck. Those wedding invitations—and every other social invitation—had come to a complete halt when Gage was arrested.

That's why it was bittersweet, sitting in the back row surrounded by an abundance of pungent flowers, listening to generic vows while the audience shifted in their seats and muffled their sneezes. It looked like the Goldstein family had purchased every pink flower in the Tri-State area and had covered every available surface. While that may serve as a good backdrop for pictures, in truth, the pollen explosion was causing half the wedding guests a great deal of distress.

Sophia was not one of the allergy sufferers, but she was developing a scent-induced headache from being seated too close to Alec. His cologne was enough to make her want to gag. *He dies tonight*, she reminded herself every time she got a whiff of the eau de teenage boy he'd doused himself with. She'd sat next to him to create a buffer between him and Chelsea. Chelsea was riding a strange high, to the point she'd cried during the vows for reasons Sophia was certain had nothing to do with the love between Jenna and the balding accountant. She hoped the tears weren't second thoughts.

"Beautiful ceremony," Sophia murmured as the interminable exchange of vows ended and the crowd shuffled off to the reception. It wasn't. It was long and boring, and the traditional glass shattering had been almost farcical, but they had to be polite and couldn't stand out. Nobody could overhear them saying anything remotely controversial. Ideally, nobody would notice them at all, and if they did, they'd be treated as Talia's single friends, and wasn't it a shame they were still unmarried? Elderly Jewish mothers would probably spend the evening sending their sons their way, the ones who were older, unemployed, and seeking a desperate shiksa to overlook their flaws.

"There are drinks, right?" Alec asked. His head was on a swivel, looking for the bar. As soon as they made it to the lobby by the reception ballroom and heard the sound of ice in a shaker, he was gone.

"Thank god," Chelsea said. Sophia nodded. They were both thinking the same thing: they wanted Alec drinking. Visibly drinking and loudly drunk would be ideal. Enough to make a small scene, but not enough to ruin the reception. Enough for people to shake their heads in disgust and say they weren't surprised when the news broke later. *Probably had it coming,* they would say privately, while publicly offering Talia and her family their condolences.

"I'm so glad Talia invited us. I've always loved weddings," Sophia said, which was true, though she was saying it as a way of blending in and establishing why they were here, for their explanation to the cops later. *We love weddings, so we turned it into a fun girls' weekend. That's why we got the adjoining hotel rooms. We wanted to give Talia her privacy if her date worked out.* The story, though it evolved and updated constantly, had to be believable.

"Me too," Chelsea lied, in a falsely bright voice so out of character that it almost made Sophia laugh. "And not just because of the drinks."

"I'm not drinking tonight. Antibiotics," Sophia again spoke for the benefit of any eavesdroppers. She was not allowing anything to damage her calm state of mind. Murder took planning. If you lost control, if you didn't think through every step, if you made one tiny mistake, that was it. Game over. Somehow, Alec had gotten away with it, but his advantage was that Max was a nobody to society, just another drunk driver who lost control. Maybe a suicide, maybe an accident, but no proof of murder. This would be different. They had to be more careful to cover their tracks.

They made their way to the three tables outside the ballroom door littered with place cards in far greater numbers than attendees at the ceremony.

"Can you say gift grab?" A man nearby said to the laughter of his friends. One quick look and Sophia dismissed them. They must be co-workers of the groom, members of the balding accountants' club.

Sophia found what she assumed was her name. *Table 34— Sophie Alden.* Close enough. She wasn't going to judge the spelling error for a last-minute guest. She would, however, allow herself a tiny smidge of judgment for the fact that they were printed, not embossed, and were not quite thick enough to stand up neatly. It was understandable that the bride's family skimped on the small details. Their money seemed to be invested in purchasing all the lace on the East Coast and wrapping their daughter in it. Jenna's skirt had been so full, she almost couldn't fit down the aisle, and the groom had barely been able to lean far enough over the flounces to deliver the first kiss, a moment that was greeted with a chorus of "Awws" from the ten bridesmaids and "Ewws" from the teenage stepchildren. Then, when the groom went to do the traditional glass stomping, it shot out from the wrapped napkin, rolled under the massive dress, and vanished for a few frantic minutes, as Jenna tried not to step on it herself. Poor Talia had to crawl underneath the layers, searching for the lost glass.

The worst part of that embarrassing moment had been Alec, who muttered, "Oh yeah, that's what I've been waiting for," at the sight of Talia's satin clad ass peeking out from under her sister's skirts as she searched.

He dies tonight, she repeated her mantra. Max's life mattered more than his. An eye for an eye, blood for blood. Death for death. Gage had told her that once, when he'd said he'd be willing to take the death penalty. *Death is the punishment for murder. It's only fair,* he'd said. Somehow, though, her brother had chickened out, serving his consecutive life sentences when he could use a simple noose fashioned from sheets to self-administer his deserved punishment. Alec wouldn't get a choice.

thirty-seven
chelsea

Holy f*cking sh*t what did I just read? Someone slide into my DMs and explain it.
   –@grishamisagod

The chaos of emotions swirling beneath Chelsea's calm exterior kept seeping out here and there. The craziest part was none of it had anything to do with killing Alec and everything to do with burning Rick Stafford to the ground.

She ordered a steady stream of vodka and crans that she never drank. She leaned in extra close to the men at the bar, added extra-wide smiles, hair flips, and even lingering touches. When a doctor from Long Island asked Chelsea to dance, she accepted with extra flair and did her best to fawn as he went into basic medical jargon that didn't impress her in the least.

Sophia arranged her face into a mask of delight when Chelsea left her dance partner adjusting himself on the other side of the floor.

"That guy is still staring at you," Sophia said through an awkward but sellable smile. "And so are all the Jewish mothers, clutching their pearls."

"He's a doctor." Chelsea needed only raise an eyebrow at the bartender who set her usual down with a wink. "As we know in the hierarchy of Jewish husbands, doctor trumps everyone else."

Sophia arched a perfectly plucked eyebrow and shifted her attention to the drink in Chelsea's hand.

"Don't worry, I've only had one. The rest are"—she swept her arm out to indicate nothing was off-limits—"around. Left behind at tables or dumped in potted plants."

"Well played. You had me convinced." Sophia ran her hand over her sleek ponytail and tossed it over her shoulder, eliciting a smile from a man nearby. She jerked her head back to Chelsea.

"You really aren't great at flirting," Chelsea chuckled, clutching the cocktail straw between her teeth. If Sophia was ruffled by the comment, she didn't show it, which continued in line with her character.

"Why would I be? I hate it. But you know what I don't hate," Sophia said, a genuine smile spilling across her meticulously made-up face. "That this whole thing is going to be over soon."

Chelsea followed her gaze across the dance floor to where Alec stood in the center of a ring of adoring onlookers, including Talia's mom, whose eyes sparkled like an anime character's.

"Lawyer trumps accountant," Chelsea said. "We probably should have given Talia a safe word for tonight, just in case ..."

Chelsea had pondered every possible direction tonight could go, including south. Talia was emboldened by doing Max justice. But there was still a chance she'd fuck things up.

Her phone buzzed against her hip, and Chelsea withdrew it to find a string of fresh messages popping in from Brad. Seeing his name shot adrenaline through Chelsea's middle like a lightning bolt. Something about him heated her insides. She turned away from Sophia so her friend couldn't see the smile that pulled at her cheeks.

> Thanks again. Remind me never to get on your bad side.

> I thought maybe we could meet up again. Not about the story. I don't need you anymore for that.

> That came off bad. I meant I want to see you for reasons that don't include trying to get something out of you.

> Shit, that came off even worse. I'm out of practice at asking anyone out on a proper date. I'm better at one-nighters.

> God, I suck at this.

> I'd like to see you again. Not in a professional or a one-night-stand sort of way.

> Anyway, I'm going to dive headfirst out of my window now. Bye.

The three dots lingered, as did Chelsea's smile. What was this reaction? She wasn't a teenager with some crush. She was a grown-ass woman who had no time for this bullshit. She was about to help murder a man. Crushing over one—

The dots disappeared.

> FYI the link to the MF Ascher reveal is live. I'm nervous you won't think I did Max justice, so I hope you like it. I'd hate to disappoint you.

Chelsea's heart stalled for a solid thirty seconds as the words sunk in.

"FUCK!"

It didn't matter that the rabbi who performed the ceremony was at her elbow. Or that the doctor from Long Island was two steps away with drinks. She whirled around to the dance floor, her radar locking in on the target. If Alec saw the story—if someone sent it to him—this whole thing would blow up.

"What's wrong?" Sophia said.

"The *Times* article about Max is live," Chelsea rasped back between clenched teeth without taking her eyes from Alec's sweeping hand gestures. She needed to act fast and do whatever it took to keep him from seeing the story.

Sophia's eyes widened. "Already?"

Chelsea nodded absently, her brain running through every possible scenario until it landed on one that made sense.

"I need to get his phone," she said, grabbing the drink from the Long Island doctor's outstretched hand and setting off across the dance floor to her intended target.

She wouldn't let this go off track, not after she'd done the impossible in finishing Rick. If she could do that, she could get a cellphone out of Alec's horny hands.

Three steps away from him, Chelsea slowed her gait and added a little sway to her steps. She took a sip of her drink, which was heavy on the vodka, so the burn saturated her breath.

Alec turned his red face in her direction. "There's one of my girls," he slurred, moving his gaze down to her feet. "Nice shoes." The smacking of his lips sent a wave of disgust into her mouth. She had a job to do. She needed to be sure.

Chelsea stumbled into his space, putting her lips against his ear.

"Talia showed me the pic you sent her last week," she whispered, noting the goose bumps popping along his neck. "*Quite* impressive."

She leaned against his stiffening body, patting his chest with her free hand, confirming his phone was tucked into the interior pocket of his jacket.

Alec fumbled to recover. "I—uh. Listen, if things with Talia—"

Chelsea drew her glass up to her lips and tipped it the opposite way, sending the cranberry, vodka, and ice streaming down the front of Alec's pristine, hand-tailored, Armani jacket.

"What the hell!" Alec jumped back and raised his arms as the liquid soaked into the navy blue twill.

"Oh my god, I'm so sorry. Let me ... let me help," Chelsea said in her best drunk-girl slur. She pulled down the back of the jacket, slipping it from Alec's shoulders.

"You're a sloppy drunk, Chelsea, you know that?" He brushed down the front of his tie and regained his composure under the weight of all those eyes.

"I'll go put some soda water on this ... maybe get the hotel to clean it if that's what it takes. So, so sorry." She turned away, righting her face from the fake concern and desperation. Before she made it across the dance floor, Chelsea pulled his phone out, swiped her finger down from the right corner, and tapped the airplane mode button. Within seconds, the phone was safely tucked back in Alec's jacket pocket, Chelsea was on her way to get that soda water, and their plan was still in motion.

She would make sure Alec had the jacket back just before he left to die.

thirty-eight
talia

This was the kind of book that as soon as you finish it you want to go right back in and read it again. Plus, it brought me back to my husband. Conjugal visits are scheduled and on track.
—HybristophiliaSupportGroupLeader

Talia flitted about the reception with the energy of a windup toy. Throughout the evening, she'd consumed nothing but virgin espresso martinis. They'd gone down like coffee milkshakes, one after the other.

Alec, to his credit, behaved reasonably well. Chelsea and Sophia, keeping low profiles, helped Talia keep him in check, ensuring he drank plenty of scotch—but not too much. They didn't want him passing out in her room and rendering himself unable to do the dirty deed of licking Talia's honey-laden toes clean.

A few nosy relatives questioned Talia about her handsome date, but she played it cool. *We're not in a relationship, at least not yet; yes, he is a successful lawyer; so good-looking, yes I know.* She spoke highly of the man who would soon be dead, wanting her gossipy family members to see that her plus-one was quite the catch.

When it came time for the newlyweds to cut the cake, Alec sauntered over and grabbed Talia around her waist with one strong arm.

"Stop that." She wriggled and giggled to put him off.

He nuzzled closer. "What if I gave you a hickey right here and now, in front of everyone?"

"I would have to kill you." She was growing bolder as the minutes passed.

"I think you'd like it—your judgmental Jewish family seeing you with a man like me."

His implication was clear. "So, you think you're quite the catch, huh?"

Alec hemmed. "Let's just say, if things work out between us, your mother will tell all her friends you're marrying up."

"Fine by me." Talia cozied up against his strong arm and pretended to enjoy stroking his muscle. It twitched beneath the thin fabric of his shirt. She hoped his death would be painful, tortuous, agonizing.

A waiter came by with champagne, and Alec grabbed two flutes. Talia accepted. She needed something to help her tolerate her insufferable date. By this time next week, she'd be at a health resort in the Hudson Valley drinking herbal concoctions, meditating, and snoozing by a pool. With Alec dead and the news breaking that she had been the best friend of the illusive MF Ascher, Talia's life would take off in a whole new direction. *Carpe Diem!*

She downed the champagne as her sister and new brother-in-law sliced into their three-tiered, white frosted cake adorned with pink roses. They fed each other messy bites, swaying to the tune of "*How Sweet It Is (To Be Loved by You).*" Ugh, so corny.

Alec wobbled beside her. He'd had way too much to drink and needed something to absorb it. "Let's get cake," Talia said, guiding him back to their seats. "It's from the best bakery in town."

"I like cake," Alec slurred.

The elevator pinged when it reached the 14th floor. With her sister's bouquet in one hand, her shoes in the other, and a plate with a slab of cake balanced on one arm, Talia padded down the hallway. So far, everything had gone according to plan. Alec was in her hotel room waiting for her. Chelsea and Sophia would be right next door. The hardest parts were over. Now, all Talia needed to do was offer Alec Pendergrass the very thing he could not resist: her feet.

She swiped the key card over the panel, and the green entry light lit up. Talia entered the room slowly, her chest rising and falling with every quick breath. A silent clock ticked in her brain.

The bathroom door was ajar, and steam drifted into the room through the opening.

Alec's navy Armani suit lay haphazardly over the back of one of the swivel chairs, his shoes and socks beside it. Talia scanned the luxurious suite—the sumptuous cream-colored bedding, the smooth hardwood floor covered by a thick, cushy area rug.

It reminded her a little of Max's new apartment, the one she'd rented with the money she made off their book. The windfall that should have improved all of their lives, but ended Max's. Even with Talia's massive and overactive imagination, she never would've anticipated the dark, deadly turn their story would take. But now that it had, she embraced her fate.

There was no doubt Talia would be punished, even if they never got caught. Guilt would gnaw at her insides, like termites chewing on wood. Not for killing Alec—that wouldn't faze her in the least. But the guilt over everything she didn't do to protect Max. That would eat at her forever.

So be it, Talia thought, slipping out of her dress. She hung it in the closet, put on her sexy lingerie, and propped her feet on a towel atop the coffee table. With the wooden dipper stick from her favor, Talia drizzled honey onto her toes. It felt pleasantly gooey. On top of the honey, she spread a thick layer of frosting, pleased with herself for enticing Alec with the idea. And a much better coating than the Hershey's chocolate sauce she had in her bag. Talia wiped her hands on a towel and envisioned how it would play out ...

Alec emerging from the bathroom in a white robe. The sight of her waiting for him with her toes deliciously dressed would give him an immediate erection. Talia would close her eyes and imagine she was with a new lover. Or better yet, think of herself as a sexy spy charged with taking out the operative who'd betrayed her country. Yes, she was the one with the power, the control, the commitment to a mission. She would hear the allergens begin to take effect as the enemy struggled and gasped for air ...

The sound of voices in the hallway outside her door halted the fantasy.

Jesus, what was taking him so long? The shower was still running. The frosting on her toes was dripping down the front of her feet.

"Alec," she called out. "I'm ready."

thirty-nine
sophia

Ascher is the death of literature as we know it. This book, this author, this breath of fresh air in the stagnant world of publishing ... this changes everything. The entire publishing industry has been upended. Now, with Ascher's success, it is clear that [Content available for subscribers only]

Sophia and Chelsea waited five minutes after Talia left the reception before they followed. Sophia could feel a thrum of excitement building inside her, but she kept her face impassive. This was it. It was time.

"I'm exhausted. I might fall asleep before my head hits the pillow," Sophia said as they unlocked the door to their room. It wasn't likely that anyone was listening, but she wanted all her bases covered, just in case. *I heard the ladies next door returning from the wedding. They sounded tired*, that's what the neighbors needed to say, if anything.

"Me, too," Chelsea agreed, for the benefit of the neighbors. At this stage, the plan on their end was simple: get into pajamas and wait. Talia would alert them when it was time, and they would join her in watching Alec die, his throat closing from anaphylaxis, as they stood over him, holding up a photo of Max. The last thing he would see would be Max's face. Talia had chosen the photo to use, quintessential Max, sneering at the camera, but with a brightness in her eyes, a look of knowing, like she was posing for just this moment, staring down her own killer.

Chelsea stopped so abruptly when they entered that Sophia ran right into her back. "What are you doing?" Sophia asked, but then she looked around her friend to see Talia, in the middle of their room, wearing lingerie and balancing on her heels, honey and frosting dripping down her feet.

"I ... he ..." Talia was shaking and gasping. She was not cut out for a life of crime.

Sophia carefully locked the door behind them. "What happened?"

"Come see," Talia managed to say. "He's in the bathroom!"

"No, that isn't the plan," Chelsea hissed. "You need to wait for him to come out, get him to lick your toes, and then we'll come in."

Talia was on the verge of hysterics. "I can't—it's not—please, right now!" She gestured frantically for them to follow as she hobbled awkwardly through the adjoining door back to her room.

For the briefest of moments, Sophia considered what would happen if they didn't go through with it tonight. Talia had already screwed something up. They could go back down to the wedding, have some real drinks, and try again some other time.

"It doesn't sound like our plan is working," she began. "We should ..."

"You're right," Chelsea said. "We should see if we can fix it." She grabbed the framed photo of Max and rushed after Talia. With a sigh, Sophia followed.

———

Alec wasn't dead. Sophia wasn't sure if she was disappointed or relieved. He wasn't dead, *yet*. But there was something seriously wrong with the situation. She observed it dispassionately, as a writer, not as a participant. If this were a book, she'd focus on the details, the steam billowing from the bathroom, the drips of water, the tangled shower curtain Alec must have grabbed as he fell, the uneasy obscenity of his flaccid pride, the organ that had lured him to his fate so easily.

"Help me," he said from his contorted position in the tub. His voice came out a rough whisper. "Call 911. I can't feel anything."

"How did this happen, Talia?" Chelsea asked, the first to recover from the surprise.

"I—I don't know! Maybe because I took a bath earlier. He must have slipped on the bath oils. What do we do now?" Talia was whispering like Alec, even though there was nothing wrong with her vocal cords.

"We have to change the plan." Chelsea's voice was controlled.

Sophia stared at the man in the tub. What would Gage suggest? He'd make a bloody mess, that's what he'd do. She had to focus on what someone who didn't want to go to jail would do. Pillow over the face? Pour the honey down his throat? Wait it out?

"Plan? What do you mean, plan?" Alec's eyes, the only things he seemed able to move, widened in fear.

"This," Talia said, lifting one messy foot to show him the deadly allergen. "It was going to be sweet."

"Is that honey?" He sounded more confused than scared.

"Death by anaphylaxis." Sophia leaned over him. "We were going to use your allergen against you." *Like you used Max's alcoholism against her,* she wanted to add, but she held her tongue. This was meant to be a triumphant vengeance for a horrific crime; mentioning the flaws of the deceased weakened it.

"I'm not allergic to honey; I just say that because I don't like it." Alec closed his eyes for a moment, and Sophia hoped it would be for the final time, that death was finally taking him. But no, he opened them again.

"Call an ambulance," he repeated his earlier plea. "Help me."

"Did Max beg for help when you killed her?" Sophia asked.

Gage always talked about lack of control, but Sophia felt totally *in* control. Like she could do anything. She stepped past Chelsea and reached up to the shower nozzle, still blasting hot water on the injured man. One little push, and it moved, the outer edge of the stream reaching Alec's chin, drops splashing at his mouth.

"That was your idea." Alec's lips twitched as he tried to move his head to escape the stream. "I did it for all of us."

"You know damn well we were joking! We would never have harmed her. You took it upon yourself. And we can't let you get away with that." Chelsea removed the showerhead from the mount and held the nozzle like a gun, directing the water so it hit Alec full in the face. Paralyzed, he couldn't turn his head.

Sophia backed out of the way. She wanted to watch. This might make a good story someday. She'd never witnessed someone die before, not while they were conscious. Grandpa had been stolen by a swift heart attack, and Grandma's end, while slower, was peaceful and morphine-aided in a hospice with Sophia holding her hand, watching to see what changed when her grandmother crossed out of existence. Nothing happened, except for a slight relaxation in her facial features and the smell of final release. Alec would be different, she hoped.

Talia shoved herself between them so that she could place her hand next to Chelsea's, the two of them keeping the water trained on Alec's mouth. They could have placed it on the mount and stepped back to observe, Sophia thought, but something about touching the physical showerhead seemed more empowering.

There was one other person who needed to be involved, so instead of adding her hand to theirs in solidarity, Sophia picked up the photo of Max. She lifted the two-dimensional witness, holding Max over Alec's face, ensuring the last image seared on his fading brain would be Max's sneer.

"Just like Max," Sophia said, "you were alive when you went into the water."

And they made sure the last thing he heard was three voices repeating Max's catchphrase, "motherfucking asshole."

forty
everyone who isn't dead

I'm closing this book in literal tears. I want to hit myself over the head with a hammer and give myself amnesia so I can reread it and rediscover it all over again. I have never encountered a book that evoked so many deep and powerful emotions before. MF Ascher is a gift to the literary world.

–prayingformoreAscher

SOPHIA

It didn't take as long as Sophia had expected, mere minutes. Alec had gurgled and made gasping noises, but his broken neck prevented any sort of fight. Then there was nothing. His eyes went from angry to empty, and he was gone. It was almost anticlimactic. Sophia had expected to feel something, witness something, but ... no. It was nothing like Gage had described.

"Is he dead?" Talia asked. She removed her hand from the showerhead.

Chelsea turned off the water and dropped the showerhead in the tub on top of Alec's body. She leaned in, placing her fingers on the side of his neck. Her smile was almost scary as she confirmed the lack of a pulse. "He's dead. It's over."

"Almost over," Sophia corrected. It wasn't supposed to go this way. He may have drowned, but his paralysis meant he didn't feel enough, didn't suffer enough. It wasn't as painful as he deserved, but at least he had been conscious. At least he knew it was them.

However, since their entire cover-up scheme was focused on the allergic reaction, they needed to rethink their next steps. They'd been planning to set the stage as an accident; now that there was an actual accident, they needed to make sure it couldn't be interpreted any other way.

Talia stared down at Alec's body, mesmerized. Chelsea still knelt, hands on his neck, as if maybe he might suddenly start to breathe again. That left Sophia to take control. She took a deep breath. She knew crime scenes. She'd seen far too many photos of them.

"Okay, new plan." Sophia carefully picked up the shower-head, avoiding contact with Alec. She didn't want to touch him. She wiped the fingerprints off the chrome with a washcloth, secured it in place, and positioned it so that the spray would hit Alec directly in his face. "Talia, you need to get wet."

"Get wet? Why?"

"This wasn't how it was supposed to happen, so we have to improvise. Turn the water on, lean over him like you're checking on him, then start screaming as loud as you can."

"I have to clean up first! I don't want anyone to see me like this!"

"You can't. The way you're dressed right now makes this whole thing far more believable. You were waiting a long time. He said he was going to clean up while you dirtied up. He took too long, you finally went to check on him, and you found him like that. Scream. Get hysterical. React the way you would if you wanted him alive." Sophia had expected Talia to see the rationale and obey, but Talia wasn't the best in stressful situations.

"But I have honey and frosting on my feet!"

"Yes, and you'll leave footprints in the bathroom. It's not real-istic that you'd clean up or get dressed or anything. You're in a panic. If it helps, you can put on a robe after you get soaked. I don't think you'd have had one on before."

"The paramedics won't care," Chelsea added. "I did ride-alongs with EMTs in college. They're always removing things from people's rectums and penises. Your foot stuff is comparatively tame."

Talia finally did what she was told, turning the water back on, leaning over Alec's body, and then covering herself with a robe before screaming. Her screams were fantastic, realistic horror-movie type screams that would definitely bring two friends running from the adjoining room.

Sophia gave her a thumbs-up and placed the call from the room phone.

"911, what's your emergency?"

Sophia made herself sound scared and nervous. "He's dead ... oh, my god, Alec is dead. We found him, we need help ..."

"Okay, ma'am, I can send someone there to help you. I see your location; what's your room number?" The operator had a smooth, calming voice. If Sophia had actually been upset, he would make her feel better.

"Yes, we're in ... I don't know, this is my friend's room, we're staying next door. Ours is 1420, so this must be 1418. Please help, he's dead and I don't know what to do." In the background, Talia carried on, appearing to enjoy it. She wasn't screaming anymore, but her sobs provided the perfect background accompaniment to the phone call.

"Alright, ma'am, I've got help coming. I need some more information from you. You said someone is dead? Do you know the person?"

"Yes, he's dead, it's Alec, he's ... he's a lawyer, we were all at a wedding, and he was Talia's date, it was her sister's wedding ..." Sophia knew panicked people gave extraneous details, so she kept going. Chelsea was watching her, so Sophia gave a wink to show it was working perfectly.

"Can you check and see if Alec is breathing? Can you find a

pulse?" The operator spoke slowly, soothingly. "You can check his neck or his wrist or even put your hand on his chest."

"I can't reach. The phone cord doesn't stretch to the bathroom, but Chelsea already checked. That's the first thing we did. She went to med school. She's not a doctor, she dropped out, but she checked, and he's dead, he's completely dead." She took quick deep breaths, so the operator would think she was holding back sobs. In the background, Talia kept wailing. "Chels, please give her a bathrobe; the police are coming. Talia, sweetie, they'll be here soon. Get out of the bathroom, go sit on the bed. Don't look at him anymore."

"Ma'am, do you know what happened to Alec?"

"I guess he fell? I don't know, Talia's not making much sense. They were going to, well, you know, it was after the wedding, and they were kind of into each other, and he's in the bathtub, I think he slipped and hit his head; I don't think it was an overdose or anything. I mean, he did have a lot to drink at the reception. He was showering and she was waiting for him, and he took too long, and she found him, and she's really upset." By this point, Talia had moved her performance to the bed, leaving squelchy honeyed footprints on the hotel carpeting. Sophia was enjoying herself. She felt like she was doing a radio play, like Orson Welles, creating a scene to scare others.

A knock on the door sent Sophia's heart rate spiking. It was time for a live performance. "I think they're here, the police are at the door, thank you, thank you so much."

"Ma'am," the operator said. "That's probably hotel security. They get notified when a guest calls 911. The police are a few minutes away. I promise, they'll be there shortly. Please ask everyone to stay back from the body." The operator's voice held a touch of annoyance now, probably directed at security guards who might mess up the scene before the police could properly investigate.

It wasn't hotel staff at the door. There was someone much worse.

Riva Goldstein swept into the room. "Talia, I could hear you all the way down the hall. What's wrong with you? You're making a spectacle of yourself!"

CHELSEA

The entire scene unraveled like a high school play. Talia (who was in full-on theatrics) forgot her lines the second Riva stepped into the room.

"Mom!" Talia cried out between faux sobs. "You can't be here."

"Why are you carrying on like a banshee?" Riva cast a stern look towards her older daughter, hands plastered to hips. Her gaze moved from the river of makeup streaming down Talia's cheeks, past the loose belt of the robe draped across her lace teddy, until they landed on her honey- and frosting-caked feet. Riva stepped forward, bent at the waist, and squinted down at Talia's toes. "What in the world is all over your feet? And why are you wet?"

Everything they worked so hard to make happen was about to fall apart, all because they'd failed to consider that Riva Goldstein was also staying on this floor. Even if their original plan worked, Talia was always going to become hysterical, and Riva was always going to come running in.

A hand jolted Chelsea's right shoulder blade. She turned toward Sophia, still tethered to the 911 operator. Her lips wrapped around her teeth, her eyes undulating between wide and wider. Chelsea couldn't process what the hell her friend wanted or what she was doing, until Sophia huffed out a breath and yanked Chelsea by the shoulder, pulling her in close and whispering, "Do something. *Now.*"

Right. She needed to stop watching and start acting. Chelsea turned back toward Talia, who was now standing and scuffing her feet along the carpet in place.

"Mom, you need to leave." Talia shouted at her. "I—we—there's been an accident."

"Not until you tell me what is going on. If I didn't know any better, I'd think this is some kind of attempt to upstage your sister on her special day!"

The fear in Talia's face spoke to Chelsea without words: *My mother is going to blow this whole thing up because she can tell I'm lying.*

Chelsea's mind rolled back through all the times Talia complained about her mother. Because she knew her daughter better than anyone, it was impossible for Talia to fool her about her weight (whether she lost or gained), her chosen profession ("foot modeling" was the term coined explicitly for Riva), or her dating prospects (none). Until tonight, that is, when Talia showed up with a lawyer who was now dead in the shower of her hotel room.

Chelsea straightened herself, slipped on her best doctor-delivering-bad-news-face, and plunged ahead. "Maybe your mom needs to know what we're dealing with here."

Talia's eyes got even bigger—a feat Chelsea didn't believe possible. She shook her head with such voraciousness, the water from her hair sprung out like a sprinkler.

"No! That is the worst idea ever!"

"Talia Ruth Goldstein, tell me what's going on right now. I'm not leaving until you do." Riva's volume matched Talia's and doused the room with silence.

It was now or never. If Chelsea couldn't get Riva out of here, Talia was going to lose whatever was left of her mind. She sprang into action, moving close to Riva, whose dark eyes shone with skepticism.

"I'll show you, Mrs. Goldsten. But I need you to be prepared because what you're about to see isn't pretty."

"Considering what I've already seen here …" Riva glanced back at Talia's feet. "I think I'll manage."

Talia sank onto the bed and buried her face in her hands. Chelsea escorted Riva into the bathroom and showed her the tub.

Talia's mother clamped her hands over her mouth. "Is that Talia's date?"

"It is," Chelsea said. "Or was."

Riva stomped back into the bedroom. "Talia! What have you done?"

Talia opened her mouth, but any attempt at words was drowned out by the pounding from the other side of the door.

Chelsea opened it to reveal an entire fire brigade poised for action. She couldn't help but think this would be one hell of a meet-cute in one of Talia's books if not for the dead body in the bathtub.

A tall lumberjack-esque man stepped to the forefront, his onyx beard framing perfect pale pink lips. "We have reports of a—"

"You killed him with your sex games!" Riva's shouts echoed off every wall in the suite and beyond.

"MOTHER, PLEASE LEAVE!" Talia stood up on quaking knees, took a step and crumbled in a heap.

The EMTs rushed in and tended to Talia on the floor.

Sophia and Chelsea drifted together. Chelsea put a hand on Riva's shoulder. "Let's give them space, Mrs. Goldstein."

Riva, for her part, looked nervous as the men poked and prodded Talia's head, chest, and wrists. She was wringing her hands as Talia began moaning. Chelsea could feel the woman's shoulders collapse beneath the weight of her breath as she exhaled.

"See, she's going to be okay. I think you should wait outside until they're done." Chelsea nodded at Sophia and began leading Riva towards the door. "She's in good hands." *Really good hands* ...

They made it to the door just as four police officers and two hotel security guards came pouring into the scene. The entire room was now teeming with enough testosterone to fuel an NFL franchise.

Before she left, Riva cast another glance into the room. "And to think he was a lawyer. He was perfect for my Talia!"

TALIA

When Talia came to, a dreamy fireman with a fiery gaze stood over her, his face only inches from hers.

"There you go. How are you feeling?"

"Uh, fine." She reached up and stroked his bearded cheek. "You're beautiful."

He chuckled and tucked her hand beside her body. "Still a little loopy. That's okay. People sometimes pass out when they're stressed. We're going to transport you to the hospital."

Talia sprang up, recalling everything that had happened. "No, no hospital. My friend Chelsea's a doctor, sort of, almost. Chelsea! Tell them I don't need to go to the hospital. Oh, my god, where's my mother? Did you get rid of my mother?" She used his arm, which was as thick as a tree trunk, to stand up.

"I'll take care of her," Chelsea said, muscling in between Talia and the hot man.

"Are you a physician?" he asked.

"Excuse me, but shouldn't you be assisting the paramedics in the bathroom?" Chelsea deflected like an expert. "After all, there's an *actual* dead man in there!"

And just like that, Talia's dreamboat vanished. But at least there was no more discussion about her going to the hospital.

For the next three hours, Talia huddled on the bed while hotel security and police investigators filled the room. She couldn't believe how long Alec's body remained in the tub. Finally, the coroner arrived and confirmed the cause of death was an accidental slip-and-fall and a subsequent broken neck. They zipped Alec into a big black body bag and rolled him out on a stretcher.

What a perfect send-off for a man who deserved the most unceremonious ending.

As for the three friends, Talia believed they'd performed their roles like seasoned actors. No matter which way the police asked questions, they stuck to the story. It played out exactly the way they had planned. Only better.

one year later

This book inspired me to make some changes in my life. Big changes. I gave notice at the law firm where I've been slaving away for 12 years, and I filed for divorce from my husband the same day. I'm selling everything I own, downgrading from a BMW to a Subaru, and traveling around the country for the foreseeable future. I don't want to be tied to anything. Thank you, MF Ascher, for inspiring this change. I can't wait to experience Death Valley in August.
 −Lawyer No More

TALIA

Talia sat in the swivel chair in front of a giant mirror with bright, round light bulbs. The makeup artist finished touch-ups and sent her down the hall to wait for her interview with Susanna Price, the queen of daytime talk. In the year since the "true" identity of MF Ascher went viral, Talia was the new media darling. She, and she alone, had become the spokesperson for Max DeLeon, the deceased author of one of the biggest bestsellers in history.

In her new signature look—dark pantsuit (usually black or charcoal), silk blouse, peep-toe pumps, hair pulled back in a tight bun, and oversized hoop earrings, Talia followed a production assistant into the studio.

"You'll be sitting right here, Ms. Goldstein." The PA, a perky college student, motioned toward an upholstered club chair. "I want you to know that you're kind of my idol. I've watched all your interviews."

Talia glanced at the credentials hanging on the lanyard around her neck. "Thank you, Jessica. I appreciate that."

The young woman, just starting her professional career, reminded Talia of herself at that age. Naïve, idealistic, full of the exuberant enthusiasm one holds onto until life takes a turn and humanity's cruelty makes you into a cynic. After Alec Pendergrass died from an accidental slip and fall (evidently, a not-so-uncommon cause of death), Talia had become a different person. She was proud of the role she'd played in his demise.

Sometimes at night she'd lie in bed and picture how he had likely fallen backwards, his feet flying into the air in a cartoonish mishap, the back of his head smacking the tub, neck snapping in just the right place to render him paralyzed. With the image of him lying helpless and the shower spray flooding his nose and mouth, Talia would fall into a deep, dreamless sleep.

"The engineer will be right over to set up your mic and earpiece," Jessica said. "May I get you anything? Coffee, tea, soda, Perrier. Or we have juice. Apple, cranberry, orange—"

"I'm fine with my water," Talia said with a soft smile. "But thank you for your attentiveness."

Susanna Price, an attractive forty-something with short dark hair and large-frame designer glasses, approached with an outstretched hand. "Talia Goldstein, what a pleasure. I'm Susanna."

Talia rose, her four-inch heels just high enough to meet Susanna's height. The host's grip was firm. Talia, an expert at shaking hands these days, matched it.

They exchanged niceties and got started. Susanna rushed

through the usual softball questions about Talia's friendship with the elusive MF Ascher, a.k.a. Max DeLeon, the novel's unexpected success, the hundreds of thousands of reviews.

"Tell me, Talia." Susanna leaned forward with intense focus. "Do you fear for your life?"

"Excuse me?" That was a question Talia had not expected.

"First the author, your best friend, *accidentally* kills herself driving drunk into a lake. Which again, I'm so sorry for your loss. Then Alec Pendergrass, her lawyer and the representative of MF Ascher, dies in a hotel bathtub. It's uncanny, don't you think?"

Talia twitched. Okay, so if that's where the interviewer wanted to go, bring it. "I hadn't considered that, but no, I'm not worried." She kept her voice gentle, almost appreciative, although she wanted to be snarky. Max would've told the cloying host to fuck off.

Susanna hummed and nodded, as if she and Talia had made a true connection. "I can't help but ask, especially since social media and all the weeklies made such a deal of it. Do you believe it's a possibility that Max DeLeon died by suicide?"

Talia crossed and uncrossed her legs, formulating an answer that would meet Max's approval. "Max had demons. She despised any system that took advantage of the vulnerable or flattered the undeserving simply because of beauty or money or status or—"

"That's not what I asked," Susanna interrupted, peering at Talia over her stylish glasses.

"I wasn't finished," Talia said with a lift of her chin. "But she had put all that behind her. She found happiness. I can tell you with certainty that she did not die by suicide. Her death was a tragedy. And Mr. Pendergrass's was an unfortunate accident."

"Both accidents, then." Susanna sounded disappointed, as if she'd hoped to break Talia's composure.

"Yes, accidents." Talia let the word settle on her lips. Everything that happened in the last two years had been caused by an accident: four old friends used AI and accidentally created a book.

Then one of them published it, and they all made shitloads of money—by accident. If not for those accidents, MF Ascher would never have existed. And Max DeLeon would not be dead.

A slight whimper escaped Talia's throat. She looked away, embarrassed. As hard as she tried to exude confidence and toughness, when it came to Max, the wound cut too deep.

"Let's move on then." Susanna flashed a sympathetic smile, as if she sensed Talia's emotion. "You've become a best-selling author. Congratulations."

"Thank you."

"I just read *Love in the Swamp*. I must say, it is, well, quite clever and compelling." Susanna sounded surprised.

"I appreciate that. You know, many authors never achieve success until they become known for some unrelated reason. I'm fully aware that most of my readers had never heard of me until I became the voice of MF Ascher, but I'm delighted they're enjoying my work."

Talia knew deep inside that although she hated the way she achieved notoriety, she had earned her success. Her books were good, and they deserved readers. And she deserved her time in the sun, for however long it lasted.

"Now," Susanna said, interrupting her thoughts, "you promised us an announcement of sorts." Her lashes fluttered with anticipation.

"Yes, I did." Talia rested her hands in her lap, her chest expanding. "I am proud and pleased to announce that the MF Ascher Foundation has been established with a $500,000 gift from the estate of Max DeLeon." Talia paused for a reaction, but there was none. The talk show host had probably hoped for something salacious. "Our mission is to pluck talented, struggling writers out of obscurity and help them achieve their publishing dreams."

"Well, that is something, isn't it?" Susanna turned toward the camera. "And that concludes our interview with Talia Goldstein, the voice of MF Ascher. Coming up next, a segment on summer foot care you won't want to miss—I'll be sinking my bare feet into a tank swarming with nibble fish!"

Talia stood the second the producer gave the wrap-up signal, and the cameras pulled away. Susanna gave her a hug, as if they were best friends, and whispered into her ear. "God, that was dull." She positioned herself beside Talia so the photographer could take a few stills and walked off, her stilettos clicking on the hard floor.

What a fucking phony. Max would've hated her.

Jessica, the perky PA, appeared out of nowhere and led Talia to the green room. "Your driver should be here shortly, Ms. Goldstein. Can I get you anything while you wait?"

"No, thanks. I'll help myself. Good luck to you."

Jessica reached for a handshake that morphed into an awkward hug. "I'm so honored to have met you."

The young woman disappeared, taking all her exuberant energy with her. Talia withdrew her phone from her purse to text her publicist and tell her exactly what she thought of Susanna Price.

Her phone jingled and the screen lit up: *Mom cell.*

"Oh, hell no." Talia tapped ignore. A moment later, the texts began:

Just saw your interview

Hmm, no punctuation, what did that mean? Would she ever stop craving her mother's approval?

What'd you think?

I think you should've worn a dress or at least something more colorful. You looked like you were going to a funeral

Fuck you, Mom.

> Actually, my publicity team helped me design my look. The bloggers love it. And my personal shopper at Saks curates every outfit. So I'll stick with her style advice, thank you very much. Talk soon, bye!

There was a long pause. Hopefully, the exchange had ended. Then the dots started up again.

> Please wear something bright and cheerful to your sister's baby shower next week

> Won't be there. Interview in Chicago. See you at the bris if I'm not out of town. 🙄

Talia shut off her phone and slipped it into her bag. Max would be proud of her.

She checked her watch, a Cartier Tank with diamonds, and hoped the limo driver would arrive soon. Interviews always drained her.

The smell of fresh coffee beckoned. Talia went to the counter, took a paper cup from the stack, and poured herself a steaming cup of coffee. She turned and crashed into a wall. Not a wall. A man built like a wall. The paper cup crushed against his chest.

"Youch! Shit, ow!" The man ripped open his shirt to escape the burning liquid, buttons flying.

"Oh, my God, I am so sorry!" Talia was mortified.

"No, nope, it's okay." The man splashed cold water on himself as a large red blotch rose on his muscular torso. He made grunting noises, obviously because of the pain, but they still sounded erotic.

Talia couldn't turn away from his rippling muscles and the way his dress pants rested on sculpted hips. The rousing sounds continued, sending Talia's fantasies into overdrive.

"You're burned."

"What?"

"Your hand," the man said. "It's blistering. Here, run it under the water."

His touch was so gentle it felt like the flutter of butterfly wings. He cupped her right hand and held it beneath the cool stream. "It's my fault," he said. "I saw you were pouring coffee. I should've announced myself."

Talia's knees almost buckled. "Who are you?" she asked, breathless.

"Dr. Maxwell Weiss."

Maxwell? Weiss? Doctor?

"You're a doctor?"

"Cardiologist. I was Susanna's guest before you. She interviews me every time some young celebrity or athlete has a heart attack. Anyway, I watched your interview, and well, I was so taken by your confidence."

"Confidence?"

"Yes. And your devotion to your friend, your charitable work, and, if I may be so bold, your beauty."

She had to be dreaming. Had to be. This was the best meet-cute ever.

CHELSEA

In the scheme of things, everything turned out as it should. Her friends were living large, writing, publishing, and promoting, which warmed Chelsea's heart whenever their smiling faces crossed her feed. But it had been a year since the three of them had been in the same room, and as Chelsea zipped up her carry-on, an excitement shivered over her skin at the prospect that they'd all be together at the lake house the next day. To take care of Max.

The wheels of her bag glided over the tile floor as she made her way from her bedroom, stopping to close the windows on her way out, deflating each billowing curtain as she went, pausing before the open sliders in the main living space and allowed herself to soak in the breeze. The realtor who showed her the house did so reluctantly, swearing it was too large for a single woman. Chelsea fired the man on the spot and made a cash offer to the sellers that day, adding an extra incentive to get them to vacate sooner.

Sure, it was more house than she ever needed, but after living so many years crammed into a box in a gray world, she wanted space to breathe in life. And that she did, every single day since. The guilt she entertained from time to time over what she'd done paled in comparison to the life she'd created as a result.

Alec got what he deserved. The death was ruled accidental, which was mostly accurate. Had she finished medical school and taken her Hippocratic Oath, she would have been obligated to try to save him. But, fortunately for them and unfortunately for him, life hadn't led Chelsea down that path.

Alec's slip and fall freed them from too much culpability. Had they not returned to the room when they did, he very well might have drowned and died all on his own. And really, what kind of life would Alec Pendergrass have led if he was paralyzed from the neck down? They did him a favor, taking mercy like they did.

And Rick—even now as she stood at the edge of her infinity pool overlooking the cerulean blue waters of the Caribbean Sea, his name did nothing to disturb her peace. After news of Rick's plagiarism came out, the studio did everything to stomp out the spreading wildfire. They ceased production on the MF Ascher film completely, paid the estate compensatory damages, and started negotiating with Chelsea to atone for their sins.

She didn't make it easy. She could have, since the money she made from the MF Ascher book alone was more than enough to sustain her new life in Costa Rica. But she wanted to squeeze every dime out of the studio before turning her sights on Rick. He declared bankruptcy soon after she filed the civil suit, only paying a fraction of what the judge ordered, but that didn't matter. She didn't need it. It was satisfying enough to know that

Rick wound up in an apartment worse than the one she'd left in Newark.

Even her parents reached out after the news about Rick broke. She'd let her finger hover above her mother's number for a beat too long before sending the call to voicemail and then deleting the contact. Chelsea had learned to let go of things that no longer served her, and her parents had certainly not done that in a long time, if ever.

Most days she didn't give them or Rick or Alec a second thought, her time consumed instead with meditation, yoga, runs on the beach, hikes through the rainforest, and writing. Her passion for the craft had returned in a way that made every other desire pale. She wrote for herself for the first time since her world had been turned upside down four years ago. Three books in one year, all different yet threaded together with the common themes of friendship and found family. Of course, all three had a bit of an edge, something about loyalty, and righting things when someone was wronged. Happy endings can only come with elements of revenge, or so the three books purported.

Chelsea could have used her real name for the first time but chose not to. Instead, she paid tribute to her three friends by creating the pen name TS Maximilian to publish the first book months after stepping into her new life. *The Write Way to Commit Murder* rocketed up Amazon and bestseller charts everywhere. It took BookTok by storm, fueled in part by its timely topic related to AI in the publishing world and how it destroyed the four friends at the center. It was relevant, something agents and editors were fighting to find. Chelsea had been fielding offers of representation and Big Five publishing promises since she released the book eight months ago. But there wasn't a shot in hell she would share any of her hard-fought success with those motherfucking assholes.

Sophia and Talia were the only ones who knew what she wrote or where she lived. Even Brad, who she'd grown *very* close to over the last year, only knew she lived somewhere down south. They'd met up once a few months ago at a conference in San Diego. The way they collided those three nights scared the hell out of Chelsea. Not because she needed him to fill some vacant space within her, but because she didn't. For the first time, she was whole and happy just the way she was. But she wanted Brad in her life. They talked daily, and he begged to see her again, confessing that he didn't know what he was doing either and had never before felt the way he did about her. She'd finally agreed to meet him tonight for dinner before heading out to the lake house tomorrow. The anticipation of being with him fueled her excitement. Maybe she was finally ready to tell him where she lived. Maybe she wanted him to see the person she was in this space. Maybe she wanted to see him here with her. She swung the porch doors shut and clicked the locks as the car waiting to take her to the airport honked out front.

So much of her life had changed this year. Instead of dwelling in the past, Chelsea leaned hard into the now. Her happy place sprung to life, all of it because of the work she'd done. The plot she'd planned. The Revenge Story that worked itself out in real time.

She had fought so hard to get here and lost so much in the process, but to find herself, it had all been worth it.

SOPHIA

The dock creaked beneath their feet. Sophia made a mental note to have a handyman come out and check on it, see if the boards needed to be replaced. That was another small joy in having money, the ability to hire someone to do her dirty work. Grandpa had built this dock by hand; Sophia had not inherited his DIY skills.

"This is it," Chelsea said. She stood tall on Sophia's left side, holding a bottle of Beluga Epicure Vodka. She'd changed so much over the past year that Sophia hardly recognized her. She hadn't realized how much stress had bowed her friend's strong shoulders and muted her personality until the real Chelsea had emerged, bright and shining, unburdened by the pressures of poverty and family disapproval. This new version was healthy and smiled readily, glowing with a Costa Rican sunshine tan and the secret smile of a woman who'd just met up with her lover, a fact that she blushingly denied. But Sophia had seen Brad's Instagram post.

"It's over," Sophia confirmed. She held a small bowl of ashes. Not Max's; those were in Talia's hands. Sophia held the ashes of a copy of *Deep Within the Discontented Dreaming of Dorian Dimwitty*. They'd burned it ceremoniously in a metal bucket to keep the remains separate. The book that kicked everything off, putting Max—and Alec—on the paths to their own destruction. It was only fitting that the three remaining friends burn a copy to cast into the lake with Max.

Sophia had considered an additional tribute, burning a copy of each of their books, Chelsea's thrillers, Talia's romances, and her own beautiful novel, her precious literary baby. But that idea had been in her mind *before*. Before her author copies arrived and she was able to trace her own name, Aldren, on the spine. She hadn't realized how possessive she would be, how obsessed. She carried a copy with her almost everywhere, so she could pull it out and admire it. Her book had already been chosen for a national book club, the September book of the month. It had also been selected for a prison book club, because Gage promised lots of sales, though he also promised that each prisoner who got a copy would be carefully removing her author photo and giving it to him. He would allow no pictures of his sister in any bunks.

It hadn't felt real to her, the bidding war, the two-book deal. Until the box of author copies arrived, with a bottle of champagne from her agent. Dom Perignon, a trivial gift given how much her agent had made off her commission. Even now as the glowing reviews—and one unnecessarily snarky one—came in from advance readers, she still had to pinch herself. It was real. It was all real. Next week she'd even be featured in the *New York Times*, though Brad's interview may have been more inspired by his love for Chelsea than by his love for Sophia's book. Didn't matter; his review was flattering.

At this moment, she had almost everything she wanted. It would be better, of course, if Max was at her side rather than in an urn in Talia's hands. And of course, her wildest fantasies placed her brother on the dock, freed via presidential pardon, the only way he'd ever leave prison. He'd come home to her, and they'd share the lake house. He'd be reformed, and she would never have to worry about what he was up to, never come home to see him digging a large hole or burning something in a bonfire that smelled like pork and left human teeth behind.

"Should we do this?" Talia interrupted her thoughts. Much like Chelsea, Talia had changed. She was stronger, tougher, channeling Max, whose death had made her more assertive. She also, Sophia noticed with a sniff, no longer smelled of rose oils. Talia had given up her fancy baths in the wake of Alec's death.

"On three," Chelsea said, and they all extended their hands over the lake, a reflection of the way they'd stood in the hotel bathroom one year ago, sharing an unpleasant task. Then it was a solemn moment, hastening—but *technically* not causing—Alec's ending.

"One," they said together, holding their tributes over the lake.

"Two." They tipped their individual burdens.

"Three." As the vodka splashed out, a sudden breeze carried the ashes of Max and the book away from the dock, scattering them where they floated on ripples before sinking into the inky blue water.

"It's all over," Chelsea said.

"All over but the money," Sophia added. Sales of the book had slowed, but each monthly deposit was still more than they had ever expected to see in their lifetimes.

"For now," Talia chuckled. "But what if we were to discover a sequel on Max's computer? It wouldn't take us long."

Chelsea and Sophia exchanged a glance, and an understanding passed between them.

"Over your dead body," they said in unison.

THE END ... for now

about the author

Ivy H. Booker is the pen name of four authors who came together through the Women's Fiction Writers Association. While they've all published under their own names, this work of dark friendship fiction is their first collaboration. It does not mirror their real-life friendship.

Sara LaFontain lives in Arizona, where her husband lovingly supplies her with chocolate to fuel her writing habit. She is the author of the romantic women's fiction Whispering Pines Island series, and the Corbitt Calamities pop star thrillers. Prior to becoming an author, Sara held a variety of jobs ranging from the unusual (wildlife tour guide in the Brazilian Pantanal) to the emotional (domestic violence case advocate) to the respectable (attorney). She also works as an Author Accelerator certified book coach.

Julie Mayerson Brown is an author, essayist, and playwright. Her Clearwater Series, five novels and a YA novella, takes place in a charming town in California Wine Country. The books all feature lovable, quirky characters, adorable dogs, best-friendships, and delicious sticky buns. In addition to feel good stories, Julie writes book club fiction that delves into darker themes of family dysfunction, betrayal, and suspense. She lives in Los Angeles with her family and a pack of rescued boxers.

Marina DelVecchio is an award-winning author of the YA novel, Dear Jane, named in Kirkus' list for Best Indie Books of 2019. She is also the author of The Professor's Wife (2021), The Virgin Chronicles (2022), and Unsexed: Memoirs of a Prostitute's Daughter (2024). Her essays appear in Ms. Magazine, HuffPost, The New Agenda, The Tishman Review, WE Magazine for Women, and Vast Literary Magazine, among others. She teaches writing, literature, and women's studies as a full-time professor in North Carolina.

Jen Sinclair pens personal essays and contemporary fiction that explore complicated relationships, love, loss, and all the messiness of life. She lives in Saint Augustine, Florida, with her husband, kids, and spoiled puppy. When she isn't working out story elements, belting out songs from one of her many Spotify playlists, or having conversations with imaginary friends, she enjoys spending time outside walking beaches and trails, paddling waterways, or driving around with the top off her Jeep.

instagram.com/ivyhbookerauthor

also by ivy h. booker

Books by Sara LaFontain

The Corbitt Calamities Series

Unexpected Encore

Concerted Chaos

Matchmaker Mayhem

The Whispering Pines Island Series

That Last Summer

Say the Words

No Longer Yours

Cherry Christmas, Baby!

If This Were a Love Story

Books by Julie Mayerson Brown

The Clearwater Series

Long Dance Home

Road to Somewhere

The Lonely Sommelier

The Everywhere Girl

One Last Dance

A Clearwater Christmas

Books by Marina DelVecchio

Dear Jane

The Virgin Chronicles

The Professor's Wife

Unsexed: Memoirs of a Prostitute's Daughter

Books by Jen Sinclair

There's Always a Price

According to My Science

www.ingramcontent.com/pod-product-compliance
Lightning Source LLC
Chambersburg PA
CBHW031317280626
47169CB00019B/1867